WARRIOR RISING

LINDA WINSTEAD
JONES

Warrior Rising, Copyright 2016 by Linda Winstead Jones. Print Edition, 2016

ISBN-13: 978-1530137305
ISBN-10: 1530137306

Cover design by Elizabeth Wallace
http://designwithin.carbonmade.com/

Print formatting by A Thirsty Mind Book Design
http://www.athirstymind.com/

PROLOGUE

She had waited for years, years of planning, of intense preparation. At last the time was here. Victory was just beyond her reach, hovering so close, so near to the fulfillment of her plans, that sometimes she wanted to scream in frustration because no matter how close it was, she still didn't quite have it in her grasp.

How could *any* vampire be against her? She didn't understand that. Vampires were superior to humans in every way; it was logical that they be in control, that humans serve their betters. It was also logical that she, the most powerful of her kind — save Luca Ambrus, damn him — be the one in control.

Marie insisted on being called Regina. *Regina,* Latin for *Queen;* it had a nice ring to it. Her ego was huge, but ego wasn't the sole reason for the sobriquet. Small details produced huge results. Forcing people to call her queen, to acknowledge her as such, was the first step in becoming so. As they became more familiar with the idea, they also became more malleable to her rule. She had been born to rule, and everything she did led to ensuring her absolute rule was recognized.

She had confirmation from one of her soldiers that the sanctuary spell had been broken, but she was angry and she was hungry, and she wanted to see — to *experience* — the result of her hard work for herself. The battle in the Potomac mansion that had been her headquarters for many years had drained and infuriated her, but she was still powerful.

Until tonight, she had never seriously considered that her plans wouldn't be executed without flaw, but now with some bitterness she saw that her self-confidence had been a critical error. Her worst mistake was that she'd put too much faith in the loyalty and competence of others. She had allowed herself to trust, because she'd thought she knew her people. She'd assumed that most vampires would follow her, that they would *want* to subjugate the humans.

She'd been wrong. So many had failed her, had been afraid. Vampires, afraid! She was appalled on so many levels, and for so many reasons.

The sanctuary spell — the old curse that kept vampires from entering a home uninvited — had been broken, but she hadn't been able to stop the influx of Immortal Warriors. Worse, she had lost her headquarters and her right hand man.

Lost, hell. That bastard had *run* to the other side. But Sorin would pay, sooner rather than later. She would make him her special target; the one she would most enjoy killing.

WARRIOR RISING | 5

She'd learned a painful but important lesson. From now on, she would rely on no one. She would not allow anyone to share her rule. Her power was beyond compare. As a rare blood born, a child conceived and born to two vampire parents, she possessed gifts most others only dreamed of. She would hide those gifts away no more.

She tore her thoughts from the ugly taste of failure and betrayal, because in the main quest she hadn't failed at all: she had forced the witch to break the sanctuary spell. For her personal test of the witch's success, she chose a two-story house along a tree-lined street well away from the Potomac mansion where the initial battle had taken place. The Virginia neighborhood not far from Washington D.C. was modestly prosperous, the houses far enough apart that it was unlikely screams would be heard. And if they were heard, she wouldn't care. Nothing could stop her now.

Marie strode up the sidewalk, past well-manicured bushes and a low growing red flower that looked black in the moonlight, and stood for a moment looking at the dark green door that in the past had been all a human needed to keep her out. She lifted her hand to knock, then paused. Instead of knocking, she kicked the green door in. A savage thrill surged through her as she stepped, uninvited, inside the house. For a moment she was dizzy from the sheer ecstasy of success, of power. Three loyal vampires came in behind her. They moved so quickly, drawn up the stairs by the scent of human flesh, that the residents of the house had no chance to call for help, by phone or otherwise.

Marie moved up the stairs more slowly, savoring every moment. Her pace was regal, the long train of her fine but bloodied gown trailing the stairs behind her. Much of that blood belonged to Chloe Fallon, Luca's pet, the pet she had taken from him with a sharp knife and great pleasure.

There wouldn't be any more hiding away who and what she truly was. She would make no further effort to blend in to these jarring, modern times. When she was acknowledged queen by vampires and humans both she would wear fine gowns and jewels. Her home would be luxuriously furnished. She would surround herself with loyal servants and soldiers and subjects, and if they were not loyal enough they would suffer and die.

Forget about the Council; she wouldn't be returning to Council headquarters, the Georgetown home where her plans for this war had begun and grown. The remaining Council members would be wise to decamp. The Council headquarters would be the first location given away. She had no doubt that the humans would win *some* of the battles, simply because there were so many of them, so these first days would be perilous.

But even though tonight hadn't gone as planned, nothing of importance had changed. Her plan was simple enough: Take D.C., and from there, take this country. The world would follow.

Not that vampires all over the world weren't enjoying her gift tonight. There was no more haven for humans, no place for them to hide.

She entered the master bedroom. In the big bed situated against the far wall were two bedraggled humans, both elderly and frightened. Each was held in place by one of Marie's soldiers, while the third soldier busied himself pacing, waiting for one of them to attempt to fight so he'd have an excuse to strike. The humans had no way of knowing exactly what kind of invader they faced. How could they? As far as these ignorant humans knew, vampires were legend, not real. They would soon learn differently.

The woman's gray hair stuck out to one side in a rather comical way. Her husband wore wrinkled striped pajamas and had no hair at all.

Marie smiled, but didn't show her fangs. "What are your names?" she asked politely.

The woman opened her mouth, but no words formed. She croaked, then choked on her unspoken response. Fear had stolen her tongue. The man cleared his throat and said, "Honeycutt. John and Cynthia Honeycutt."

Marie walked closer. She realized her movements were unnaturally smooth and silent and might alarm the couple in the bed, but she didn't care. She would never have to care about such things again.

"I'll open the safe for you," John offered, his voice shaking with age and with fear. "There's no reason for anyone here to be hurt. We don't have much, but you're welcome to it. Just... take what you want and go."

She smiled. Now that she knew there *was* a safe, she didn't need him to open it. Access would be easy enough, and additional wealth was always welcome.

Marie glanced at one of her soldiers; at the moment she couldn't remember his name, and didn't care. "Drain them," she said calmly, and then she watched as her soldiers did as she commanded. They made surprisingly little mess as they drank their fill. The Honeycutts died without much fuss, too old and weak to put up a good fight.

Once the previous owners of her new house were disposed of, Marie turned to her soldiers and commanded, "Bring me a man. Someone young, and pretty. And clothes." She wiped two fingers at a spot of blood on her left sleeve. The blood didn't bother her; the scent of Chloe Fallon's death still gave her a silent little thrill. But her gown was sticky, and she had to present a regal appearance.

Her soldiers left to do as she had ordered. While they were gone, Marie took a few minutes to explore the house. It wasn't a castle, but it would do for now. She located a comfortable red velvet wing chair in the formal living room, and sat, spreading her bloody gown around her. In the silence of the house her thoughts rapidly returned to the night's events and the anger she'd been holding at bay surged forward.

It was bad enough that she hadn't been able to convince Luca to join her, but for Sorin to betray her, for her right hand man to turn on her... it was unthinkable. How *could* he? Of all the vampires she'd chosen to fight with her, he was the one she'd trusted most. Sorin had always seen first to his own self-interest, and it was clearly in the best interest of every vampire to be able to feed at will, to have free access to the human sanctuaries. But he'd turned on her, had chosen to ally himself with Luca. She would make him pay, and pay dearly, so all who saw would understand what became of those who betrayed her.

When the soldier returned with a suitably pretty young man she rose to her feet and smiled at her obedient child, and at the terrified boy who couldn't be much more than twenty. He wore blue jeans and ridiculously brightly colored tennis shoes. His t-shirt, too large and badly wrinkled, bore the logo for a band she had never heard of. But his face was handsome, in a clueless sort of way, and his blond hair was well styled. He hadn't come from his bed, he'd been out at this late hour. Drugs or alcohol or both might account for part of the dullness in his eyes. The rest, the rest was fear.

She showed him her fangs, and before she could touch the pretty boy, he fainted.

He would awaken soon enough, and she would

soothe him. She would make more of her own soldiers, to add to those who already followed her. A soldier of her own making would never turn on her, would never betray her.

The boy regained consciousness, swimming back to reality. He looked around, his eyes wide with fear and confusion. As soon as his eyes reached her she smiled, without displaying her fangs this time, and the young man relaxed. She caught his gaze with hers and delved deeply into his brain, seizing control. "Come here, pretty."

He did.

CHAPTER ONE

Chaos ruled. He should be thrilled.

Sorin paced the cellar hallway where the night before an epic battle had taken place. An itch danced up his spine, the same itch he always got when everything was about to go to shit around him. What the hell was he doing here? It wasn't his war, though for a time he'd believed it was. He should go — *now*. He should get out of here and let the other idiots fight the battles still to come. His mouth twisted wryly as he realized he'd just called himself an idiot, but if the shoe fit... yeah, he needed to leave. He wasn't necessary for this war.

Proof of that was in the number of Immortal Warriors who were now roaming the mansion along with Luca, his newly turned woman, and a handful — a very small handful — of vampires who didn't want what Marie wanted: complete rule over the human world.

There had been a time when he'd been right there with her. He was older, stronger, better than any human. Why should he hide? There was no logic in the inferior race — humans — being the ones in charge and making the rules. He didn't deal well with rules, never had. Centuries of hiding who and what he was had shredded his patience. He brooded over the recent decisions he'd made, wondering what the hell had come over him.

Nevada, the little red-haired witch, had to have cast a spell on him. Long before she'd touched his face and instructed him to remember, she'd ruined him. Otherwise why would he have spared Phillip Stargel, the child conduit? So what if he was a child with Down syndrome? He was still a conduit, and Sorin should have taken care of business. But he hadn't. If there was no spell, why else would he have abandoned the cause and fought alongside that damn Luca Ambrus?

Moreover, why hadn't he killed Nevada when he'd been ordered to do so?

A witch's spell explained it all. But — damn it! He couldn't use that excuse. He wanted to, but he couldn't. He'd grown fond of Nevada long before she'd developed her witch skills to the point where she could cast even a simple spell. Her delicate scent reminded him of his mortal daughter, dead hundreds of years ago, but his memory of her smell came roaring back when he was around Nevada.

Maybe Nevada had hidden her skill for a long time, stalling them when she could have removed the sanctuary spell weeks, months ago, before the Warriors could come through in sufficient numbers to put up a good fight. He should confront her. But not now. Nevada had a difficult job ahead of her and she needed to focus her considerable talents on reinstating the sanctuary spell.

Those were words he had never thought would pass through his brain. He'd cursed that spell for hundreds of years, and he should rejoice that it had fallen. Without it, he could go into any human home at any time and feed whenever he was hungry. He wouldn't have to scheme and hide and wipe away evidence of his existence. At the moment, though, he felt no joy. Perhaps, after all these years, he was going soft.

No fucking way.

"You should stop that senseless pacing and save some of your energy for fighting your queen."

He turned and gave the Warrior — Indikaiya — a narrow-eyed look. Now, there was a woman. Tall, strong, a face like an ancient queen, with a thick blond braid that was long enough to bounce against her very curvy ass. What was the saying? *They don't make them like that anymore.* No, indeed they didn't.

He had the feeling she was keeping watch on him, because he couldn't imagine she enjoyed his company. She was sitting on the floor with her back against the wall, slowly running a cloth up and down the gleaming blade of her sword. Indikaiya's voice was both soft and hard, the voice of a woman who would do what she had to do, regardless, who would take on any adversary if she deemed the fight worth it. She didn't trust him and he returned the sentiment. She'd as soon kill him as look at him, and only the twisted circumstances had landed them on the same side. At least for now. It remained to be seen if the uneasy alliance of vampires and Warriors would hold.

He flashed what would have been a charming smile if he hadn't extended his fangs. "She isn't my queen."

"Any longer," Indikaiya added, verbally jabbing at him. "A day ago, she was."

"A day ago she *thought* she was. Now she knows differently." Maybe he'd have stayed with the rebellion, but the odds were he'd have walked away. Marie's ego was hard to take for any length of time, and when she'd needlessly killed Jonas, that had pretty much done it for him. He didn't suffer fools gladly, and that had been a foolish act. Not only that, he didn't like to lose.

The war wouldn't be an easy one, but now that the Warriors had joined with Luca and the humans, his instinct was that they would tip the balance of fate against Marie. Marie was an incredibly powerful vampire, a blood born like Luca, but though she had studied warfare and strategy, she hadn't been steeped in battle for centuries the way the Warriors had been. Or Luca, for that matter. The vampires following her rightly feared her, and some of them were powerful in their own right, but again, were they as experienced as the Warriors? He didn't think so.

Perhaps he should be noble enough to be true to

his chosen side, to truly believe in what he was fighting for, but nobility was a fine sentiment for people who had the luxury of safety and stability. Since he'd been turned vampire, he'd had to fight for his existence, and nobility took a back seat to survival. To survive, he'd had to become powerful in his own right, to look at the world with clear, pitiless vision and make his decisions based on what was best for *him.*

And yet here he was.

"You had your share of responsibility in bringing about this war," Indikaiya said, her tone cool and even.

He studied her, not rising to her bait. She had — all of them had — been drenched in blood from the battles that had been fought in this house. At least he'd had his own clothes here to change into, and he'd loaned Indikaiya one of his shirts on a devilish impulse, because he knew she wouldn't take even a handkerchief from him, had she any other choice. She was also wearing a pair of poor Jonas's trousers. Neither shirt nor pants fit her well, but she didn't seem to mind.

Why should she? Indikaiya was a Warrior. She could be dressed head to toe in *haute couture* and she would still look other-worldly. It was her bearing, the feral beauty of her strong-boned, sculpted face, the weapons she wore or carried or wielded that marked her as *more.*

Much as he wanted to, he couldn't argue with

her. He'd followed Marie for far too long. He had been a part of bringing her and her rebellion to this point.

Sorin had killed conduits to stop them from bringing in their Warriors. He'd kidnapped Nevada, and he had taken her family as well, in order to force her to cooperate. No, he couldn't plead innocence. He *had* followed Marie, even when he had his doubts about her decisions.

He shrugged and changed the subject. "Tell me about this place you come from. This... other world."

She gave him another of those cool, scornful, regal looks that told him without words exactly what she thought of him. A finely shaped eyebrow twitched and rose. "Why?" she asked. "It is a place for heroes. You will never see it."

He winked at her, hoping he could annoy her out of her coolness. "I'll probably never see Disneyland either, but I don't mind hearing from someone who's taken a spin in the Teacups."

Her expression was one of puzzlement. Of course it was; he might as well have been speaking a foreign language. Indikaiya wasn't of this time. Even in borrowed clothes, instead of the short leather shift she'd been wearing when she'd crossed the plane into this world, she was different. She continued to wear two daggers strapped to her waist, and sensible short boots that had seen better days. Jonas's boots. Her face was free of makeup, but why would a Warrior worry about something like that? Probably she'd never worn it, even in her earthly life. Not that she needed any, not with that bone structure. Didn't Warriors watch this world, always alert for danger? If she had, she hadn't paid any attention to the current slang or modern culture.

He could relate. Now and then he caught himself slipping into phrasing from long ago times, manners from another century. It was the price of living so long, a price he had never minded paying.

"Humor me," he said, taking a step closer to her.

Her eyes flashed a warning, telling him to give her room. Gracefully, effortlessly, she rose to her feet with that sword in her hand, ready for an attack.

"Why should I?" If she could, would she have stepped back to maintain the space between them? He didn't think so. Warriors didn't retreat. The only reason she would step away would be to get enough room to swing the sword.

"I'm curious." He was curious about a lot of things, and he was vaguely surprised to find one of those things was... her. He'd never met a female Warrior before. Truth to tell, he'd always tried to avoid the bastards. Warrior or not, she wasn't like any woman he had ever known before, and he'd known a lot of women, both biblically and otherwise.

"Satisfy your curiosity some other way. We should go to the meeting now."

Ah yes, the meeting, where the uneasy alliance of vampires, Warriors, and humans tried to form some sort of organized resistance to Marie's savage attacks.

"Luca can run the meeting. I don't give a shit." He said it flatly, because he was still so royally pissed at himself, at Marie, at Nevada, at this whole damn rat's nest.

Her voice sharp with impatience, she said, "So you don't care about the red-haired witch? Killing her would be the obvious way to reinstate the sanctuary spell, as she so foolishly tied the spell to her heartbeat. Some of the others, both Warrior and human, think that sacrificing her would be acceptable, as it would instantly reinstate the sanctuary spell and prevent countless vampires from entering human homes. Those of us who are against the plan are in the minority. I thought you might want to have a say in the matter."

"Why should I care?"

"I don't know, but obviously you do." Her gaze was shrewd; she'd noticed the protectiveness he felt toward Nevada, though he'd tried hard not to betray it.

Because it's my fault she's here, he thought savagely. Nevada's scent reminded him of his daughter, Diera. Damn her, Nevada had made him remember what it was like to be human. She made him remember what it was like to live and love, to be loved. She'd slipped into his head and he couldn't shake out what she'd planted there.

Shit. Now he had to argue for Nevada's life. The irony was unmistakable. He'd killed so many humans over the years, but now he had to protect her. Why her? Why now?

"What if we kill Nevada, and find out what she said about the breaking of the spell being tied to her heartbeat is bullshit?" he snapped. "What if she thinks that's the way it works but she's wrong? Without a powerful witch to recast the spell, we're screwed."

"Screwed?"

"Fucked. Up a creek without a paddle. In a world of —"

"I understand," she interrupted tersely. "That is a valid argument. You should present it to the others."

"You can argue for her."

"No." Perhaps that twitch at the corner of her mouth was a smile, but surely not. "I do not have your charming way with words."

Frustration gnawed at him. He stalked toward the Warrior, moved in dangerously close. She was tall for a woman, especially for a woman of her time, whenever that had been. If he went by the clothes she'd been wearing when she'd arrived, it had been a very long time since Indikaiya had walked this earth as a human. Because he wanted her to be as annoyed as he was, he kept prodding. "Where are you from? *When* are you from?"

She didn't back away. "Save the witch and perhaps I will tell you."

He leaned down slightly, sniffed her throat. She stiffened at his nearness, at the inherent threat of his action, but again she stood her ground. Her scent was warm and female, and she smelled human enough, though that was open to question. She'd been human once, as had he. He knew what he was, but he wasn't completely certain exactly how the Warriors would be categorized. Superhuman? Paranormal? Or just humans from another plane? They were puzzling. He inhaled again, because human or not, woman was woman and he liked the smell. "Why do you care if I save Nevada?" he murmured.

Narrow-eyed, she took her own investigatory sniff. He was so taken aback he almost laughed. Damn if he didn't like that he couldn't intimidate her. He also liked how close they were standing, so close that with each inhale his chest almost touched the tips of her breasts. For a second, just a second, temptation raced through him, the temptation to touch her, to feel her bare skin under his hands.

He jerked back to attention when she said, her voice low, "The world does not hold enough strong women. I would hate to see one so powerful snuffed out on the mere chance that it might save us a bit of trouble."

"Well, that's interesting," he said. "You like a bit of trouble, don't you?"

Her mouth quirked. "On occasion."

That he could relate to. He smiled. "So do I."

She tipped her head back and looked him in the eye. The movement sent the thick blond braid of her hair swinging down her back, brushing back and forth across her ass. She had a powerful gaze, bright and intelligent and forceful. Her eyes were blue, but not a blue like his own. There were swirls of green in those deep depths, as well as an unexpected spark of gold. "Your flirtatious manner is a waste of time, vampire. You can't charm me into your bed."

"I didn't ask."

"You did not have to. Your manner speaks for you. I admit, you are handsome and strong. I suspect you are talented in sexual ways, and I have been a long while without a man. But — no." For a second her gaze turned inward, as if she was looking back across the endless years with longing and... grief? Then her body shifted as if she couldn't stand still, as if thinking about the possibility of having sex with him had caused an itch down her spine similar to the one he was feeling.

He was too experienced to miss the signal, as unexpected as it was. His entire body sprang to attention. "So, why not?"

Impatiently she said, "You're a vampire. You have chosen to fight on the side of right, for now, but that does not change who, *what*, you are."

Sorin didn't say a word. He caught Indikaiya's

gaze and held it. Neither of them looked away, neither spoke. There were many beautiful and willing women in the world. Human and vampire, tall and short, voluptuous and thin, sweet and not so sweet. Each woman was special in her own way.

At the moment, no other appealed as this one did.

"Never," she whispered, even though he hadn't spoken. Perhaps his expression said more than mere words.

She turned and walked away from him. "Come to the meeting or do not. I will try to argue for your witch, if I can."

Sorin watched her walk away, then impatiently swore under his breath and followed her. Leaving would be easier, it would be more in keeping with his character, but he wasn't going to abandon this war he'd helped to set into motion. And if he wasn't going to leave, he damn well needed to be in on the decision-making.

It had been well more than two hundred years since one of her descendants — a conduit like Chloe Fallon — had called her into the world to fight. Indikaiya had been a rebel, of sorts, during the American Revolution. She had fought in a number of skirmishes, rather than the more well-known battles, but at the call of a man in her bloodline she had played her part in securing the victory for the revolutionaries. Many of her fellow Warriors had been on this earth since then, in war, in minor battles. She, however, had not been needed or called.

Never before had so many Warriors been summoned to the same fight. It was difficult, in an age where no one knew of their existence, to find a way in, to be invited into the world to do battle for the human race. In the days when the Immortal Warriors were not only known but revered, it had been much simpler to be called. That time had been gone a long time now. As years passed, the Warriors became more myth than fact, and then… they had disappeared from memory entirely, and had not even existed in tales. The little witch so many now wanted to kill had cast the spell that made the unprecedented influx possible.

Indikaiya would enjoy fighting alongside her fellow Warriors, and she would enjoy fighting alongside the humans who had been called here. Inevitably some of them would find themselves in her world, the world of Warriors who were dedicated to protecting humankind, when they died. Most people who died in battle truly died, went to earth, but some special ones instead crossed the plane to abide with the Warriors, immortal until they chose not to be, willing to come to the aid of humans who were fighting for the right causes, sometimes for humanity itself. She would gladly fight back to back with any of them without a second thought.

She did have second thoughts about fighting alongside vampires, no matter how good they were in battle. Luca Ambrus was an extraordinary fighter, true, but he was a blood born vampire and, even worse, he had turned her descendant Chloe into a vampire, too. The only thing that had saved him from her sword was that being turned had been Chloe's choice, and his act had saved her life.

It stung that her blood descendent, her conduit, had been turned into one of them. It had been that or death, for Chloe and the child growing inside her. Indikaiya couldn't kill Luca and, in truth, at this time she could kill none of the vampires who were fighting with them. They needed every sword — every fang — at their disposal.

Chloe's pregnancy was disturbing. Part of Indikaiya was appalled that one of her descendants was half vampire, but another part was worried sick that the child wouldn't survive. Human/vampire pregnancies were extremely rare, all but unheard of. She could not imagine that the results would be good for either mother or baby.

She wanted Chloe to live; to see the end of such an unquenchable spirit would be devastating. But there was no precedent for Chloe's circumstances, so Indikaiya had no idea what to expect. Chloe was a conduit. Luca was a rare blood born. With both mother and father being so different, would that change the outcome for this pregnancy?

If either Chloe or Luca realized that she was carrying his baby, neither had made it known, but the pregnancy was so new and they'd been so embroiled in one crisis after another that she doubted either had had the opportunity to even think of the possibility. Luca would soon notice, though, because Chloe's scent would be different... perhaps. Now that she was a vampire, perhaps not. Indikaiya had no intention of telling them, because words spoken aloud could always be overheard. They would have good reason to keep the news to themselves for as long as possible. There were those who would see the child as an abomination, an unnatural thing who should not be allowed to live. The unknown was always frightening, and the child... the child was most definitely unknown. If the babe survived to see the world, would she come into it human or vampire? Would she be strong or weak? Would she be able to walk in the sun? Would she need blood or milk to thrive? That — and more — remained unknown.

Indikaiya entered the room where the meeting would soon begin, and instinctively moved close to Chloe's side. As a newly made vampire, Chloe hadn't been able to resist the overpowering urge to sleep while the sun was up, even though she exhibited unusual control for one so young, but now that night had fallen again she was wide awake and ready to take on the world. Her cheeks were pink with healthy color; perhaps Luca had fed her with his own potent blood, giving her strength. Indikaiya felt a surge of unwelcome gratitude for the vampire, because without him Chloe would be dead.

The room was crowded with vampires and humans and Warriors, the unusual alliance uneasy but necessary. As they were settling down, the door opened once again and Sorin came in. Indikaiya didn't want to notice his presence, but she couldn't help it. She knew he was in the room, was aware of his location even when she wasn't looking at him. There was an electricity about him, the force of his personality blasting out in all directions.

Sorin, along with Rurik and the human Jimmy, argued for the witch's life. Why? A creature such as he cared for no one but himself. Did he love Nevada? It seemed ludicrous that a vampire could love a human, but Luca had fallen in love with Chloe so it was not impossible. Did Sorin lie with his redhead? Did she offer him comfort and release? That made more sense than love. Perhaps lust was why he argued so passionately for the witch's life.

No, Indikaiya decided when the witch entered the room uninvited and unwanted. Sorin did not look at Nevada the way he had looked at her, just moments ago. He cared for the girl, he was protective of her, but his caring was not of a sexual nature.

Rurik, on the other hand...

Indikaiya thought the young woman might plead for her own life. She did not. In fact, she looked ready to accept her fate, no matter what it might be. She possessed bravery of a different sort, a bravery that should be respected.

The petite redhead held her head high. There were dark circles under her eyes, and she was wearing the same clothes from last night. She had not rested, that much was clear. "I have been working on recasting the sanctuary spell. I can do it, I know I can, but it will take time. A few days, at least." She took a deep breath. "I want to live, I will not lie about that, but if my death is what's best…"

"No," Sorin said, and with that he placed himself in front of her. As they had last night, Rurik and Jimmy did the same.

It was Rurik who put forth, "If we murder this girl to make our battle easier, if we sacrifice her, then we do not deserve to be called Warriors."

Many agreed with him. Indikaiya caught a glimpse of the witch, as Jimmy swayed to the side. The human was tired, so it was only natural that he would be weakened. That movement revealed that the witch was relieved. She was willing to sacrifice her life, but she wanted to live, as she had said.

Sorin turned, looked down, and whispered to the girl. She scampered off, back to her chamber to work on the spell that would save countless humans.

And if she could not recast that spell?

The attitudes of many in this room would change, if that were the case. How many could be sacrificed in order to spare the life of one witch?

As talk turned to plans of strategy and of leaving this place, Sorin walked across the room to join Luca, Chloe, and their vampire friends. She had not known vampires were capable of friendship. She looked to Luca. Or of love.

That knowledge was a complication she could do without.

Nevada was so tired, she was literally seeing double. Four books on the worktable instead of two. Two piles of small, multi-colored stones instead of one. She gripped the edge of the table to ground herself.

It had been almost two days since she'd murdered countless innocent people. The ancient spell she'd broken had once given humans a safe haven, a place to hide even on the darkest night. The sanctuary spell. The protection at the doorway of a human's home. She was the one who'd broken it, who made it fall. She was to blame...

She wasn't surprised when the familiar knock sounded at the door of her room, which in the past few years had been prison, workshop, and — on occasion — home. Rurik's knock was both gentle and strong. Like him.

"Come in," she said softly, knowing he would hear her even if she whispered.

Rurik opened the door and stepped into her room. For a large man, he was eerily silent in his movements. A Warrior thing, she imagined. Some of the Warriors had adopted modern clothing since coming into this world, but not Rurik. His plain shirt looked like it was made of coarsely woven dark linen. The pants were much the same. And the sword that hung at his side was massive and extremely sharp.

"What do you want?" she asked.

"I wanted to see you. That is all." His accent — Russian or Russian-like, since she didn't know exactly where, or when, he had come from — was both harsh and harmonious. "I will be outside your door, should you need anything. Anything at all."

Unlike most of the men Nevada had known in her lifetime, Rurik was simple and straightforward. No games, no riddles. He liked her; he had made that clear from the moment he'd laid eyes on her. She barely knew him, and yet he'd stood up to his own in order to protect her.

"I should've been stronger," she said. "I should've told Sorin to go fuck himself when he kidnapped me and put me to work on breaking the spell. I should've stood up to him and given him the finger. Yeah, he would've killed me, probably. Likely, anyway. Okay, he definitely would've killed me." Six foot plus, no telling how old though he'd always look thirty-ish, all muscle and fangs, long blond hair like some kind of Viking, he was one scary dude. He was fond of black leather and massive swords Nevada couldn't lift with both hands. Even now, when he was on the right side... scary.

"He is on our side now," Rurik said. How could he stay so calm?

Our side was the only thing that gave Nevada real hope. This mansion which had once been quiet as a tomb was now teeming with, well, people, for lack of a better word. People of all sorts. Humans who knew what was going on and wanted to stop it as well as vampires who liked the status quo and didn't want to see that sick bitch Regina take over the world. Marie, her true name was, not Regina. She looked like a pretty teenage girl, but she was an ancient sociopath with fangs, and somehow she'd decided she was supposed to take over the world. D.C., at least. D.C. to start.

And then there were the Warriors. *Immortal* Warriors, like Rurik. They looked human, but then so did the vampires, most of the time. Their existence had been as much of a shock to Nevada as the truth about vamps. When a room was full of these Warriors, it was like a history book exploded and the pages came to life. From every age, from every country, they'd been called to battle. The way Nevada understood it they had once been human, but they'd all been soldiers, fighters, protectors. After death, they waited in another world, an alternate universe of some kind. They waited to be called by blood descendants. Conduits, those descendants were called. The Warriors waited for a fight like this one. They'd been here before for smaller battles. Some of them, anyway. Rurik seemed to know a lot about this world. Indie — which is what most of the humans called Indikaiya — seemed much more *not* of this world. She was older than Sorin, probably. Hard to tell, since she didn't talk much.

In so many ways, the Warriors were more of a mystery than the vamps.

"You look very tired," Rurik said. "Have you been traveling?"

"Traveling?" It took a moment, but Nevada soon realized what he was asking. "Oh, no. Remote viewing takes too much energy, and I need every ounce I've got to get this spell fixed." She'd used the newly found gift to check on her family when they'd been held in the large, dungeon-like basement of this mansion. Rurik had first seen her that way. Humans and vamps couldn't see her when she traveled, but Warriors were another matter. Something about traveling between worlds.

She did not want to talk about herself. It was easy enough to change the subject.

"I've heard about people who don't understand how they survived a particularly hairy situation. Like, maybe they were invisible to their enemies, or they thought they were going to be hit by a bus or a bullet and then they weren't. Was that you?"

Rurik raised a hand to his chest. "Me?"

"Well, Warriors. Do you... pop in often?"

"Sometimes. Sometimes not." There was that smile again. It was so heartbreakingly *real.* "I would gladly return to this world to end your enemies."

Nevada shook her head. Was this his way of flirting with her? "Why? Why are you being nice to me? I'm such a colossal screwup!"

"No. You are a fighter, as we all are. You are a brave and noble woman."

Brave? Noble? Something inside Nevada snapped, and she could see clearly once again. "I'm a wimp. The vampires threatened my family, they held me hostage, they forced me to cancel the sanctuary spell. And I did it. I should've let them kill me and my family. I should've sacrificed us all to save the world." The words spilled out. "I didn't. Sacrifice sounds noble, in theory. You know what? It's damn hard. Besides, maybe I have the right to sacrifice my own life, but my parents? My brother and my sister? I don't see nobility there, not at all."

"You did what you could. You were willing to die..."

"I still am," she whispered.

Rurik's expression was suddenly both angry and sad. Even he knew there might be no other choice. "They will have to come through me," he said, his words a solemn promise.

The spell she'd cast to end the sanctuary spell

was connected to her heartbeat. She'd been so certain she would die as soon as it was done! With her family away from this prison, and the original spell once more in place, they would be safe. Everyone would be safe.

But they hadn't killed her, even though Regina, self-proclaimed queen, had ordered Sorin to do it. Nevada had made Sorin remember his past, his time as a human, and he'd let her live.

She should've left well enough alone, but it was too late for should'ves and might'ves.

"Do you need anything of me?" Rurik asked.

She shook her head, then turned to business. "I'm making progress on the new spell." She wanted someone to know. Anyone. "I'm still days away from finishing it but... but..." Her voice broke, a little. "I have to fix this! I unleashed hell on the world, and even if I can reinstate the original spell or come up with an entirely new one, nothing will be the same again. Nothing. Too many people know now. Too many people have seen."

Rurik seemed unconcerned. "They will forget."

"How?" Her hands fisted. She wished she could forget!

"Dark days come and they go. Life continues on, and people believe what they wish to believe."

"You make it sound so simple. Everything has changed. Everything! You will eventually go back to wherever it is you came from, but for humans, for people like me, death and destruction is knocking on the door." That was not entirely true. Thanks to her, death no longer needed to knock.

Rurik knew that as well as anyone.

"As I said, if you need anything I will be near." He gave her a kind of formal and old fashioned bow, a gesture so out of place, so unnecessary, that she laughed. It wasn't a pleasant laugh, but was more of a short-lived hysterical cackle.

Rurik left the room, closing the door behind him. In a weird way his visit had revived her. She felt a rush of energy, and was no longer seeing double. Anger and desperation were as good as caffeine, maybe.

Nevada turned her mind to her work. Nothing else mattered, not even a hunky man from another world, a protector with a Russian accent and a killer smile. A man who winked at her in the midst of chaos.

She could do this. She figured vamps didn't have a newsletter or a phone tree, so the news that they could now enter any home uninvited couldn't have spread far and wide. Not yet. It would. Soon. In her head she could see a map of the country, of the *world*, where reports of violent deaths grew and grew and spread outward like something out of a movie about a world-ending epidemic. The movies had it wrong. The world wouldn't end thanks to a virus or a nuclear bomb. Humanity didn't need to worry about an alien invasion. Life as humans knew it would end when the vampires took over, the way some of them had wanted to do for a very long time. If they were to win, they'd probably keep some people alive, enough to produce blood for feeding, and be servants and produce the luxuries that they enjoyed. But most would die.

Nevada wondered how many people would ever know that this all happened because a naive college girl who didn't realize she was a witch by blood was willing to sacrifice the world in order to save her family. A family now no more safe than anyone else, so it had been a stupid thing to do. She wondered where her family was, if they were safe. Sorin said he'd find them, but even though he'd spared her she still didn't trust him. She didn't trust anyone, not entirely.

Nevada almost lovingly touched the two books on her worktable, readying to dive back in, ready to try to make sense of words that all too often meant nothing to her. She whispered to herself, "If I were like Indie, we wouldn't be in this predicament. If I was strong and determined and knew how to carry a sword like it was a part of me, Sorin never would've taken me in the first place, and the world would still be safe." But would it be, really? Vampires had been around for a very long time, and they hadn't been getting by on tomato juice and beer. No, humans had been their food source for hundreds — *thousands* — of years.

Nevada knew she needed to be as strong as Indie, in her own way. She had to find a way to reinstate the spell that gave humans a refuge. That alone wouldn't stop the sick bitch from trying to take over the world, but it would be a start.

She would allow herself a few more days to get it done. If she couldn't recast the spell, if she couldn't make things right, then she would have to die.

CHAPTER TWO

By day the vampires slept, or else huddled in the dark below stairs. Luca could withstand daylight better than most but Chloe could not, and the blood born never strayed far from his woman. There were only five vampires in their army, at least so far. That included Chloe, who was so new as to be worthless when it came to war. Warriors and humans spent the day above stairs, preparing for the battles that would soon come. Swords were sharpened; ammunition was stockpiled. Guns and rifles were cleaned and loaded. Indikaiya herself preferred the sword. It was the weapon she had fought with in her human life, the one that felt most natural in her hands. She was also quite talented with a bow and arrow, but she preferred steel. She could and would kill a lot of vampires with that sword when the time came. The time was near.

The Warriors didn't need as much sleep as the humans, though they did rest when their bodies demanded it. Indikaiya had grabbed a few hours of sleep in the late night and early morning hours. She preferred nighttime for that rest. Not because her body was set to sleep while it was dark, as the humans' were, but because that was when the vampires among them were most active. During the day, humans and Warriors had to be on guard, on the lookout for the more powerful vamps that were able to travel at any hour, those who could withstand some degree of sunlight as Luca could. Sorin? She could not be sure. So far he had not exposed himself to daylight, but that didn't mean he was incapable. But at least at night she could trust Luca and the rest to guard.

During the day, the humans among them took some delight in playing popular music on small devices. That music was unlike any Indikaiya had ever heard. Some of it was jarringly unpleasant, but on occasion someone would play a song that appealed to her. She found she was particularly fond of songs the youngest among them called "oldies." She'd asked Jimmy about a couple of the songs that most appealed to her. He had laughed at her and said it made sense that she liked Joan Jett and Aretha Franklin. They were powerful women. She wondered if she'd be in this world long enough to get herself one of those devices, then dismissed the silly idea. She was here to fight, not to enjoy herself.

She'd cleaned her leather shift and had gladly disposed of the shirt that smelled like the vampire Sorin. The boots, she kept. They were a little large, but they were also sturdy and more suited for battle than bare feet or the insubstantial sandals she'd been wearing when she'd been called in.

Indikaiya kept her distance from the vampires, as much as was possible. She did not wish to see her blood relative, Chloe, adjusting to her new body, her new vampiric demands. Sorin was simply irritating. Luca was disturbing in many ways. It was a particular annoyance that the humans kept forgetting him. Only the elder vampires and the Warriors — and Chloe, of course — remembered Luca when they turned away from him. She supposed that talent, if it could be called such, came in handy during ordinary times, when it might be convenient for a bloodsucker to be forgotten as soon as he was out of sight, but when one was planning a war it was damned inconvenient.

Exploring the second floor, Indikaiya found Rurik standing guard outside the witch's door. Warriors did not fight one another; it simply was not done. But she suspected Rurik would take on his own to protect the girl, if he had to. Rurik would be a fearsome adversary. He was as tall as the vampire Sorin, all muscle and sinew, a strong man who, like she and many others among them, preferred a blade to more modern weaponry. Rurik was not as handsome as Sorin, his smile was not so annoyingly charming.

Not that she should be comparing one man to another. Sorin did not even deserve a sliver of her attention, though he was a man — no, a vampire — who could definitely capture and hold a woman's attention in this or any age. Why was she thinking about him at all? Had he put a vampiric spell of one kind or another on her? As a Warrior who was not of this world, she should be immune to his trickery, as she was immune to Luca's.

"I need to see the witch," she said.

Rurik's eyes narrowed. "I will allow no one to do her harm."

"I give you my word, I will not harm her on this day." She would give no promises beyond this day, and he would not expect it of her.

He nodded, then knocked on the door and opened it slowly. "Her name is Nevada," he said in a lowered voice. "Nevada Sheldon. Not *the witch*."

Indikaiya had never had much time or any sympathy for witches, but she felt sympathy for this one as she stepped into the large bedchamber. The girl stood before a long table which was worn with age, and on that table massively thick, ancient books lay scattered about. Some were open, revealing brittle yellowed pages; others were closed, perhaps already discarded, perhaps yet to be explored. There were small piles of stones in a variety of sizes and colors, as well as vials of powders. Some dull, others disturbingly sparkling. Nevada's face was pale, her clothes misshapen, her red hair mussed.

Indikaiya had never cared much for pampering herself. Her clothing was chosen for comfort and freedom of movement. She wore her long pale hair in a braid because it was easiest. Nevada could do with a neat braid at this moment.

As if such matters were of any consequence.

"I need your assistance."

Nevada turned tired — no, desperate and exhausted — eyes on Indikaiya, and it was easy to see that the young girl was on the verge of surrender. The fear there was an indication that she wondered if the Warrior in her chamber had come to kill her.

"I'm trying, truly I am…"

Indikaiya stepped toward the table and the girl. "You need to turn your attentions elsewhere, for a time."

Nevada slammed a massive tome shut. Her expression was fearsome, for one so small, or would have been if the dust that rose up from the old book didn't make her sneeze. Twice.

"I can't afford to turn my attentions elsewhere," Nevada argued as she swiped at her nose. "I can't sleep, or shower, or eat…" Tears filled her eyes.

"You have been at this for three days," Indikaiya said.

"I know, I'm sorry… God help me, I'm almost there but I can't see the end. It's there… it's *right there!*" She swiped out a hand that knocked a few stones from the table. Those stones flew through the air, catching the light and glimmering.

"Have Rurik and Sorin and the human Jimmy seen you this way?" Indikaiya snapped.

"What way?" Nevada sighed and turned away, dipping down to gather the displaced stones from the floor.

"Never mind." Indikaiya opened the door and snapped at Rurik. "Soup and bread, quickly. Ale, if it is available." She slammed the door hard, and looked at Nevada. "Men of every age and species are fools. Have you clean clothes?"

"Yes." Nevada stood with the stones in her hand, glancing down and back, toward her bed and the closet beyond, searching for stones she might've missed. "I just don't have the time to worry about…" Her words, and her thoughts, faded away, as she spotted an errant stone and scrambled to collect it.

It was no wonder Nevada had not finished her task. Her brain could not possibly be functioning at anywhere near full capacity. "You will bathe, you will eat, and you will sleep," Indikaiya ordered in her most commanding voice.

Nevada carefully placed the retrieved stones on the table. "I can't…"

"You will do all of those things, and you will also turn your mind and powers to another problem."

Nevada's hands curled into fists and her mouth thinned before she snapped, "Dammit, Indie, I can't handle *this* problem! How do you expect me to take on another?"

"Indie?"

Nevada shrugged tiredly. "Sorry. It's what Jimmy and some of the others call you. I think they're afraid they can't pronounce your name correctly. I hope it's okay." She unclenched her fist and rearranged the stones on her worktable, taking a moment to make sure they were correctly positioned. Perhaps checking to make sure they were all there.

"I do not care." Indie was what Chloe had called her, as she'd tried to capture and hold onto the name Indikaiya. The shortened name would suffice, for the remainder of this journey into the world she fought for. A name was... unimportant, insignificant. Until it was time to be called by a conduit. Then a name — the correct name — took on greater meaning.

"The brain is a complicated and miraculous organ," Indikaiya said, getting back to business. "It is capable of doing many things at once. You have allowed a large portion of your brain to shut down, to all but quit working. Exhaustion and fear have taken their toll. Take care of yourself, think of other things, tap into other parts of your brain, and you may awaken what has been sleeping."

"What if the part of the brain I need is not just sleeping but is... gone."

"I refuse to believe that. You have much power inside you, Nevada. You must find and use it."

Soup and bread arrived, delivered to the second floor by a conduit who had decided to remain with this new army, then carried into this chamber by an overly protective Rurik. The ale — a can of light beer — was accompanied by two bottles of water. Nevada sat on the edge of her bed and ate. She drank all the water but left the beer sitting on the nearby night table. As she ate, the color in her face improved. Her eyes took on a sparkle that had been missing. Perhaps her brain engaged another gear. Fed, Nevada rose from her bed, collected clothing from the closet, and headed for the attached bath.

While Indikaiya paced the room, she studied the stones and vials with some interest, and peeked at the open books. She was well versed in many languages, but the writing in these books was unknown to her. She would never admit so aloud, but she was instinctively afraid of these magical books. Nevada had shown no evil tendencies, but magic could be light or dark, good or evil. These books in the wrong hands could wield great darkness.

In her lifetime, and in others she had glimpsed from the world of Warriors, magic had often been misused. Those who exercised it frequently turned to darkness, seduced by the promise of endless power. Only the strongest possessed the will to turn their backs on the lure of the dark. Was the red-haired witch that strong? So far, yes. If the day came that she was not, who would deal with her?

That was a question for another day.

Nevada showered and changed into denim pants and a t-shirt that was too large for her petite body. She exited the bathroom with pink cheeks and her hair wrapped in a towel she quickly whipped away. While she was combing the tangled strands of her wet hair, she asked, "What is this other task you have for me?"

Already, the girl looked better. Stronger. He voice was clearer. Indikaiya told her what she had in mind. Nevada nodded, and without hesitation grabbed a book from a stack on the floor near one end of the table, as if she knew instantly what information — what spell — would be needed. The book was a heavy one. When she placed it on the table, it landed there with a dull, ominous thud. For a few minutes Nevada studied one page and then another, then she closed the book and looked at Indikaiya with a new strength. "I'm exhausted. If I don't get some sleep I'll be worthless." With that she headed for her bed, pulled back the covers, and laid her head on a fat pillow. In seconds, she was asleep.

Indikaiya left the room hoping she would not have to take the young witch's life before this war was done.

Sorin slept, but not for long. His mind was restless. He knew his way around this mansion in a way none of the others did. He had lived and worked here for a very long time. As darkness fell, he slipped out of the house by way of Marie's secret passageway.

He really should tell the others about the hidden exit, but it would only remind them that he had recently been fighting for the other side. Besides, Marie would be an idiot to come back now, and while she was occasionally unstable, she wasn't an idiot. Luca and the Warriors were already talking about leaving this place, so… it was a secret he could keep, for now.

Again, he thought of leaving, of walking away from the coming battle. He had been on both sides of it, at one time or another. This war was, in many ways, of his own making. He had agreed with Marie's thinking that it was time for vampires to rule. He had embraced her vision of a world where vampires would no longer have to hide. He had kidnapped and killed. He had given more of himself to the planning of this war than he dared to admit to anyone.

He'd battled his own kind often enough, in years past. Not so long ago he'd stood toe to toe with Luca and had exchanged blows. If they hadn't been interrupted, one of them wouldn't be here today.

In any war, soldiers died. Sorin had smelled Melody, his vampire child — what was left of her — on the shotgun wielding Jimmy. He had not noted the faint odor until he'd stood close to the human, as they'd both protected Nevada. His first instinct had been to lash out, to take the life of the boy who had dared to end Melody, but fortunately for Jimmy the impulse had come and gone in a flash.

In truth, it had been Sorin who'd ended Melody. Long ago, entranced by her love of life, her exuberance, her beauty, he had thought to preserve her for an eternity. She had embraced her new life;

she had been a powerful vampire. She had been beautiful and high-spirited and incredibly bloodthirsty. She'd been a fine soldier, and she'd met a soldier's death.

This street was quiet. The mansion that had been Marie's headquarters and was now home base — though not for much longer — for a ragtag army of Warriors, humans, and vampires, was well lit and lively, but the houses all around had been abandoned. Even before the initial battle, neighbors had sensed a wrongness in their vicinity and had fled.

Most humans had better instincts than they gave themselves credit for. Lucky for him, and others of his kind, they ignored those instincts more often than not.

Humans and Warriors planned and waited, as others of their kind arrived. The fighting had not yet begun in earnest, but it would. Soon. For now they drew up battle plans and strategies, and were in the process of setting up headquarters all around, and even within, the city. They had to be able to strike from any location; they could not afford to gather all of their forces in one vulnerable house.

Sorin had never been patient enough for strategies. He'd been one for action, in his almost forgotten life as a human and since the change that had made him more than human.

If he found and eliminated Marie — Regina, the self-proclaimed queen of the kindred — the war would be a short one. Maybe he would even be called a hero. Ha. Unlikely that anyone would ever look at him as a hero.

On this dark night, he took flight. He wasn't capable of flying long distances, but he could soar in the air for a few moments at night, when his power was at its zenith.He loved the sensation of flying. The air in his face, the sensation of lightness... it was a sensual pleasure. To soar above, to look down on the world, that was freedom. Even if it didn't last... Freedom. From above, the city he knew so well looked almost normal. Almost. A handful of neighborhoods had gone entirely dark, while others were lit up as if the world had not changed. He supposed for those who were ignorant, it had not. Not yet. Even if Nevada managed to reinstate the sanctuary spell, the world had changed. There were some, led by Marie, who were no longer content to hide. They were no longer afraid of a Vampire Council that had been ineffective for many years.

He still believed that as a vampire he was better than humans, but he did not believe the human race should be eliminated. For one thing, they were a necessary food source. For another...

They were not without their charms. Some of them, anyway. He would admit, he had met humans who added nothing meaningful or beautiful to the world, but there were others who deserved to live. Who deserved to exist as more than a food supply.

Their lives were amazingly short, and yet for some, for many, there was so much joy and love in those short lives. So much wonder.

In his centuries as a vampire, Sorin had forgotten love. He had forgotten human joy. He had Nevada to thank — to curse — for the return of so many memories that had faded over time.

He touched down in the middle of a suburban street in a dark neighborhood. Not just dark, but pitch black, for anyone without a vampire's vision. A deep breath brought to him the stench of spilled blood. He listened, with his enhanced hearing, and noted a distinct absence of life. How many neighborhoods in the world were like this one tonight? Dark, blood-soaked, deserted.

New vampires were not particularly smart, normally, but they were strong. He heard the five that approached and then surrounded him long before he smelled or saw them. They were reckless, drunk on power, and hungry beyond belief. All young men, all fit and pretty. He would guess not a one of them was older than twenty. With a newborn's speed and hunger, it would not have taken the five of them a full hour to devastate this entire neighborhood.

"It's him," one of them whispered. "It has to be! He looks just like she said he would."

"Long blond hair and leather," one said in a louder voice. "Who else could it be?"

"If we take her his head, she'll be pleased with

us," another added. "So very pleased."

Yes, they were new. They did not yet know that if they took his head there would be nothing left of him but dust. It was not his job to educate them, but they were about to learn a valuable lesson. Their last. "My reputation precedes me, I see," Sorin whispered.

"What?" the dumbest among them responded.

"You know who I am," he said, speaking more loudly.

"The betrayer," one said as he came a step closer.

"Traitor," another said.

Sorin looked at one new vamp and then another. "Great. It looks like Marie is putting together a boy band."

"A what?" the dumbest one asked again.

"Sorry," Sorin said. "Before your time."

They swarmed, without a plan, without the kind of strategy Sorin had just been berating the Warriors for relying upon. They were newborn strong, but he was smarter. Older. He knew where and how to strike. A newborn with bleached blond spiked hair screamed as he attacked. Sorin thrust his hand into the kid's chest and ripped out his heart. There was a moment of surprise on a too-young face, and then there was only dust.

Two came at him at once, perhaps foolishly believing their numbers gave them an advantage. The boy with a close buzz cut lost his head, as Sorin ripped it from his body and used it — again, before it went to dust — to knock his companion to the ground. The baby vamp flew through the air and landed a good twenty feet away.

If they'd had time to develop any smarts at all, the other two would've run. They did not. But they did make an elementary attempt to learn from the mistakes of the others. They were more cautious, now. Not good. Even Sorin would have difficulty fighting against a baby vampire's wild strength. Only their lack of experience and their over-confidence would save him.

One of them knocked him to the ground, and the other tried to do what Sorin had done and take a heart. Sorin threw off one attacker and rolled away as the other's hand thrust into the asphalt where Sorin had been a split second before.

He rose to his feet, flew above them for a moment, then came down kicking. The one that had tried to take Sorin's heart lost his head first. As the other was asking, awed, "Dude, will I be able to fly?" Sorin took his heart. As he went to dust, Sorin answered.

"No."

That left one. The one remaining member of Marie's murderous boy band — the one Sorin had sent flying — stood several feet away. He'd taken a fighter's stance, but kept his distance, bouncing back and forth on the balls of his feet with nervous energy. "I'm hungry again." Great. It was the dumb one.

Sorin walked toward him. "Don't worry. That won't be a problem for long."

The kid — perhaps not as stupid as he'd appeared thus far — turned and ran. Fast. Sorin gave chase, and tackled the kid on the front lawn of a well-kept, modest two-story house.

The body of a plump middle-aged woman lay, dead and drained, just a few feet away.

"Where is she?" Sorin asked as he pressed the kid into the ground.

"Mother?"

Sorin cursed, low and in the almost forgotten language he had spoken as a human. Mother? Really? Council member, would-be queen, and now *mother*? "The one who calls herself Regina or Marie. Where is she?"

"I don't know," the kid whispered. "She found us in the park a couple of days ago. Maybe she's still there."

"What were you doing in the park?"

The new vamp giggled. "Smoking weed."

"And that's where *Mother* found you?"

"Yes. We are among the first, she said." The vamp smiled, showing his new, shiny fangs. "She's going to build an army of us."

"So, you don't know where she is, exactly?"

The kid shook his head, and as he did Sorin took his heart.

The fight had drained him, so as he left the scene Sorin did not fly. He walked. Taking long strides down the street of a dead neighborhood, he listened to the city sounds, or tried to.

If five newborn soldiers of Marie's so-called army could do this much damage in a single night, perhaps even a single *hour*, what would the next days and weeks bring? What would become of the world? Imperfect as it was, this world was his as much as it was any human's.

As he listened to the deep lifeless silence and then, in the far distance, faint, weak screams, he wondered if he — if anyone — could save it.

CHAPTER THREE

Carroll County, Georgia

Mike Harrelson sat in his favorite recliner with a shotgun in his lap. He faced the front door, vigilant to a point, but far from alert. He was sure that what he'd seen on TV was nonsense, but Ellen, his wife of more than thirty years, was scared senseless. It was the middle of the night, going on morning. They both should be sleeping, side by side in their comfortable king-size bed. Instead he was guarding the entrance to his home and Ellen slept on the couch behind him.

If there really were vampires, the way that wild-eyed man on the cable news said there were, then he imagined they were all in Washington. D.C. D.C., home of the bloodsuckers. Made sense to him.

He had dismissed the ridiculous report, figuring the violence in the nation's capital was thanks to some sort of terrorism. *Human* terrorism that had not yet been explained. Maybe a drug that caused mass hysteria, or some kind of movie special effects. Whatever it was, it had scared the bejesus out of his gullible wife.

Mike had grumbled a bit, but truth be told he'd

do anything for Ellen. She'd asked him to keep watch until dawn, so here he sat.

As a plumber, he made enough to pay his bills. This small house — three bedrooms, two bathrooms, a two-car garage — was paid for, and had been for five years. His house was on a big plot of land. It was well more than a mile, as the crow flies, to the nearest neighbor's house. Even if vampires were out there, why would they come here? What self-respecting vampire would bother with two aging folks in a small house smack dab in the middle of nowhere?

Nonsense. But he'd promised Ellen he'd keep watch until the sun came up, and he always kept his promises to her.

She wasn't as pretty as she'd once been, but then again, neither was he. He blamed their three kids, all grown and on their own now, for the gray hairs on his head. And for the wrinkles, added to his face by worry and by laughter. His youngest got most of the blame, and rightly so. None of them were bad kids, not even Steph, his youngest child and only daughter, but raising children wasn't easy. Yes, he blamed them for his gray hair, his wrinkles, and for his paunch.

Ellen had a few gray hairs of her own, but she took care of them, as women do. Maybe she had a few wrinkles, too, but not as many as he did. He seemed not to notice them on her, most days.

Now and then she got a bee in her bonnet about

one thing or another, and she just wouldn't let go.
Like the vampires. It was easier, usually, to just give
her what she wanted. That's what he was doing now,
shotgun in his lap in case monsters came calling,
and a can of beer on the table at his side.

He didn't hear anyone approaching. Not so
much as a whisper. Without warning, the front door
flew in and two people — no, not people, not really
— moved into the room so fast they were nothing
but a blur. One man, one woman, that was all he
could tell, they moved so fast. Mike stood up, too
fast and clumsy. His balance failed him. He gripped
his gun tightly as he fell back into his chair. He
bumped the table, and what was left of his beer
spilled. Ellen would be pissed...

Ellen was screaming. One of the people — no,
vampires, not *people*. One of the *vampires* — had
grabbed her by the hair and pulled her violently off
the couch.

Mike was not one to panic, but he panicked now.
Why had he thought a shotgun would be sufficient?
Two shots, that was all he had. He spun and fired at
the thing that held onto Ellen. The shot caught the
vampire, the male of the pair, in the shoulder. Like
it would've with a bear, the injury just made him
mad. The monster broke Ellen's neck and dropped
her to the floor, where she landed boneless as a rag
doll.

Mike thought it could get no worse when the
other vampire, the female, whispered in his ear.

"Daddy?"

He knew that voice; it was no trick. Mike turned slowly and looked his daughter in the eye. No, this was not his daughter, not anymore. The fangs, the weird glowing eyes they marked her as something else. Something unnatural. This was not hysteria of any kind, nor was it a special effects trick.

The angry male behind him was moving in, coming fast. Death was in the air; death had arrived. There was no time to think clearly, to take this nightmare in, though Mike did manage to say, "Love you, baby girl," before he pointed the shotgun at his daughter's heart and pulled the trigger.

Sword strapped to her side, matching daggers in sheaths at her waist, Indikaiya was ready to take part in one of the many patrols their army had decided to send out in the pre-dawn hours. Finally! A proper fight. She wondered if Sorin might be joining them, but he was nowhere to be seen. Knowing what she did of him, he'd probably deserted. Perhaps he'd even rejoined the vampires they were fighting. Just as well. She liked her battle lines drawn in stark black and white. The shades of gray in this one were troubling enough without Sorin in the mix.

Could she kill him if they met in battle?

Without a second thought.

Would she enjoy that killing? No, but to be honest she had never enjoyed killing. It was a necessary part of battle, not a joy. She would worry about any soldier who took pleasure in ending life of any kind.

She and four others were almost out the door when Rurik came up behind her and whispered, "Indikaiya, wait."

She turned, annoyed at being interrupted. She might not enjoy killing, but she did take pride in doing her job well. "We will return shortly after daybreak."

"Nevada is asking for you," Rurik said. "The matter seems urgent."

Indikaiya was antsy, she was beyond ready for this fight. "What matter?" What couldn't wait a few hours?

"I don't know, but the poor girl is near the breaking point. I will take your place with this party if you will attend to her."

A part of Indikaiya wanted to argue. She was not one to be left behind, to be given the chore of seeing to a needy female. She did not cook, clean, or care for the ill and wounded. Those activities were noble and necessary, but they were not for her. She fought. She always had.

But she remembered what Nevada had looked like a few hours earlier, and she could not forget the importance of the tasks — one to save the world, one simpler — assigned to the witch.

"Fine." The tone of the single word conveyed her displeasure.

Rurik grinned widely. Always armed, his own short-bladed sword was strapped to his back. He drew it smoothly and followed the others out the door, into the dark night.

"This had better be good," Indikaiya said as she headed for the stairs. She bounded up them, light on her feet, and ran down the hallway at a quick pace. If Nevada's need for her took only a few moments, she could catch up with the others. She was in the mood to use her sword tonight. That was her purpose in this world, after all.

"What is it?" she snapped as she opened the door.

Nevada stood at her desk. She looked a little better, in clean clothes and freshened by her recent shower and long nap. The witch had fashioned her own hair in a braid much like Indikaiya's. No shower or change of clothing could disguise the stark paleness of her cheeks or the exhaustion in her eyes, but her appearance had improved.

"I decided to try the thing you asked me to do, just for a few minutes, and when I turned my brain from one matter to another, something seemed to shift. Slip, maybe. I don't know exactly what happened, but suddenly the spell I was trying to put together just looked different."

A wave of relief washed through Indikaiya. This world might never be truly safe again, but if humans once more had the haven of home, not only would Nevada be safe from those who would kill her to see the sanctuary spell recast, the battle lines would be more clearly drawn. "Are you ready to recast the sanctuary spell?"

Nevada took a deep breath. "I just did. How can we know if it worked or not? It's not like I can ask for a confirmation email."

"A... what?"

"Never mind." Nevada waved one small, pale hand in a dismissive manner. "I need to know if I can stop working on this spell or if I'll have to tweak it and try again."

"I will ask Luca to attempt to enter a neighboring house. If it is not possible, we will know your spell was a success."

Nevada frowned. "Who's Luca?"

"Do you recall the other task I assigned you?"

"Something to dampen a vampire's magic. I haven't finished..."

"No matter. When that project is done it will go to Luca. His magic, his gift, is that when he is not in your sight you forget him. Entirely."

"Wow. That's kind of... weirdly cool."

"You will likely even forget that I mentioned his name, but please do remember what I asked of you. A dampener. A talisman that will allow you and the other humans among us to remember him."

"You seem to remember," Nevada said.

"I'm not human." Indikaiya pointed at Nevada. She didn't understand why the girl looked so alarmed until she realized she still held her sword in that hand. "Stay here."

Nevada nodded, wide-eyed and paler than before.

Indikaiya sent the first human she ran across — a female conduit who had decided to remain and help as she could — to stand guard at Nevada's door. The girl had no measurable fighting skills or magic, but she was marginally better than nothing. There were still those among this army who would gladly take the life of the witch if it meant the sanctuary spell would once again be in place. It would be a shame for that to happen now, just as she had, perhaps, succeeded in her task.

At the last moment, Indikaiya turned back, drew one of her daggers, and slapped the handle into the girl's palm. "Just in case," she said.

The girl — no, not a girl, a woman who had made the difficult choice not to run away — who was as tired looking as Nevada, offered a weak, "Thanks, Indie."

Among the humans, the nickname "Indie" seemed to have stuck. Indikaiya didn't find it entirely objectionable.

It took her a few minutes to find Luca, who was in a large, windowless room in the cellar with a satellite phone in one hand and a large map spread on the table before him. His two vampire friends and three Warriors studied the map, pointing and arguing. Luca was a leader. He snapped orders to whoever was on the other end of that call, undeniably commanding. He might be talking to a vampire on the other side of the world, or a Warrior on the other side of town, or to anyone who was a part of this war. Well, anyone who had the ability to remember him, which limited the possibilities to powerful vampires and Warriors.

She hated to call him away, to take him from his duties at such a time. One of the other vampires would suffice for the test Nevada had requested, she decided.

Chloe was also present, standing close by Luca's side. She looked different, as a vampire, but this was still Chloe. She had no place in this room, no part to play beyond remaining at her mate's side. Since she had been turned, she had always been at her mate's side.

They needed to talk. Chloe needed to know about the baby inside her. But Chloe was not just Indikaiya's conduit, she was a newborn vampire, strong and hungry and unpredictable. She would not do for this test. Indikaiya was about to ask the quiet vampire, the dark haired one, to come, when Sorin walked up behind her.

She realized it was he long before she turned to look up into his face. His step, his scent — she already recognized them. How incredibly frustrating! She looked him up and down. He'd been injured, though his wounds were already healing. His clothing — the snug denim trousers so popular among the humans, a dark green shirt that would not dare to wrinkle, and the long black leather coat that allowed him to conceal his sword — was sprinkled with ash. Vampire ashes, it appeared. He had not run away, he'd been out killing vampires.

Which was where she wished to be.

"Come with me," she said, before Sorin could make his presence known to the others.

She climbed the narrow stairs, conscious that she'd knowingly turned her back on a vampire. Did she trust him? What choice did she have?

"The witch thinks she has managed to recast the spell, but she doesn't want to announce it until she knows she's been successful. I need a vampire and a house which he has not previously been given permission to enter."

"I knew you needed me," he teased.

"I need no man," she said, refusing to engage in banter. She was not skilled in wordplay. He was. He would win that battle every time.

Thank the heavens, he turned his mind to the matter at hand. "The houses on either side of this one are empty and have been for months. The humans who once lived on this street vacated, one after another, not long after Marie made this her home away from home. Instincts drove them away, I suppose, though it's also possible Marie snatched up a few to feed her soldiers."

"You sound as if that possibility doesn't concern you," Indikaiya said, incensed that he could offer that vile suggestion so casually.

He looked down at her. "It doesn't concern me."

"You have no regrets?" About who he was, or about the power-hungry vampire with whom he had once aligned himself?

"No regrets. What's the point?" He glanced one way, then another. "I have not entered either of the houses alongside this one, so…"

She just wanted to get this over with! "Which of the two is closest?"

"The house to the east."

They stepped through the front door, into the night, and Indikaiya turned to the east. In this neighborhood, none of the ridiculously enormous homes were in close proximity. In some eras they would be called castles, with wrought iron gates and massive lawns and room enough inside those gates for a small town or a very large extended family.

Sorin could be on the doorstep of any of the nearby houses in a matter of moments, but she did not have his gift of speed, and she wanted to witness his attempt to enter the house. She wanted to be able to verify the reintroduction of the sanctuary spell with her own eyes.

Maybe she didn't trust him completely, after all.

Still coming down from the high of fighting Marie's newest soldiers, Sorin remained on alert. Was he ever not on alert? No. Never. He had spent his long life listening for the next attacker, searching for the next meal, assuring that no matter who came at him, for whatever reason, he was prepared.

He was hungry. The fight had drained him, had roused his appetite. Not that there was anyone in the vicinity who would serve as a proper blood donor. No Warrior would offer a tempting vein to him, and he did not dare to feed from one of the few humans who had decided to remain with the fight. It would be foolish to weaken the soldiers from his own army.

He had been hungry before. He'd been much hungrier than this. If nothing else, he had the gift of control.

His mind turned to more immediate matters. If Nevada had managed to recast the spell, then her job here was done. He would take her far away from this Potomac mansion, remove her from this prison to which he had delivered her, years earlier. He would take her... where? Was there any safe place in the world? Who could know? It would be safer for all humans once the spell had been put back into place. He could locate Nevada's family, reunite them, and allow her to resume a somewhat normal life.

No. She had broken the spell once before, and too many of his kind knew it. They would find her, no matter where she tried to hide. They would force her to break the spell again, and then they would kill her. Or worse, turn her.

A powerful vampire witch. The thought gave

him the shivers, and he did not shiver easily.

There were pockets of this city which had already been overrun by vampires. This neighborhood, however, was safer than most. No vamp in his right mind would want to be in the vicinity of so many Warriors. Not yet, anyway. Soon enough Luca's army would be gone from this place, and what had once been Marie's headquarters and then their own would be yet another empty house on yet another deserted street.

The space between the mansion that had become headquarters and the vacant one next door was dark and eerily quiet. No dogs barked. No night birds chirped.

"Sheathe your sword," he said in a lowered voice.

"Why should I?" Indikaiya asked, testy. Annoyed. That seemed to be her normal state.

"Unless you plan to take my head, you have no need of it at this moment."

Grudgingly, she did as he asked. A fraction of a second later, he snaked an arm around her and leapt up and forward, soaring toward their destination.

She didn't even have time to curse before he landed on the dark doorstep.

She took a step back, drew and raised her sword and pointed it at him in a threatening manner. The tip of that sword was no more than half a foot from his nose. "Don't ever do that again."

Sorin grinned. "It was fun though, right? Admit it. You liked being airborne, at least a little."

"I did not like it at all." Her voice was clear and crisp, and without emotion. The expression on her face was one of determination. She did not give in. She did not give up. "Swear to me, never again."

"Not unless you ask." Sorin said as Indikaiya lowered her sword. He turned his back to her and reached for the knob on the massive front door, attempting to turn it. He could not. He threw his weight against that door, but bounced off an invisible barrier. Unexpected relief rushed through him. She'd done it. Nevada had succeeded.

He twisted a bit to look down at Indikaiya. "You try, just to be sure."

She reached out and turned the doorknob. Apparently the door he had not been able to open was unlocked. She stepped inside, easy as you please. Any Warrior or human could have done the same. From beyond the doorway, from where she stood in an unlit, massive foyer, she said, "Two steps, vampire, and you'll be inside."

He tried, but could not.

"Come in, Sorin," she said, backing away from the doorway, blending almost completely into the shadows.

He tried, but again was stopped by a force beyond his control. It felt very much like trying to move toward Nevada when she'd cast a small protection spell around herself. It reminded him of the early days, when he had not known the rules. How many homes had he attempted to enter uninvited before he'd figured out it was impossible? It had been years longer before he'd known why. Sorin's maker had been less than attentive, after he'd been turned. It was the reason he had always taken the time to educate his own made children.

There had not been many of them, but there had been a few.

"You do not have permission to grant access to this dwelling," he said. "It does not belong to you."

Indikaiya was smiling as she returned to the front porch. She had a wide smile, true and unfettered by regret. He had not known until this moment that she was capable of producing such an expression.

"It worked," she said. "Do you want to tell your little witch that she was successful, or shall I?"

With this task done, Nevada would want to leave. She'd think herself free. Hadn't he just been considering taking her away, hiding her somewhere? Anywhere? He could not let her go, not yet. Not now. First he had to find a way to protect her as she had found a way to protect the homes of humans around the world.

Sorin had never cared about protecting anyone before, least of all a human witch who had just recast the spell which would keep him from entering a home uninvited.

She'd ruined him.

"You may have the honor, dear," he said. "I have vampires to kill."

With that he stepped onto the long-neglected lawn and shot up into the sky, away from the Warrior, the witch and the memories.

"It worked," Indie said simply. "Sorin was unable to enter the house."

The sanctuary spell was back in place. Nevada felt as if her knees were going to buckle, her relief was so great. Tears stung her eyes, and she clenched her fists. She gasped, a sound wrenched from so deep inside her it sounded suspiciously like a sob.

Indie, looking concerned, took a couple of steps into the room. "You have gone even paler than usual. Are you well?"

Well? No, not really. Nevada had thought for some time now that she might never be *well* again. "I'm fine. It's just… I'm relieved, that's all." She didn't know how many people had died in the past three days. Three days or four? She'd lost all track of time, as she'd thrown herself into her work. God, she didn't want to know how many had died.

"You must rest now," Indie insisted.

Rest, yes, that would be a good idea. A sudden worry erased all thoughts of taking a step back from her work. "Do you think he would lie? Sorin, would he pretend that the spell was back in place?" Was he truly on their side?

Judging by the expression on Indie's face, she hadn't even thought of that possibility. Maybe for a

Warrior a lie of that magnitude was unthinkable. After a short pause she answered. "No."

"He's lied before," Nevada argued. Yes, in the past Sorin had lied skillfully and often.

Indie seemed more confident than before. "Not this time."

"He's one of us now, isn't he?"

Indie nodded.

In spite of her instinctive worry, Nevada believed that to be true. Sorin could have killed her. In the past few days he'd had several opportunities. He had not. In fact, he had protected her. She pretty much had to believe him.

"We'll know soon enough if the spell took effect everywhere." The tears were gone. Nevada's knees felt steady again. "I hope the royal bitch is royally pissed." Tired as she was, she managed a small smile. "I hope she knows I'm the one who did this to her."

"Marie is the bitch?" Indie asked. For some reason, the b-word sounded odd coming out of the Warrior's mouth.

"Yep. Big time." Nevada asked the question she'd wanted to ask since she'd learned that the sanctuary spell was back in place. "Where's Rurik? Does he know?"

"Rurik is fighting, as I will soon be. Before I leave I will have someone call the human Jimmy to share the news." Indie frowned, as if she wasn't quite sure that was the right thing to do. Jimmy was very young, but he was a leader among them. He would be a leader at any age. *In* any age. "The cell phones you humans carry are convenient, at times, but they are also annoying. Jimmy's lady friend keeps calling. She wants him to come home to Texas, or else she wants to join him here. He is frantic to keep her away."

Understandable. Nevada didn't want her family anywhere near this place, not ever again. Was it even possible to keep loved ones safe in a world like this one?

"It's been forever since I had a cell phone," Nevada said. In a way she'd love to have one now. Not for phone calls. Who would she call? It wasn't like her family had their phones with them. She hadn't seen any of her friends for years. They probably all thought she was dead. But for the Internet, for news, for music, for reaching out to the rest of the world... a cell phone would be nice.

"Sleep," Indie said. "Sleep, and then eat, and then get back to work."

Ah, yes, that other thing. "I will." Nevada was sure she'd sleep deeply, and she hoped with everything she had that she didn't dream. There was no telling what she'd dream about. Nothing pleasant, she supposed.

Indie nodded again, in that weirdly formal way she had, and then she was gone. She had vampires to kill.

Alone, Nevada allowed herself a brief moment

of pride that she'd done what she'd done. Next she'd
take care of that thing Indie had asked of her, and
then she was going to leave this place and find her
family. With the spell in place again, surely they
could find somewhere to hide until this was all over.
And it would, one day, be over.

Deep in her heart she was sure that the Warriors
would win. They had to.

Marie entered the unpleasant warehouse with
her nose in the air and two of her strongest soldiers
directly behind her. She hadn't seen Ahron for a
long time. If he was angry with her for not
including him in her plans... well, he was strong,
but if it was necessary the three of them could take
him on. Perhaps.

She didn't want to kill the old, disturbing
vampire. He was a powerful psychic, and she needed
him to help her. To join her. Her plans had suffered.
In too many ways, her soldiers had failed her.
Though she would not admit so aloud, she had
failed herself. It was time to regroup.

In the last few days she'd moved from one house
to another, making each one — each larger and
more well-furnished than the last — her own. She'd
killed or turned the humans who got in her way,
settling in and then quickly becoming unsettled
and unsatisfied. No mere house was sufficient for
her needs. She deserved a castle. Perhaps a white

house. *The* White House. In time.

She'd changed her clothing as often as she'd changed her mood. While she longed for the fine gowns of another time, for a style of dress which would mark her as a queen for all to note, such clothing was not always practical. For tonight she had chosen black pants, a black silk blouse, and high-heeled boots. While her clothing was plain, she had not given up her jewels. An enormous emerald hung from her neck. Drop earrings of the same stone hung from her ears. No matter what she wore, she would always appear regal.

In the past several days she'd made a number of children who would serve her. She'd killed with glee and drunk to her heart's content.

Tonight she had been unable to take the home she'd chosen. She had been unable to cross the threshold. That damn witch. No one else could have done this to her!

Marie knocked on the narrow, metal door, which had long ago been painted a putrid green. It was a sad entrance, marked with rust and dents and... was that blood? She could've simply blown through his door and presented herself, and her frustration had almost led her to do just that. The rules that protected humans would not protect someone like Ahron. Still, she needed him with her, needed his help. It would be best not to piss him off right away. Just beyond the door, she heard him giggle. It was a disturbing sound.

The door swung open. Ahron, the most ancient vampire she knew or knew of, smiled at her. His appearance always disturbed her. He was small, with a greenish-white pale face of young features and ancient eyes. His hair had long been white, and he usually moved like an elderly man, though he did retain a magnificent strength.

She cared nothing for his odd looks. She was here for his mind; for his psychic powers.

"Marie, my dear," he said, his always-elongated fangs showing as he stepped back and waved her in. When her soldiers attempted to follow, Ahron seemed to disappear and then reappear behind her — between her and her guards.

He could move with preternatural speed when it suited him.

She had the disturbing thought that in spite of his weak appearance he could kill both of her guards instantly, if he chose to. She'd be wise not to underestimate him.

"Just you, for now," he said.

Marie nodded at her soldiers. Ahron closed the door.

The old vampire rubbed his frail looking hands together in glee. "It has begun! I'm so excited."

Even isolated as he was, of course he knew what was going on. He knew everything. *Almost* everything. Did he see her failures?

"It has not begun exactly as I planned," she confessed. Why lie to Ahron? He would know, and he hated being lied to.

He waved a dismissive hand. "War rarely follows our plans. We must adjust, we must adapt."

Marie sighed in relief. He'd used the word *we*. If Ahron was with her, if he was an ally...

"Of course I am your ally. Do you think I wish to spend an eternity hiding in this hole beneath the ground, feeding only when the Council sees fit to provide nourishment or when some unlucky bum looking for shelter stumbles upon me? No, I wish to be free, as I once was. As we all should be."

Relief washed through Marie. Finally, something on this night had gone right! "I can give you that, but in exchange I need help." She would appeal to his vanity, if she had to. "I don't think I can win this without you."

He shrugged thin shoulders. "Probably not."

She had to ask, she needed to know... "Do you see the end? Will I... will *we* be victorious?"

"There will be an end, of course there will be there's always an end, but I do not yet see it well." He closed his eyes and reached deep. "I see sunlight and blood, I see ash and steel."

That was unhelpful.

Ahron's eyes flew open and they fixed on her. She should not be disturbed by anyone or anything, but this ancient disturbed her to her core. "Every being has a weakness. That weakness is not always a physical one."

"Luca doesn't have a weakness."

"His woman…"

Impatient, Marie snapped, "I killed his woman."

Ahron smiled. "He saved her, turned her. She is one of us now."

Rage, red and hot and dangerous, rose within her. How was that possible! Chloe Fallon had been near death when Marie had fled the mansion. She fought the urge to break something. *Near* death. She should've taken the woman's bothersome head before making her escape.

Ahron had the audacity to laugh. "Be glad you failed. Without the woman, Luca has no weaknesses to exploit."

Marie had never been glad to fail, but in this case she would, at least, make the best of it.

"Sorin. I want Sorin, too."

"Yes, yes." Again, that thin, milk-white hand flitted through the air. "You must remove the three in order to win."

Luca and Sorin. "Who is the third?"

"He's just a boy, a mere human, but he has a powerful spirit. He, too, must be removed in order for you to succeed. All three are vulnerable because they love. You, you are much stronger than they. You love no one."

"Of course not."

"Sit a while, and let's talk strategy." He indicated a long, leather sofa. He rubbed his hands together and again, he giggled.

***

New York

Natasha's Blood was Kenzie's favorite band. They weren't wildly successful, but they were pretty well known and had put out a couple of songs on YouTube. The band played this club on occasion; she was lucky they were in town tonight. She liked the

heavy bass and the electric guitar and the shouted words she couldn't really understand, but didn't need to. The words were raw, sexual, and filled with emotion. She felt it. The room pulsed, it almost shook, and she felt every note.

The crowd tonight was light. Everyone was talking about the violence in Washington. Vampires? No way. Maybe a cult that acted like vampires to scare the pants off everyone else, but there were no real vampires. Murderers who made their killings look like vampires? Sure. The real thing? Impossible.

Kenzie was twenty-one years old, pretty enough to catch a man's attention, if not gorgeous, and newly single. She'd decided to embrace being single, for a while. That's why she was here on her own, tonight. Normally she'd have a date, or a couple of girlfriends, but she didn't want a date and her girlfriends were all wusses.

The lead singer of Natasha's Blood, Darin Randall, was hot. She'd noticed him before, of course, but since she'd been in a relationship (and unlike he who shall not be named, *she* was faithful) she'd never done anything more than admire Darin from a distance. There was much to admire. His talented hands flew over the strings of his electric guitar; his voice was the one that reached inside her and made a weird sort of sense, even when the words were unintelligible. He didn't have the thin, strung out look of many rockers she'd seen. He was tall and muscular, with tattooed arms and a thick head of dark hair that was a little shaggy, but not too long. She'd never been close enough to see what color eyes he had, but tonight, with the crowd light and a newly increased drive to do the single thing well, she worked her way to the front of the room — to the center of the front row — and looked up.

Green. His eyes were green.

He looked down at her and smiled. She smiled back. It was a smile that said, "Come and get me."

Not that she thought he would. Kenzie was pretty enough, but she wasn't the prettiest girl in the world. She wasn't even the prettiest girl in the club.

But Darin kept looking at her. He looked at her as if she *were* the prettiest girl in the world. At least, the prettiest girl in this small crowd. His green eyes — and beautiful green eyes they were — glowed a little bit. It was a reflection of light, she supposed, and would not last. It was beautiful.

WARRIOR RISING | 79

The glow continued. It didn't die when he moved his head a little bit. Suddenly the words he was singing made sense. She finally understood.

Come to me.

Feed me.

I need you, Kenzie.

Come to me.

She did. Without thinking about what she was doing, Kenzie walked to the steps at the side of the stage, and slowly, very slowly, walked up and onto the platform.

Darin stepped back, and another band member took his place in front. The singer she had admired for months swung his guitar up and over his head, and set it aside. He reached for her, and she met him. Gladly. In a daze, yes, but still… gladly.

He placed his mouth near her ear and said, "I don't have to hide anymore."

"That's good, I guess." She did not feel like herself at all. Her legs and feet and arms were numb, and at the same time she felt like she was floating. How had she gotten up here? What did it matter? "What were you hiding from?"

"Everyone." He looked her in the eye again. Perhaps there was a moment of alarm. Those green eyes really did glow, and for a moment — a brief moment — her brain hurt. Then once again she felt nothing.

Darin cocked his head and opened his mouth, and she saw the fangs that grew there. There was enough of her left to think, "Oh, shit. Vampires *are* real."

She didn't mind when he bit down into her throat. It was a sexual thing, a pleasure, even as she felt her life slipping away. People were watching. It was like they were having sex on stage for everyone to see. She didn't mind, not like she thought she should.

The music stopped, and Kenzie turned her head in a way that would give Darin better access to what was left of her throat. She wondered who Natasha was, if the woman behind the name of the band had fed Darin the way she now was. And she was jealous. Slipping away, dying, and jealous.

The other members of the band — there were four of them — leapt from the stage and into the small crowd. They took from others what Darin was taking from her, only they moved more quickly. They did not savor as he did.

Kenzie heard a woman scream — the scream seemed to be very far away, but she knew it wasn't — and then she heard nothing at all.

CHAPTER FOUR

Chloe took a step away from Luca, as Duncan moved in closer to study the map. Isaac had already left, off with a handful of Warriors to set up a new headquarters on the other side of the city. They needed multiple safe havens for the few vampires among them, easily accessible dark spaces that weren't a potentially deadly hour or so away. No one yet knew what this war would look like, but there would be more battles. There would be bloodshed as Marie and those who supported her attempted to take control, she knew that much.

There were moments when Chloe was still surprised that even a few vampires were ready and willing to fight for humans.

Maybe she shouldn't be surprised. She was vampire now, and she was ready to fight for humanity. Of course, it hadn't been all that long ago that she'd been human herself. Some of the others... not so much. She didn't know the details of Luca's friends' lives, but it had been a very long time since either of them had needed to breathe.

If they could reach out to friends who valued this world as they did, if they could recruit even a handful more vampires to this side, the war with

Marie might be significantly shorter. Vampires with friends. Vampires who valued humans. These were concepts she would have dismissed even a few days ago, but now they gave her hope.

Chloe was happy to leave the planning to the older vampires and the most experienced Warriors. There were times when she could barely think — much less strategize — because everything within and around her was so new and different. She had indeed been reborn.

She needed to call her parents, and soon. In the past couple of days, she'd replayed the conversation in her head, again and again, and the imagined call never ended on a good note. Maybe it was just as well that she had no idea where her cell phone was. Not that she couldn't borrow one if she was so inclined. She just didn't know what to say. *I'm a vampire, and I don't trust myself to be in the same room with you just yet.*

She worried less now that the sanctuary spell was back in place. Neither of her parents saw well enough to drive at night. They were creatures of habit, settled in before dark; in bed no later than ten. And they were well away from D.C., in Atlanta where maybe the rebel vamps were not so active.

But that conversation... sooner or later she had to figure out what to say.

It hadn't been long since Luca had fed her from his own wrist, and already she was hungry. He had told her, more than once, that constant hunger was normal for a newborn.

Newborn. She'd spent so many years of her life dying, thanks to the aortic aneurysm, that to be a newborn with an endless life ahead of her was beyond amazing.

Everything looked *different*. Normal sounds were like music to her ears. The simplest view was like a master's painting, the colors brighter, the lines sharper. Had she really seen the world she lived in as a human? Not like this. She hadn't wanted to be turned, not until the moment when she'd literally had to choose between leaving this world for good or staying in it with the man she loved. Luca.

There might be days to come when she regretted her choice, but today she did not.

All day she'd felt uneasy in a new way. Something was wrong. Something inside her was different. Well, a lot was different, but this... yeah, something was off. She'd adjusted quickly to the change from human to vampire, much more quickly than normal, according to Luca and his friends. Maybe it was Luca's blood that made the difference. Maybe it was her. Perhaps beneath what she'd always thought of as an ordinary body and brain something that made her special had lurked. She'd been a conduit, after all, and not every human was capable of hearing the call of an Immortal Warrior.

For the first time in days Chloe stopped, closed

her eyes, and took a deep breath. She didn't need to breathe, not really, but there was something normal and calming and ordinary about breathing in and out. She listened, calling on her newly enhanced hearing. She focused on the faint heartbeats of those in the room. Vampires, humans, and Warriors all had beating hearts. It was perhaps the one thing they had in common. Thump, thump. Luca's heartbeat was slow, the slowest in the room. His two vampire friends also had slow heartbeats. Jimmy's heart rate was dangerously high. It raced, but at least it raced steadily. He was in no danger. The two Warriors who also stood over the map had heart rates somewhere in between.

Then there was her own heartbeat, which was not as slow as Luca's but was in line with the other vampires in the room.

And...

Chloe cocked her head to one side, closed her eyes again, and took yet another deep breath she did not need to take. Another heartbeat, one faint and fast and new, came from *inside her.*

How much sleep could one human need? Indikaiya, tired of waiting, pushed past Rurik and into Nevada's room, where the girl had been sleeping for going on ten hours. "Bring food," she instructed sharply.

Rurik was not accustomed to being ordered

around, but he huffed a bit and then left to do as he'd been told. Indikaiya called after him. "Meat! She will need protein."

Even her raised voice didn't rouse the girl.

Indikaiya stood beside the bed and called the witch's name. The girl still didn't stir. She would think the witch dead if not for the healthy pink of her cheeks and the gentle, steady breaths. She called again, louder, and then she reached out and shook the bed.

That did the trick. Nevada came up in a shot, with a sharp intake of breath and a shake of her mussed red hair. "What's wrong?"

"We have no time to waste," Indikaiya snapped. "You have a task and you need to see to it." Luca would be leaving this place soon. He needed something to dampen his annoying *gift*.

"I'm starving," Nevada said as she rolled out of bed. She wore the most ridiculous nightwear. Short pants, small shirt. And was that... ducks? The creatures on Nevada's wrinkled pajamas looked like no living thing that had ever existed in reality.

"Rurik is bringing food."

Nevada headed for the bathroom. "I don't think it will take long to finish up. This job is much easier than the last one." She glanced back. "The sanctuary spell is holding?"

"Yes."

Her relief was evident. "Good."

The girl spent several minutes behind closed

doors. Indikaiya heard the flush of a toilet, running water, the brushing of teeth. There was an annoying long wait before the door opened and Nevada stepped out, dressed casually, and with her hair pulled back into a hastily formulated and somewhat messy braid. It was a sensible hairstyle, which is why Indikaiya herself had adopted it long ago.

Rurik arrived with a plate of eggs and bacon, along with a piece of toast. "Protein," he said, a testy aside to Indikaiya. He looked at Nevada with... longing? Lust? Caring? All of those, it seemed. As if they could afford such complications!

"Never fear, pretty witch," he said. "It was one of the conduits who did the cooking. I am not what anyone would call good in the kitchen."

The girl smiled at Rurik. She was too sleep-muddled and stressed to show much in the way of interest in anything or anyone, but her eyes did spark a bit.

Indikaiya turned her head away. It was as if she were intruding on a private moment. She frowned. It would be beyond foolish for Rurik to get involved with a human. When the time came, when this war was over, the Warriors would return to the burial grounds of others of their kind, and they would walk back to their own world to wait for the next time they were called. That was what they lived for. The next battle.

Rurik placed the tray on a small desk near the window and left the room — reluctantly, it seemed

— and Nevada sat to eat as if she had not consumed solid food in days.

Before she finished, the vampire Sorin walked into the room. He did not knock, but then Rurik had left the door open. So he could peer in now and then? Perhaps.

"I have found your family," he said, directing his words to Nevada. "They are all well."

The witch dropped the piece of bacon she'd been carrying toward her mouth, sprang to her feet with a girlish squeal, and ran to the vampire to hug him. The hug did not last, and the girl moved back and away as quickly and sharply as she had moved in. "Sorry," she said. "I'm just excited. First the sanctuary spell and now this. Where are they? Are they safe? Did you talk to them?"

Sorin looked taken aback. By the hug or by all the questions? "I located them shortly before sunrise. I didn't drop in for tea."

"You didn't even..." Nevada began.

Sorin's words were sharp. "I kidnapped them, in case you have forgotten. I suspect they have not. Not one of them would be so foolish as to throw their arms around me."

The girl blushed. "You've changed," she said softly.

"You put a spell on me," he said, accusation in his voice.

Nevada glanced to the side, as if she had been caught doing something she should not. "Maybe a little one, but you had begun to change before that."

He waved an impatient hand, ending the conversation. "I have much to do. Vampires have finally made the news. For days our existence has been dismissed as rumor or mass hysteria, but the truth has come out. One of our human fighters, a conduit I believe, strapped on a small camera and recorded his kill of one of Marie's soldiers. The fool went to dust before many witnesses, live on television. We can no longer be denied." Was that a sigh? "There will be no real hiding for the kindred, probably not ever again."

Indikaiya watched and listened. Sorin seemed truly distressed. Wasn't this what his kind wanted? What *he* wanted? No matter what side of the fight they found themselves on, an endless existence in the shadows was not desirable.

"Vampires on the news?" Nevada repeated.

"There's been nothing else on television and radio all day," Sorin said. "We have been well and truly outed."

The petite girl, young and without doubt the weakest being in this household — physically speaking — stood tall and began to issue directives. "Rurik!" She caught his eye beyond the doorway. "Coffee. I will need lots of it." She looked then to Sorin. "As soon as it's dark and safe for you to be out, I want you to tell my parents that I'm okay. I know they'll be worried, and I don't want them venturing out to try to find me. They will only place themselves in danger." Her eyes shifted. "Take Indie with you."

"What?"

The response was in discordant harmony, Sorin's deep voice and Indikaiya's echoing.

"There's still work for me to do here. I want to leave, I do, I want to join my family and hide until this is over, but I can't." She steeled her spine. "I trust the two of you. I don't trust anyone else."

"What of me?" Rurik asked from his post just beyond the doorway. There was a touch of humor in his voice, so no one believed that he was truly offended.

"Sorry," Nevada said, sounding not at all apologetic. "Of course I trust you, as well." She continued with her instructions to Sorin. "Tell my family I'm fine, make sure they know to stay inside, especially at night. They should get out of D.C., they should go as far away as they can. This area will be the most active, I expect. A place in the country, maybe? Make sure they have enough food to get by for a while." She sighed. "I don't know how long they'll need to hide." She lifted her head and caught Indikaiya's eye.

"God help us," she whispered, her fear showing. "What if this never ends?"

"I can't believe I'm allowing myself to be commanded by a human, a witch who has not yet seen her twenty-fifth year. Is she even *twenty*?"

Sorin smiled, as they left the mansion and walked into darkness. No, Indikaiya had probably not taken orders from anyone other than a general in... hundreds of years? Thousands? "Nevada is twenty-three years of age. You're welcome to go back inside and argue with her, if you'd like."

The gentle huff that followed that suggestion was low and unexpectedly feminine in nature. Yes, Indikaiya was a Warrior, but she was also a woman.

"She has work to do," Indikaiya argued. "Work I want finished as soon as possible."

"What kind of work?" It sounded as if the sexy Warrior had been giving orders as well as taking them.

"The humans among us must be able to remember Luca after he walks away. His gift, if it can be called such, is beyond frustrating."

She refused to fly in his arms again, and to be honest his abilities in that arena were not powerful enough to carry the two of them a long distance, so he headed for the vehicle which was parked at the curb. He could've taken any of the cars or trucks that were parked around the mansion and up and down the street, and a wise man probably would've chosen a more nondescript ride. But Sorin had never been nondescript, and he saw no reason to start now.

The shiny black Mustang was sleek and it would be fast. He didn't know which of the Warriors — or conduits — had been driving it when they'd arrived, but for tonight it was his. The army, such as it was, had taken to leaving the keys to all vehicles under the driver's seat, so that whoever among them had need of transportation would have it without delay.

Sorin opened the driver's side door and reached down for the keys, which were precisely where they should be. Indikaiya hesitated. Maybe she hadn't visited this world for a while, but surely she recognized a car when she saw one. She'd been watching from the other side. They all had.

"We can ride or I can carry you," he said, knowing which method of transport Indikaiya would choose. He tossed the keys into the air. As they landed in his palm she opened the door, placed her sword into the tiny back, and slipped into the passenger seat.

His sword joined hers, then he settled in and started the engine, which roared and purred. Out of the corner of his eye he saw his passenger grip the door handle. Tight.

"You've never been in a car before, have you?"

"No, why would I have been?"

"No cars back home in Warrior world?"

"We have no need."

"Pity." He took off, made a squealing u-turn in the road, and floored it.

"Have you no horses?" Indikaiya raised her voice to be heard above the magnificently roaring engine.

"I have no need," he said, throwing her words

back at her. "I actually prefer a motorcycle, but since I'm not sure how long this will take and the windows of the car are darkly tinted, this is a better choice."

She relaxed a little as she became accustomed to the motion and speed of the car. They left the quiet neighborhood and pulled onto a main road. That road was straight and wide and deserted. Perfect for this fine vehicle.

Sorin turned on the radio, searched, and finally found a station that wasn't talking about vampires. The rock and roll station seemed appropriate enough for the state of the world, at the moment. Indikaiya didn't pay the music much attention — though she did seem to be relieved that she didn't have to talk to him — until a particular song came on. Her reaction was instantaneous and electric. She even leaned toward the speaker and listened closely.

"Who is that?" she asked about halfway through the song.

This was a question he could answer. "Janis Joplin." He could even provide the name of this one. "Cry Baby."

She leaned back in her seat. "I find that I am intrigued by much of the music from this time."

"Janis Joplin isn't exactly current," he said. "She died years ago."

"Yet her music survives," Indikaiya said in a lowered voice that was almost reverent.

"Yes, it does." They drove on, Indikaiya paying

WARRIOR RISING | 93

closer attention to the music as one old song followed another. Of course, *old* was relative.

A song came on that she didn't like, and her response was to immediately turn the radio off. The woman liked what she liked, and she also knew what she didn't like.

Did she like him? A little, he could tell. Would she admit it?

Never.

After a while, she said, "You mentioned avoiding the sun. Some vampires can withstand a little sunlight, yes?"

"I can withstand some, but it isn't pleasant."

To be honest, that was what he missed most about being human. Sunlight. The warmth of it on his face, the shadows created by a late afternoon sun, the blaze of an orange and red and pink sunset. He had never admitted that to anyone, and saw no reason to start now.

"You have truly located Nevada's family?"

It was an unnecessary question to fill the silence between them, he supposed. Maybe she thought if he was carrying on a conversation he would give less attention to his driving and slow down. He did not. "I know where they were last night. Whether or not they're still in the same place... we'll find out soon enough."

"How did you find them?"

Another unnecessary question.

It was the overwhelming stench of them. The

mother and the little sister smell like Nevada. They all smell like Diera. Will that damned odor never abate? "I know their scent, and I suspected they would not go far from the mansion. Well, not far from Nevada. Locating them was not difficult."

"Why would you know their scent so well?"

There was so much Indikaiya didn't know. There was so much he would never tell her. At the same time, he would not lie to make himself out to be more or less than he was. He was not noble. Sacrifice was not in his blood. "I'm the one who kidnapped them. I'm the one who used them to force Nevada to break the sanctuary spell."

He could feel her eyes on him. "And yet now you fight with us. The witch trusts you." She shook her head. "So much gray in this battle that should be black and white. You are a *vampire.*"

"Do I need to worry about you trying to take my head or my heart?" His tone was light, teasing.

Hers was not. "I have not decided."

CHAPTER FIVE

"Impossible," Luca said.

Chloe reached out and touched him, laying her fingers against his cheek. She'd never seen him look truly surprised, but the expression on his face... yes, that was definitely surprise.

"Not impossible at all."

"But..."

"Listen."

It had been a while since they'd been alone, but at the moment they had this small basement room to themselves. The room was directly next door to the larger space they'd been using as a war room, of sorts. It wasn't much better than a large closet, but here they could be alone. Wonderfully alone.

Like the other rooms on this level there were plain concrete walls and floors, and no windows. Thank goodness. There was a single folding chair that had been pushed into one corner. The lopsided thing had seen better days. Chloe didn't want to think about what this room had been used for when Marie had run the place. Food storage, she imagined. People, not rice and beans.

Luca did as she instructed and listened, and very soon he heard what she'd heard earlier.

A third heartbeat. The faint, fast heartbeat of their child.

"Tell no one," he said as he took her into his arms and held her close, his hand cradling her head, his heart beating close to hers.

"Why?"

He paused a moment, stroking her hair. "This is unprecedented, a child conceived when the mother was human yet nourished after the change. There are those among the kindred who would not be pleased to see such a child come into the world."

"That's rather short-sighted," Chloe argued. "The baby might be like you. Strong, powerful, the best of the best. Hasn't this sort of thing happened before?"

Instead of acting like a thrilled, soon-to-be father, Luca seemed determined to focus on the facts. His voice was distant, emotionless as he said, "There is no documented evidence of a surviving half-breed. If there is a human pregnancy, which is rare enough in itself, there will be a miscarriage."

"That's sad."

"Would any human female want a half-vampire child?"

She moved away and looked up. "Don't snap. And the answer is... maybe. If it was the child of a man she loved."

Luca sighed. He *never* sighed. "I have heard the story of *one* half-breed that came into the world. It lived only a few hours. The mother did not survive."

His voice, his expression, was no longer emotionless. He was afraid. For her.

Chloe was washed in a new fear. "Will I... will this baby..."

"There is no way to know," Luca said. "If the child survives will it be a vampire with human tendencies or a human with the occasional thirst for blood? Will it be one of us, or will it be more, or will it be less? The kindred don't normally embrace the unknown."

Again, shortsighted! "These days everything is unknown," Chloe grumbled. She wasn't pleased to find out that her pregnancy was a history making event among the vamps. She would much rather have had Luca assure her that this kind of thing happened all the time, that she and the baby would both be just fine.

"We must protect the baby, while we can," Luca said softly. "For now, we protect him with our silence."

She leaned back in and rested her head against his shoulder. *Him* was better than the earlier *it,* and still, it was wrong. "Her," she whispered.

He did not question how she knew. Her single word was enough.

"Will I carry the child for nine months, as if I were still human?"

Luca spoke words she suspected had not often passed his lips. "I don't know."

"Will the baby survive the change in my body?"

According to him, if she were still human she'd lose the baby. Could a vampire nourish a fetus? Obviously the answer to that was yes, since Luca had been born to a vampire mother. But his father was also a vampire, and both parents had been vampires when he'd been conceived.

Her daughter had been conceived when she'd been human, and still grew beneath her heart.

Their time alone together had been rare these past few days, and this day was no different. A solid knock sounded on the door next to this one. A moment later, that same sharp knock sounded on the door to this small room. Luca snapped, "Enter," and the Warrior Rurik did. Only then did Luca release her.

"Nevada requests your presence immediately."

Luca looked annoyed. He had much to do, and he was not accustomed to being summoned by anyone. "The witch? Why? And how would she even remember enough to ask for me?"

The Warrior smiled, a wide, real grin. "She needed a bit of help, I'll admit. There were many scribbled notes before her."

The three of them left the room and climbed to the first floor, then to the second. There was much activity as Warriors, humans, and vampires prepared to move their headquarters elsewhere. As their forces spread out, effectively setting up stations all around the city, the number in this large mansion continued to decrease. The battle that had taken place here had left the once-fine house more than a bit of a mess, but they had managed for several days. They would not stay much longer, though.

Two Warriors guarded Nevada's door. As Chloe walked down the hall, following in Rurik and Luca's footsteps, the scent of human blood grew stronger and sweeter and more tempting. Heaven above, she was hungry!

"No," Luca said softly. "I will see that you're fed later."

It wasn't easy, but she trusted him. Besides, Nevada was on their side, and Chloe was far too new to have the kind of control that would allow her to stop before draining a human past the point of death. But oh, the witch smelled good.

The two Warriors parted to allow the threesome to enter. Nevada stood at a worktable that literally glimmered with remnants of magic. Chloe wondered if everyone could see it, or if that glimmer was for her eyes only.

"This is him?" Nevada asked, her eyes on Luca, her question directed to Rurik.

"Yes. This is Luca. Shall we test your latest spell?"

Nevada lifted her hand and impatiently instructed Luca to step forward. He did so, and — eyes on him the entire time — the witch offered a ring on her outstretched hand. Chloe's eyes were drawn to the blue veins on the witch's pale wrist, to the heartbeat, to the scent of blood. She stopped well short of the table, as Luca continued on.

"Put it on," Nevada said as Luca plucked the ring from her hand. At his expression — raised eyebrows, hardened eyes, thinned lips — she added, "Please, sir."

Luca looked to Rurik, who nodded once. Only then did he slip the ring onto the middle finger of his right hand.

When it was done, Nevada turned about, presenting her back to them all. A moment later, she completed the circle.

She would not remember Luca now. He had been out of her sight. The witch smiled widely and even did a little happy dance that included clapping her hands twice. "Luca, nice to see you again."

"Clever." Indikaiya said as the conveyance Sorin had been guiding stopped in front of a small building. The front of the business was constructed almost entirely of glass. They had passed pockets of complete darkness on their way here, but electricity was still being supplied to this area.

A neon sun shone brightly in the front window, along with the bright flashing words, "24-Hour Tanning."

"Yeah, clever. It's not sunlight, exactly, but even the artificial stuff hurts like hell. It'll kill most kindred if they're exposed long enough, and incapacitate even the strongest for an undetermined period of time. Especially if the light hits the eyes."

"Have you been burned or blinded by this artificial sunlight?"

Sorin shook his head. "Not yet."

To business. She did not care if Sorin had been burned or not, so she wasn't sure why she'd asked. "Is Nevada's family still here?"

"Yes. The smell is too strong to be a lingering one. They are here."

He sat, his attractive face lit by bright colored flashing lights from the window before them. For a moment, she wondered where he'd come from, when he'd been turned. Viking she would guess, given his build and coloring, but it was impossible to be sure. She was tall and blond herself, and she was not Viking.

And again, she *did not care*.

"Are you going inside?" she asked, as she tried to figure out how to open the door. Her eyes went to his hands. When he opened his door, she'd know how to open her own. She would not ask; she would not admit that she was effectively stuck in this vehicle.

"I'm thinking about how I might speak to them without getting burned."

"Considering what you've told me, that might be impossible."

"I'm aware," he said in a lowered voice.

"Come," she said in a strong voice. "If I must, I will protect you."

He evidently found her offer funny. His laugh was harsh, as he reached for a recessed handle all but hidden in the door and pulled upon it. She did the same, then reached into the back seat for her sword. She probably would not need it, but she would not trust her life, or the life of the humans here, to a *probably*.

Sorin did not collect his weapon from the rear seat of the vehicle, even though the long black leather coat he wore would've concealed it well enough. Why did he continue to wear the leather? He did not need to be warmed, and it wasn't as if many others weren't carrying weapons at this stage of the game. He slammed the car door, and she copied his action, hefting the sword in her right hand as she took long steps toward the glass doors straight ahead.

He looked at her weapon and held up a hand to stop her. "I'm grateful for the offer of protection, I truly am, but don't hurt anyone in there. Odds are I'll survive any injuries I sustain. If I'm lucky, I can deliver Nevada's message before they hit me with a dose of that light."

Sorin could leave without speaking to Nevada's family; he could toss a note tied to a rock through the glass window. He showed no indication of doing either of those cowardly things. She asked, "Why do you care so much about delivering the witch's message?"

The question annoyed him. "I have a debt to pay. Can we leave it at that?"

"Of course." She tried to see inside the building. Even with all the glass, it was difficult. Bright lights shone in the windows, but beyond all was dark. "Your conveyance is quite loud. I suspect the humans inside realize we are here."

"Yes, I suspect so."

"They are likely terrified of you."

"Likely."

"Trust me, and do not move." She swung her sword around so fast it was a blur. Surprisingly, Sorin did as she'd instructed and remained in place. The blade of her sword rested against his throat.

"Family of the witch," she called in a voice loud enough to carry. "We come to you with a message from Nevada. This vampire has sworn not to harm you, but for your peace of mind I will keep my sword at the ready."

A man came to the glass door, turned a key in the lock, and opened the door. "Is Nevada all right?"

"Yes," Sorin said. "May we come inside and talk?"

The man — Nevada's father, almost certainly — looked at Indikaiya. "As if I would invite two vampires into what has become my home."

Indikaiya was insulted, and that insult was evident in her voice as she responded. "I am not a vampire."

The man looked her up and down. "What the hell are you, then?"

She glanced toward Sorin. "Why does he not think me human?"

"The clothes. The sword. Maybe he has some magic like his daughter and can see that you are not like him."

He looked to the man in the doorway. "She is not a vampire. She's a Warrior here to fight for humans. For you. We do not need to come inside. Nevada wants you to know that she's all right, and she wants you to be aware of what's going on."

"We've been watching the news."

"The news," Sorin said lightly, "where half of what you hear is true and half is not and it's impossible to know which is which."

"I've seen enough to know what you're trying to do."

Sorin shifted his weight. He clenched and unclenched his fists. It was obvious he was impatient to have this chore done. "A lot's happening, and D.C. is going to be one of the world's hot spots. Get out while you can. Travel by daylight and stay in the sun. Take the tanning lights with you, if that is possible. When you get to where you're going and have power, they will make fine weapons. Get out of the city, and find an isolated place to lay low until this is over."

"Will it be over?" the man asked, almost wistfully.

"Eventually."

Nevada's father did not relax. Behind him, Indikaiya saw three other figures in the shadows. "Why are you here?" the man snapped. "You did this. You were working for the other side a few days ago. You threatened us, and you threatened my daughter. Why should I believe you now?"

"Believe me or don't," Sorin said, and then he moved. He shifted — a blur and nothing more — away from her sword so quickly, Indikaiya had no chance to follow. He could have removed himself from the threat of her blade at any time. The man in the doorway had never truly been safe.

Sorin returned to the car. He started the annoyingly loud engine.

"I cannot answer your questions," Indikaiya said to the human who looked as surprised as she felt. "I cannot tell you why, but I do know that Nevada trusts him. The message he has delivered is a true one, it comes from your daughter's lips. You have my word."

She saw such pain on his face, such longing and distress. "When will she join us? If we go far away, if we find a secluded place to hide out until this is over, if it ever is over, how will she find us?"

"That is a problem for another time," Indikaiya answered pragmatically.

With that, she returned to the blasted car and opened the door. She slid into the seat, then carefully placed her sword in the rear seating area.

106 | Linda Winstead Jones

"Now what?" she asked as the conveyance got underway. "We have many hours still until dawn." And Sorin's dreaded daylight.

"I don't know about you, but I feel like killing some vampires."

She caressed the smooth grip of the knife at her right hip. "That is a fine idea."

Sorin drove toward the center of town. He knew D.C. well. He had walked, driven, and flown into all corners.

"Have we a plan?" the Warrior asked from the passenger seat.

"Council headquarters, in Georgetown," he answered simply. "Even if the Council members themselves have fled the city, as I expect they might've, others might flock there." Maybe even Marie, who'd been a Council member herself and would know the place well. With the sanctuary spell back in place, her options were limited. Not that he didn't think she had her own hideouts in this town she'd called home for so long. Still, she might be back at headquarters. If he could kill her, if he could remove the leader of this revolution...

Unfortunately, she would not be easy to kill. Blood-born power hungry psycho that she was.

If he could get some of her followers, if he could kill more of her soldiers — old and new, strong and weak — he *could* hurt her.

"We need to get you some new clothes," he said as he turned down a deserted street. There were too many deserted streets for this hour of the night in this city. People were fleeing, or staying in what they believed to be safe places.

"Why? My tunic is comfortable and offers freedom of movement."

"You don't blend in."

"Why should I wish to blend in?"

She was stubborn, and full of questions. He didn't need her beside him as he fought, didn't need the distraction. And yet, he did not once think of putting her out of the car and going on alone. "Humans will be on alert for anyone different. I'd hate for you to be mistaken for a vampire who never moved on, fashion wise, by a frantic human with a gun or a sword or a grenade." He looked to the woman who rode beside him. "What happens if you die?"

For a long minute or two, he thought she would not answer. Then she said, "I would return to my world, my home."

"Handy. Could you come back?"

"Only if I'm called by a blood descendant." She turned her head and looked at the city flying past. "Chloe can no longer call, as she is no longer human. I could not locate another receptive blood relative when I was speaking to her, so I would likely have to wait until called for the next battle. That can only happen if the human race survives, and a descendant has the gift of hearing."

"Do you have a lot of descendants?"

"Quite a number, but not many with the ability to serve as conduit."

He tried to imagine Indikaiya as human. Obviously she had been a soldier in her time, but also obviously she'd had children. Otherwise, there would be no descendants to hear her call. She had not always been a woman who knew nothing but the sword.

"Where were you, when you lived in this world?" Like it or not, he wanted to know. He wanted to be able to imagine her as a human, in her place, her time.

"Why does that matter?"

"It doesn't. I'm just curious."

"Where were you, when you were human?" she asked.

"Romania." He didn't often talk about that place. It was so long ago, that time seemed almost like a dream. "I was a farmer and a soldier. A husband and a father." That had been a simple time, and he had been a different person.

"How long have you been... what you are?"

Her distaste for *what he was* was evident in her tone, but he did not take offense. "Seven hundred years or so. Your turn."

There was a long pause. Maybe she'd answer; maybe she would not. He supposed it didn't matter, but he was curious.

Soon they'd reach Council headquarters. If it was deserted, they'd keep looking. He didn't think it would be deserted. When they left this car their attentions would have to turn to war. There was no time for curiosity in battle.

As he pulled to the curb and parked, Indikaiya said, "Atlantis. I lived in Atlantis before my death in battle."

"No shit!" He actually smiled. "I thought Atlantis was just a myth."

She caught his gaze and held it, something very few were brave enough to do. "The world thought the same about your kind, until a few days ago."

"True enough." He laughed. "Man, you're *old.*"

"Is that an insult or an observation?"

"Observation." He would love to sit down for a long conversation with her about her home. What had happened to Atlantis? Who had she done battle with? "At a mere seven hundred years old, I feel like a kid again."

He stepped into the night. The street was eerily deserted, unnaturally quiet. And yet he knew they were not alone. "Let's go kick some vampire ass."

If he died in the process? That was more than possible, it was damned likely. And if a final death came to him, he wouldn't wake up in another world to another life. No reincarnation, no warrior's reward, and certainly no heaven. Not for him or for any of those he planned to send from this world tonight.

CHAPTER SIX

Indikaiya was more than ready to remove a few vampires from this world they had been foolish enough to invade. She was anxious, *eager*, having gone too long without a battle.

Time moved differently in her world than it did in this one. Years for a human might pass in days for the Warriors. Time was fluid, uncertain, moving at a pace determined by the need for Warriors in this world. But time did pass. As she waited to be called she trained; she painted; she studied and she watched. The training was necessary, and she threw herself into it wholeheartedly, even though practicing swordplay could not hold a candle to an actual battle. She painted landscapes more than anything else, though on occasion she had tried to capture the faces of her children from memory. Painting was a hobby. She wasn't very good, but there was something about putting a paint-filled brush to canvas that was soothing. And frustrating, when the results were not pleasing. She was a bit impatient, with herself more than with anyone else.

It had never been her habit to spy on her descendants for purposes of amusement or curiosity, but she did watch over them, on occasion.

She had seen Chloe as a child, and again as a teenager. She had watched over her descendant when she'd been in the hospital, after the car wreck that had revealed her aneurysm. There were other descendants, those who had not been able to see or hear her when the time had come, and she had looked in on most of them a time or two during their lives.

It had been easier to keep watch when only her daughters had still lived, but it had also been painful. Her love for them had been so fresh, and she had been so sad and angry that she could not be there to see them grow, to see them become fine women and mothers. There had been more of her blood descendants to spy upon when her daughters' children and then their grandchildren had come into the world. That had been less painful, since the bonds were so distant. She had not held them as infants, fed them from her breasts, protected them night and day. From there, the number of descendants had grown. They had spread out, moving to all corners of the world. Over time some lines had died out, but most had survived and a few had thrived.

Those Warriors who watched their descendants more diligently than she had were more well-versed in modern ways and language. Indikaiya knew enough to get by, but she was too often confused — even lost — in a world which had grown and changed so very quickly.

Sorin was like her in that way. He was a part of this world, he lived and moved within it, but on rare occasions she saw the age in him, the years that had passed. In an out of place phrase or a too-formal and old-fashioned gesture, he gave himself away. He was no more of this time than she was.

The building Sorin approached was red brick, sporting more than its share of ivy. The windows were shuttered. Though some lights shone along this quiet street, the Council building was dark. At first glance it appeared to be lifeless. Her instincts warned her not to approach. Was that truly an instinct that sensed the darkness of the place, or did some kind of vampire magic meant to keep the unwanted away surround the building? She should be immune to such unnatural magic. Surely it was nothing more than her own good instincts that warned her to stay away.

She scoffed, silently. Even if the building was filled with vampires, it could be deemed lifeless. They were an abomination, not *life* at all. They were walking dead things.

She glanced at Sorin and frowned. The few vampires she had met since Chloe had called her into this world were making her question her knowledge of the bloodsuckers. Was it truly possible that vampires were no different from humans in that some were good while others were evil? How could a being whose sustenance came from the blood of others be considered good in any way?

Again, gray. She preferred her battles to be black and white, but looking back — were they ever?

Sorin stepped to the massive double doors of the red brick building, turned to her and said, "Wait here."

"I will not," Indikaiya answered.

For the first time, she saw his anger. Fangs, glowing blue eyes... and she could swear that his already broad shoulders grew broader, that he grew impossible taller. Instinctively she took a step back. She recovered quickly and moved back toward him. In the distance, she heard faint gunfire. Someone somewhere had joined in a battle in his city under siege. Soldiers from this time? Law enforcement? An armed citizen?

"If you are attempting to glamour me, save your strength," she said. "I am immune to your... charms."

In an instant he shifted back to the Sorin she knew. "I only want to make certain it is safe for you. There are two of us. If Council headquarters is teeming with Marie's soldiers, we won't make it out alive. I have a chance, if word that I betrayed Marie has not spread too widely. You, on the other hand, will be attacked on the spot."

"I can defend myself," she argued.

"Against a dozen panicked vampires?"

"Yes." Her voice was strong and certain, even as her stomach turned at the thought.

"A hundred?" he offered in a lowered voice.

She was brave, but she was no fool. "As you wish, then."

His head turned toward the next round of gunfire. It seemed to be closer than the last.

"You are a powerful witch," Rurik said.

Nevada sat on the top step of the stairway which was just a few steps beyond her bedroom door, her feet on the step below, hands clenched in her lap. Rurik stood behind her. He was often close, she had noticed, nearby more often than any of the other Warriors.

Just a coincidence? Maybe. Maybe not.

"I suppose," she said softly.

"Be proud of your abilities," Rurik insisted.

He moved around her, and she scooted over a few inches to allow him to pass. Instead of walking past and down the stairs, he lowered himself to sit beside her. Rurik was a big guy, so it was a tight fit. Not that she minded.

"The sanctuary spell has been reinstated," he continued, "and you managed to make a talisman that will allow Luca to be remembered. That was no easy feat. Everyone is impressed."

"He's wearing the ring, but I don't think he likes it much." She couldn't believe she'd met a vampire like that before and didn't remember! That was some seriously powerful magic.

Rurik laughed, a little. "No, he does not enjoy being remembered by the humans. I suspect he will remove the ring when he no longer leads us in battle."

His arm pressed against hers. She could lean away, but she didn't. She liked it, the warmth and the strength and the solidness of him. She'd been isolated for so long, held prisoner, left alone with her books and her fear and the occasional terrifying vampire. And her magic. Always her magic.

"I'm done now," she said. "There's nothing else for me here. I should leave."

Rurik tensed. "Why? You are one of us. You belong here."

Nevada shook her head. She didn't belong anywhere, and that was the problem. "I'm no solider. In a physical fight, I would be worse than useless." She'd been in this house, in this room, for years. The vampires had tried to force her to unleash her inborn magic, to bloom so she could do as they wished. It had taken a while, but eventually it had happened. A dam had burst within her. In the past few months she'd discovered many things about herself. She could wield magic. She was a witch. No pointy hat or wart on the nose, and so far she hadn't turned green, but still, she couldn't deny who she was.

As Rurik said, a damned powerful witch.

Tempting as it was, how could she leave now and hide away when she could be an important part of this war? She'd learned to travel remotely, and had placed a protection spell on her family so they could escape this place. She'd ended the sanctuary spell and then recast it, and she had cast a spell to make it easier for the Warriors to come in. Well, easier for the conduits to hear and understand. Same thing. She'd charmed an ordinary ring in order to dampen Luca's magic. She could do amazing stuff. If she put enough of herself into the task, she could find her family on her own. Until now, all her talents, all her energy, had been used for unselfish magic. She could not afford to think only of what she wanted for herself. That had not changed, and could not. Not yet.

Maybe there was a spell she hadn't even thought of that could mean the difference between winning and losing. Maybe she could weaken Marie somehow, or find a way to give the Warriors an edge. Tempted as she was, how could she leave?

"What news of the war?" she asked, eager to change the subject. After all, it wasn't like she knew anything she wasn't told. There was no TV in her room, she didn't have a computer or a cell phone, and even if she did, how could she trust anything she might see on the news?

"Marie's efforts are not particularly organized," Rurik said. "There are skirmishes each night, packs of vampires on the streets. We eliminate all we can, but there are always more."

"The military has to be on this, right? Police, too.

Right?"

"Some, but they are not equipped to do battle with Marie and her monsters. They do not yet understand, though we have warned them, we have told them how to fight against Marie's soldiers." Rurik shook his head. "They seem reluctant to believe us. The White House and the Capitol Building are being heavily guarded, and so far those within them are safe. For now, the more dangerous areas are in the outskirts, where ordinary people live."

Ordinary people would have no idea how to fight against vampires. None. "If Marie and her soldiers can turn enough people, if more vampires flock to the city, how long before they can take on any army?"

Rurik shrugged his broad shoulders.

Nevada took a deep breath. She was decided. "I'll stay, at least for now. I have books to study. Spells to try. I can always experiment on you." She meant it as a tease, but it came out sounding a bit creepy. Still, he smiled.

"You may experiment on me any time." With that, he stood. "We're moving to a new headquarters soon."

"Where?"

"I do not know."

In all honestly, Nevada didn't care where they went. She wanted out of this place. Marie had been here, in Nevada's room, in these hallways. Marie and some of her most disgusting, evil henchmen. She wouldn't mind being in a place where those vampires had never been, a place where the air she breathed had never been tainted with the scent of an evil self-proclaimed vampire queen.

"Marie will find me wherever I am, if she sets her mind to it," Nevada said.

Rurik looked her in the eye, then. Nevada felt his determination to her very bones.

"She will have to come through me, if she is so foolish."

Those dark eyes smoldered, and Nevada's stomach fluttered. She was pretty sure he liked her. Either that, or he was a big flirt and she was the only unattached girl around for him to play with. He wasn't what she'd call cute, but he was definitely a stud. In the past, she'd always fallen for skinny nerds, brains over muscles, glasses and smarts over swords and brawn. That Nevada had been a different person. Sorin might as well have killed her back then. The naive college student whose dreams were simple — a good job, a smart husband, a couple of beautiful kids one day — was gone.

She could hope she and Rurik might date when this was over, to see if there was really anything between them, but when this was over, if it was ever over, he'd go back to wherever he'd come from.

Too bad.

***

The door was unlocked. That in itself was unusual. Sorin stepped into the open entryway, his eyes adjusting instantly to the darkness. He stood very still. He listened. Someone was here, but the place wasn't filled with the kindred as he had suspected it might be.

"Sorin, thank the heavens."

Pablo stepped into Sorin's line of vision. Wearing the ceremonial robe of the Council, Pablo wrung his hands in evident dismay. "I had begun to think no one would come. This is a disaster, a disaster, I tell you."

"I agree. Are you here alone?"

"Yes. The others all fled. Cowards," he muttered. "They were afraid of this uprising. They're afraid that vampires might be emboldened to attack the Council members who have guided them for so long."

Guided? Not the word Sorin would've chosen. The Council had been a collection of power-hungry dictators who didn't hesitate to end anyone who got in their way or did not follow their set of rules to the letter. Marie had been one of them. It was no wonder Luca and the others hadn't bothered to try to include the Council in this war. He was a bit surprised that other vampires had not come here looking for protection or assistance. That alone was enough to tell Sorin how unpopular the Council had become. Not only unpopular, but insignificant.

"Well, I'm not entirely alone," Pablo said with a

wave of his hand. "There are a few humans in residence. I must be nourished, and I dare not leave. Someone has to maintain a semblance of order. This is our home. I will not desert."

Sorin suspected Pablo simply had no place to go. He had been a Council member for far too long.

"How many is a few?" Sorin asked. The humans Pablo kept here were prisoners, as he himself had kept Nevada and her family prisoners.

"Four. Five if the elderly woman with the unfortunate limp has not yet passed. She didn't look well the last time I saw her."

Pablo and four or five weakened humans. Council headquarters was not a dangerous place, after all. Sorin was disappointed. He was itching for a fight, and he'd thought to find one here. "I have a companion on the front steps. I'm going to let her in now."

"A companion?" Pablo asked.

Sorin ignored the question. What else was he to call Indikaiya? He could hardly refer to her as a friend, and it would not do to tell Pablo that the Immortal Warrior was here to take out the kindred.

When Indikaiya stepped inside at Sorin's invitation, eyes sharp and sword drawn, Pablo backed away in fear.

"He's the only one here, and he is no danger to us." Sorin said. "Leave him be."

She did not sheathe her sword. "We should find the fight that is moving closer and join in. There are only a few hours until sunrise, and…"

Sorin turned to Pablo. What the hell? If he was going to fight for the humans, he supposed it wouldn't hurt to throw himself whole-heartedly into his new role. Hero. Rescuer. Truth be told, he knew Indikaiya would be pissed if she found out people were being held here and he had abandoned them to Pablo.

He shouldn't care what she thought, but he did.

"Show us to the humans."

"Of course, you're hungry." Pablo led them to a stairway that wound down. The three of them moved quickly, efficiently. Faint lights lit the way at intervals of perhaps six feet. It was enough that even Indikaiya should be able to see. When they reached the proper level, Pablo led them down a long hallway, reaching into a pocket in his robe for a set of jangling keys. "Would you prefer male or female? Female, I suppose. I have a particularly tasty teenage girl in room six. The glamour is wearing off so she might fight you, but I'm sure a man of your stature will have no problem with that." He chuckled. "Even I have no problem with her."

He unlocked an unmarked door and swung it open to reveal a young, terrified girl who was half dressed and chained to her narrow bed. When the door opened, she screamed and yanked at her chains. Her eyes were dull and unfocused. If he passed her on the street he'd think her to be high on drugs.

How far gone was she? Had she been glamoured so many times her brain was gone? Had Pablo been feeding her his own blood, so that she might be on the edge of becoming what she so despised?

"Shut up, girl," Pablo snapped. "Sit down and shut up and offer all you have to offer to your betters."

Those were his last words, in this world or any other. Without warning, Indikaiya raised her sword, swung it, and took Pablo's head. He had a moment to look surprised before he went to dust. Just a moment.

The pale, thin girl on the bed had a clear view of the beheading through the open door. She stopped screaming; she relaxed, her shoulders dropping slightly and her hand unclenching. "Please, please, let me out of this place. I want to go home, I just want to go home."

Indikaiya retrieved the keys Pablo had dropped, keys that were sitting on top of a fine robe now filled with gray ash. "We will free her and the others before we move on to battle."

Sorin took the keys from her and quickly found the one that fit the lock that held the girl's chains. "How long have you been here?" he asked. He was careful not to show his fangs — even though he was hungry and she smelled tempting. It would not do for him to drink from a girl who'd been serving as a food source. He did not want to take the risk that she might be turned.

Besides, Indikaiya was watching.

"A few days, I think," the girl said. When she was free she rubbed her wrists. "Time is weird here."

In other words, she did not know.

"I shouldn't have run away," she whispered. "I never should've run away. I just want to go home now."

Indikaiya took the heavy key ring from him and moved down the hallway, opening doors, searching empty rooms and those that housed prisoners, and releasing those prisoners.

Most seemed not too badly damaged by their time here, though there were a couple who were dazed into incoherence. The elderly woman Pablo had mentioned was indeed dead.

Four. There were a total of four living prisoners on this level.

Sorin explained what was going on, as simply as he could. He suggested that they wait in this building until the sun was up, before making their way to a safe place. He explained about the sanctuary spell, sunlight — the heart and the head. He and Indikaiya led the four up to the main floor, after gathering some food from a makeshift kitchen located on the prison level. Crackers and peanut butter. Bottled water. Stale bread and a jar of mixed nuts. It was better than nothing, but not by much.

He turned on a few low lights on the ground level. The humans were much happier when they could see into all corners. Indikaiya had also collected a lighter and a stack of old newspapers and magazines someone had left on the counter in that kitchen down below. He did not ask why. He did not have to.

"Eat," Indikaiya said as the humans made themselves comfortable. They sat on the floor not far from the front entrance, holding onto food and water and one another. All were still dazed and damaged, but it was possible they would regain their minds. One day.

Indikaiya placed the newspapers and magazines beside a young man who looked slightly less far gone than the others. She handed him the lighter with some care. "Gather your strength and your courage, and stay here until the sun rises." Her eyes grew hard as she added, "And as you leave, burn this unholy place to the ground."

The man — a boy, really — nodded. He did have some of his wits about him, still. He added, in a lowered voice, "I believe I saw a propane tank in the kitchen. A small one, but still…"

"I'm not going back down there," the girl Pablo had offered to Sorin said in a sharp voice. "Not now, not ever, not going back down."

The man with the lighter seemed no more eager to retrieve the propane tank than the girl from room six did, and the other two were dazed beyond caring.

Sorin had once been beyond caring himself, but no more.

He reached into his coat pocket, retrieved the car keys, and tossed them to the boy who was, like it or not, now in charge of himself and the others. The kid caught the keys in the air. "Black Mustang, one block down," Sorin instructed. "Get yourself and the others out of the city. Today."

CHAPTER SEVEN

After Sorin collected the small propane tank located in the kitchen area on the level where the prisoners had been kept and gave it to the young man, Indikaiya and her vampire partner departed Vampire Council headquarters, leaving the former unwilling blood donors there waiting for the sun to rise. In this large city tonight, how many humans were doing just that? Waiting for the sun to rise. Hiding, cowering, believing — hoping — themselves caught in a nightmare that would soon end.

Indikaiya wondered if she'd ever get the unpleasant stench of the place she'd just departed out of her memory. No one else had seemed to notice the overpowering smell of blood and bleach and scented candles, but she had. Vampire Council headquarters was a place of nightmares.

Until he'd inexplicably given the keys to his vehicle to the former blood donor and instructed the boy to get out of town with the others, she'd assumed that she and Sorin would travel in that way to the site of a battle. Instead, they walked crisply, side by side, toward the sound of gunfire. Surrendering his vehicle had been out of character for Sorin, one that made her question everything she thought she knew of him. She had never seen him as one for self-sacrifice.

To be honest, she preferred walking to speeding along in that car Sorin seemed to enjoy. In the passenger seat she was out of control, entirely in his hands. She had rarely been comfortable in anyone else's hands, least of all a vampire's. She would also admit, it had been an effective mode of travel. Perhaps if someone taught her to drive and put the steering wheel in *her* hands...

But for now, they walked, following the sounds of war. Echoing gunshots and distant screams. It was more than sound that drew them, it was a particular energy in the air, an indefinable call she and Sorin both responded to on a soul-deep level. Indikaiya did not know precisely what they would find when they reached their destination. A battle, yes, but would it be a battle large or small? Soldiers or civilians against the vampires? Would any of her kind be there? The fight had begun, but this was a young war. Neither side was yet well organized. That would come.

She and Sorin did not speak for a while. They listened, aware of all that was taking place around them and of what was ahead. The battle grew closer with every step they took.

Finally, Sorin said, "I would have killed Pablo if you had not."

Was that relief rushing through her? Why? Why

did she care? "I'm glad to hear it," she said, her voice flat. She did not want him to know that she cared at all for what he might or might not do.

"You have to know, a few weeks ago, that would not have been the case." Sorin's voice was not emotionless. He was angry. "I would've fed from that girl, no matter how close she was to turning or madness or death."

Was it a confession? If so, why? His words revealed an unexpected honesty from him, and though he was obviously angry, she heard no regret. Had he not said that he had none? Sorin did not apologize, not for who he was or what he had done. Still, he was not the same man he'd been, not so long ago.

"What caused this change in you?"

He shrugged, as if gently throwing off the question, as if doing his best to make it unimportant. "I don't know, not entirely. The revolution seemed like such a good idea, when I aligned myself with Marie. I've been hiding for hundreds of years, as my kind has done for so long. Why should I live in shadows when I'm stronger, longer-lived, *better* than any human?"

She heard the frustration in his voice, saw it in the tightening of his jaw. "And yet, you shifted to the other side. Your allegiance is no longer to that freedom which you profess to desire. Is it the witch? Have you come to care for her?"

He didn't answer for a while, and then he said,

"Yes."

Of course. Why did that answer disappoint her, a little? To be honest, she was more than a *little* disappointed. Nevada was not much more than a child.

"Not in the way you imagine, though," he added after a short pause.

"Explain," she said simply.

"No."

Even if she were inclined to push him to answer, which she was not, the time for conversation had passed. A human ran toward them. The man was dressed in a black uniform. No, dark blue. She had seen such a uniform on one of the conduits who had accompanied his Warrior to the mansion. The man gripped a weapon, a small gun, in his hand. He raised that gun, pulling the trigger as he screamed, "Fucking vampires!" Indikaiya and Sorin both leapt away, but that was unnecessary. He had already expended all the bullets.

"I am not a vampire!" Indikaiya shouted indignantly as the police officer ran past. How could the human have made such a horrible mistake?

Sorin laughed.

"It's not funny! Why would he think I'm like *you?*"

He was not offended, or at least, appeared not to be. The anger she had sensed in him earlier was gone. "You look as if you stepped out of another time," he said.

"I did!"

"When we get a few minutes, we really do need to take you shopping."

Shopping? Ridiculous. She was ready to argue the point, but there was no time. Straight ahead, yet another police officer was doing battle with a vampire. And losing. He fired a shot from one of the small guns. The bullet entered the vampire's shoulder. A wasted shot.

Sorin leaped in, wrapped his arm around the vampire's neck, and neatly separated it from the body.

A body covered with the blood of humans.

The policeman watched the vampire all but disappear, leaving nothing but ashes. He took a deep breath, then thanked Sorin. "Where did you come from?" he added, his voice tired and more than a little suspicious. "You're not... one of us."

"We will talk when this is done," Sorin said, and then he rushed forward to join the fight that had been edging closer. Indikaiya did the same. Many humans had fallen here. In the beginning, they'd had the numbers against the vampires, but no more. The bloodsuckers were winning.

It was a small battle, likely one of many taking place on this night. Humans battling monsters. Monsters delighting in their violence and their blood. The sidewalk and the street were littered with bodies, with blood, and with dust. There was not nearly enough dust.

A vampire with long greasy hair and a blood-stained mouth grinned as he ran toward Indikaiya. She ducked, spun, then rose up and with a single swing of her blade took his head. Sorin was quickly engaged in a similar battle, drawing his short, heavy sword from his leather coat and taking down one of his own kind.

Together they turned the tide. Soon the police officers and the handful of civilians who had joined them for this fight realized that the newcomers were on their side. Knowing they had help seemed to energize them.

"Take the head or destroy the heart!" Sorin shouted. He had a voice that could be heard above the noise of battle. "Don't waste your bullets!" He threw himself into battle as if he were fighting for his very existence.

Soon he was truly fighting for his life. The vampire rebels who had been near victory when Indikaiya and Sorin had arrived on the scene soon realized that they were now fighting one of their own. In many cases they turned their attentions from the humans to the vampire. And to her. The humans were easy to kill. The two newcomers were a much bigger and more immediate threat. Many of the humans eased back, into shadow, some dropping to sit or lie on the ground. They were almost done in, after what was only the first of what might be many such encounters.

Indikaiya would never ease into the shadows.

She never had, not even as a human. At last, she had the chance to do what she had come to this world to do. Kill vampires. She was skilled with a sword. She knew how and where to strike, and she knew just as well how to avoid the blows of her opponents. Her movements were quick and they were deadly. Any who thought they had an advantage because they faced a woman were soon disabused of that notion.

The tide turned. The few surviving vampires fled.

And Indikaiya and Sorin found themselves surrounded by weary and wounded humans who were grateful but also suspicious. Those who had allowed themselves to rest rose wearily to their feet. She wondered if they would last more than a few days in this war.

One stepped forward. His uniform was torn. Blood, his own, ran from a small but deep gash on his forehead. It had stopped bleeding, but she could see that it needed tending. Soon. But that concern was for later, as they all recovered from this fight.

"Why would two vampires join us to fight against their own kind?" the man asked.

Indikaiya responded hotly. "I am *not* a vampire!"

"You don't look human," another fighter responded.

"I am a vampire," Sorin said. "She is not." He looked to the east, where the sky was lightening. "I don't have a lot of time, but I can tell you this. There are some of us who are fighting for you. With you."

He explained about the sanctuary spell falling and then being reinstated. One bloodied fighter was so relieved, he burst into tears. Sorin explained again about the few ways in which to kill a vampire, and about most of the kindred being vulnerable to sunlight — natural or artificial.

That done, he looked to her. "We don't have time to make it back to the house before daylight."

If he'd kept the powerful vehicle with the darkly tinted windows, they might easily make it back to the mansion. That was not an option. She thought of Council headquarters — a place she did not wish to see or smell again — and then, from that direction, she heard an explosion. The propane tank. Council headquarters would soon be no more. Just as well. It had been a place of true evil.

Sorin offered her a tired smile. "I have an idea."

Indikaiya needed new clothes — otherwise humans would be mistaking her for kindred again and again — and he needed to get indoors before the sun truly rose. She didn't like it when he flew with her clutched in his arms, but at the moment it was necessary.

Such language, from a lady.

Normally Sorin could stand enough sunlight to get from one place to another during the day. Direct sun made him feel ill, and his powers were greatly diminished, but he could function. At the moment he was drained from the fight, and it had been too long since he'd fed. He wasn't sure what would happen if he tried to brave the sunlight, but he didn't want to test it. Once the sun was truly upon him, he would not be able to fly at all. In his current condition, he would hardly be able to walk.

He didn't have to carry Indikaiya far. They dropped down near the glass doors of an upscale department store situated among trendy cafes and boutiques on a tree-lined street. It would do. The store was large, deep, and it was unlikely that there would be even a single window in the rear of the building. They both needed rest. Sleep. They also needed to feed. Indikaiya could likely find nourishment in any of the establishments along this street. He could not, not if it remained as deserted as it was at this moment.

Besides, he was hungry, but far from desperate.

Indikaiya walked toward the doors with her sword raised, as if she intended to burst inside. Sorin moved past her so quickly he would be no more than a blur, and he opened the unlocked door. As he had suspected, many normal precautions had gone by the wayside.

Indikaiya stopped, lowered her weapon, and walked inside. Behind her, the sun peeked over the horizon. The sunlight wasn't full strength, not yet, but he'd just as soon not stand around and see how he'd react to it after he'd spent the night fighting his own kind and passing up one human after another when he was hungry and needed nourishment.

If he fed from a soldier, a much-needed fighter, they'd be weakened. Those unable to fight had gone, or else were hiding. He could take the blood of a fighter and it might come to that, eventually, but... not yet.

He walked down a wide aisle toward the rear of the store. Indikaiya followed. The lights above were on and the front entrance had been unlocked, but there were no humans within these walls. Hungry as he was, he would've smelled them immediately. Someone had left in a hurry last night, or else had been taken. The latter was most likely.

The lights were bright, showing the fine merchandise at its best. Glass cases sparkled. Thin, well-dressed mannequins stood guard along wide aisles.

His companion studied the racks of clothing as they walked by. Her head swiveled toward the jewelry counter, and then, with a snap, toward the shoes. Sorin smiled. Women of any age and time...

"Will there be food here?" she asked, her thoughts closely following his own.

"Probably." Food for her, anyway. "If not, you are welcome to leave."

"But you must stay until dark."

"Yes."

"Will you sleep?"

"Some."

She took a deep breath. "You have proven

yourself useful, so I will not desert you. We will sleep in shifts, one guarding the other. These are uncertain times, and even though we are not of the same world we must stick together."

He was surprised. He'd thought Indikaiya would be glad to leave him behind.

She wouldn't like it when he told her he needed to feed. He knew how to take just enough, he knew how to drink without killing. The process would still disgust her, he imagined. Too bad. Perhaps he had come down on a side of this war he had never imagined, but he was who he was. That wasn't going to change. He'd hidden his true self for too long. He might have changed, but his reason for joining Marie in the first place had not.

When they were well away from the windows and any hint of sunlight, he turned to her and said, "I need to feed."

Indikaiya did not look startled, as he'd thought she might. She simply said, "Don't look at me." She followed that statement with a raised hand and a pointing, accusing finger. "And don't think you can glamour me into agreeing to offer up my throat as your dinner troth. As a Warrior, I am immune to your magic."

"Some women find the experience quite pleasant."

"I would not."

"How do you know unless…"

"We are soldiers with a common enemy, that is

all." She placed a ready hand on the handle of one dagger. Judging by the intensity in her eyes, she knew he was talking about more than feeding. Warrior, Atlantean, beautiful and strong woman. Sex with her would be amazing.

He might even let her be on top.

CHAPTER EIGHT

Rubble. Lingering smoke. Ruin. Council headquarters was gone.

Marie's first impulse on this morning had been to start throwing breakable things against the nearest fire-charred wall. Normally she indulged all her impulses, but on this occasion she refrained. She didn't want the followers around her to witness even the smallest break in her self-control.

Not that they hadn't seen her at her worst, as well as at her best.

She'd lost too many soldiers in the past two nights. It was true, humans had greater numbers than the kindred, but that should not matter. Vampires were superior in every way. She should be winning!

Flamethrowers. She had not expected the human army to have so many of them. The oldest among the kindred could withstand some fire, but the healing process was longer and more painful than it would be for a more ordinary wound. And the new ones, the children, they went to dust in the flame far too quickly, and with terrifying screams.

She should be in the White House by now, lounging in the ultimate seat of power, issuing orders to humans and vampires alike. Orders which would be followed to the letter, thanks to loyalty or fear or both. Marie admitted to herself that her initial plan had been old-fashioned. There had been a time when sitting on the throne was enough, when rebellion was a matter of taking physical possession of a castle, and with it an army.

In those days, the peasants had not been so well-armed, and they had certainly not been so damned independent and willing to fight for others of their kind. She had not taken into consideration the modern mindset, the annoying and relatively new belief that all were equal in this world. Equal? To her? No.

The leaders of this country had gone underground. Perhaps literally, but then again, perhaps they'd been whisked away from the city altogether. She could not take the White House, not yet. It was too well guarded, by soldiers with impressive weapons — including those damned flamethrowers. Even if she made it to the front door, she couldn't go *through* that door.

Now this. Council headquarters, where she had expected to be able to set up her own command site, had burned to the ground. The damage was primarily on the first and second floor. There were certainly many rooms beneath her feet that were habitable, but dammit, she refused to hide in rubble! She needed and expected better. More. She needed and expected the best of everything, and this was far from the best.

For now, she needed to focus on more immediate concerns. She was going to take her Potomac mansion back.

The vampire army's numbers had grown, through newly made children as well as older and more powerful kindred who'd flocked to her, who embraced her cause and wanted to be on the front lines. With that army she could take the Warriors, as well as any of her own kind who were foolish enough to have chosen the wrong side. She could win this, and she would. She was determined, ready to move forward.

If she were lucky, both Sorin and the witch would still be at the mansion, and she could make things right again.

This time, she would take the traitorous vampire's heart and the redheaded witch's mind. That would be much more satisfying than giving in to her earlier childish impulse and breaking a vase or a plate.

The weakest among the soldiers who were with her on this irritating morning, the new, the babies, they would have to wait here in what remained of Council headquarters. They would have to hide below ground, in rubble and darkness, until the sun set once again.

But she and any who were strong enough to survive a bit of sun would depart.

Thanks to Ahron she knew where to go. Thanks to Ahron, she had a plan.

***

Impossible. There was no way! Chloe placed a hand on her stomach — her increasingly *rounded* stomach — and turned away from a curious Duncan, who was watching her like a hawk. They were preparing to move tonight, packing up their weapons, as well as food for the humans among them. Warriors, too. The Warriors didn't seem to need to eat, but they liked food well enough. Junk food and beer and wine, for the most part.

Her baby, Luca's daughter, was growing at an alarming rate. How long before she gave birth? Days or weeks? Not months, she knew that already.

It was near noon. Chloe felt the power of the sun in the sky in her gut, in an instinct that urged her to hide, to seek darkness. She couldn't do that. If she was careful in her movements she could make her way to the stairs and up without being exposed to direct sunlight. She wasn't as strong in the daytime as she was at night, and if she passed too close to a shaft of sunlight she felt a bit queasy until she moved away.

Her weakness was the reason they were waiting for dark — or at least near full dark — before leaving this house.

She needed to talk to another woman, and the few female Warriors in their ranks gave her a wide berth. There was one female conduit who remained in the house. She cooked, she mended torn clothing, she patched up wounded humans. Chloe didn't dare go near her. The woman was terrified of the few vampires among them, and to be honest, Chloe still couldn't entirely trust herself alone with a person. The smell of blood, the sound of a fast heartbeat... dinner bell.

Nevada Sheldon, the witch among them, had tried to help when Chloe had been human. Maybe she'd be willing to help now. Chloe would still need to exercise great control, but she was certain Nevada was her best bet.

For once, the Warrior Rurik was not standing guard at the witch's door. Even he was busy with preparations for the move. Chloe knocked on the door, then opened it without waiting for a "come in."

Nevada's back was to her, as the witch packed books into sturdy cardboard boxes. Her long red hair was caught in a braid, her clothing for today was blue jeans and a pale blue t-shirt that had seen better days. She'd lost weight, it seemed. No surprise there. And oh, she smelled so good!

Nevada would likely not help at all if Chloe threatened to feed on her.

"I don't want to hear another word about this," the girl said. "Every book goes with me. Every book, every stone, every stinky vial of powder. How can I know what I'll..." Nevada spun around. She abruptly stopped speaking when she saw who stood there. For a long moment, she didn't breathe. "Need," she finally finished in a weak voice.

WARRIOR RISING | 143

Chloe held up a hand and remained where she stood, near the door and several feet away from the witch. Not that the space would be of any hindrance if she decided to leap.

"I won't hurt you, I swear."

"Glad to hear it." There wasn't even a hint of confidence in Nevada's voice.

"I need your help."

Nevada's eyes dropped to Chloe's stomach, just as the baby moved. "Holy mother of…" the witch began, and then she sat, hard, in the chair that was thankfully nearby. "I thought I'd seen everything, but apparently not. I didn't know vampires could… is that a… no, that can't be."

"I'm pregnant," Chloe said bluntly. She could use a chair herself, but didn't dare move any closer to Nevada. She didn't want to spook the girl. Everyone, Nevada included, knew how unpredictable a newborn vampire could be. "I was apparently pregnant before I was turned, and now the child is growing too fast. What's going to happen to me? To *her*?"

As Chloe watched, she saw Nevada's fear turn to amazement, and then to curiosity. The witch stood slowly, her eyes never leaving Chloe's midsection. "I'll need to do some research, and dammit, my books are almost all packed. If I start unpacking they'll rush me out of here and leave some behind."

"We have a few hours."

"You have a few hours. They'll be moving me

soon. Some Warriors and humans will start the exodus this afternoon. The vampires have to wait until dark, but..."

"But you don't," Chloe finished, when the girl floundered.

"No, I don't." She cocked her head and studied Chloe. "Our world has changed. Do you ever stop to think how much?"

Chloe found herself smiling wanly. "If I did, I think I would go crazy." A mad vampire. She doubted she'd be the first, or the last.

If she were inclined to fall in that direction, to dip toward madness, Luca would pull her out of it. Luca, who was so strong and who loved her so much, he would not allow her to go mad. If anyone could will sanity, it would be him.

"I didn't want to be a vampire, you know," Chloe confided. "There was a time when I made Luca promise that he would never turn me. But when I was dying, when my choice was to become like him or leave him, I found it was no choice at all." She lifted her chin. "I am not a monster. I'm still Chloe Fallon." A Chloe Fallon without the threat of an aortic aneurysm going off like a bomb in her chest, without the fear of growing old, or getting sick. No, she had entirely new fears now.

"Doesn't Luca know what to expect?" Nevada pointed to Chloe's stomach, then dropped her hand.

"No. This is sort of unheard of." And wasn't that just great. She'd been a vampire less than a week, and already she was making history. She caught and held Nevada's eye, and the witch flinched a little. "Help me."

"I told you no one would be here." The voice came from the front of the store. Young, with a slight southern accent, it sounded like a bell to Sorin.

He was hungry.

"Someone must be here," another voice — just as young, but with not so much of an accent — responded. "The door was unlocked. Duh. Hello?" she called. And again, "Hello? Anyone?" After a moment the voice, closer now, said, "Jeez, the store has been open for hours, and no one's here?"

"News flash," the first girl said with more than a touch of sarcasm. "Vampires. No one is out looking for new clothes or shoes or perfume."

"What are they doing, then?"

"They're home, watching the news, or else shopping for food and weapons while the sun's out. *Hello.*"

"I don't know. Some of them are bad, I saw that on the news, but really, don't you think the whole idea of vampires is kinda sexy? I read these books..."

"Sexy? Have you lost your mind?"

The girls, growing ever closer, were moving nearer and nearer to a hungry Sorin. They smelled so good. He could drain them both and be satisfied.

He might even be able to leave this place before the sun set.

Nevada had ruined him. These girls — he could smell them more keenly now, see them, though they did not yet see him — were daughters. Perhaps sisters or mothers or friends. They were not expendable. Just a few days ago he would not have given a second thought to their humanity. To their worth. Now he saw more than blood.

But he had to feed.

Sorin glanced back. Indikaiya slept on the floor behind him. She had taken no comfort, created no pillow or mattress from the clothing all around. After they'd bathed as best they could in small, white-tiled bathrooms, and she'd eaten stale crackers and drunk two bottles of water she'd found in an employee break room, she'd simply laid down on the hard floor and closed her eyes.

She slept, still. Just as well.

The two girls gasped when they saw him standing there. Immediately he caught their gaze — one and then the other — and they relaxed. They did not see him as a threat, would not, as long as the simple glamour lasted. They were pretty. One redheaded and one brunette. One thin and the other more rounded. They were nicely dressed, and wore high heeled shoes that made them look taller than they truly were.

Even in heels, they were shorter than Indikaiya.

He stepped toward the girls, smiling. His eyes

would be glowing, he knew that, but neither of them was alarmed. "I'm hungry," he whispered.

The brunette actually jumped up and down a little, then said, "Me first, me first!" She looked at her friend and waggled her eyebrows. "Just like in that book I read." She pushed her hair aside, offering her throat.

He was so hungry.

He leaned down, his fangs extended, and he bit into the offered throat. It would be so easy to drain her, toss her aside, and take the other. But as he drank he paid attention to the essence of her. She loved and was loved. She saw good in everyone and everything. Naive? Yes. Stupid? Once he would have thought so. He stopped well short of draining her, licked the wounds in her throat to facilitate a quick healing, and then turned to the other.

This time he drank slower. His fangs sunk in, he lifted the girl so her feet dangled well off the floor. She was not as sweet in essence as the first, but she was good. Smarter than she allowed others to see, as hungry for love as he was for her blood. As he had with the first girl, he dropped her well short of damaging her in any way, licked her throat, and stepped away. He took their hands, one and then another, then bent to kiss each one in turn. The redhead sighed. The brunette shivered.

A soft sound caught his attention, and he turned to see Indikaiya standing directly behind him, her eyes hard, the sword in her hand ready.

"A man's gotta eat," Sorin said.

Indikaiya didn't drop her sword. The two girls he'd fed from appeared to be unharmed. Calm even. That had to be vampire magic. "Are they damaged?"

"No."

"Swear it."

"I so swear."

"You did use your unholy magic upon them, though, did you not?"

He was the Sorin she had come to know, a man — a *vampire* — who was relaxed, casual, much more comfortable in this time than he should be, given his age. In an instant that changed. His posture shifted, became almost threatening. Almost? Handsome as he was, he presented a terrifying picture. Hard; strong; hungry. His eyes glowed an unnatural blue, and his fangs extended.

"Why is my magic any more unholy than your own?" he asked. "My life is long, and I do what I must to survive, as you do." He took a step closer, moved unwisely closer to her sword. He lowered his voice as he said, "There was a time not so long ago when I would've taken my time with these willing humans. I would've fed, and fucked, and fed some more. I would have taken them both, they would've been mine for hours, perhaps days. They would've been glad of it, *undamaged* and satisfied, if a bit weak. So don't give me any shit about taking what I need and nothing more."

One of the girls behind him said, "Did he say

fuck? I wouldn't mind. I haven't had a boyfriend in ages, which means I haven't had an orgasm in ages, and he *is* hot. In that book I read vampires are, like, really good at the sex stuff. Maybe because they've had so much practice."

"I've never had a threesome," the redhead whispered. "Oh my God! Thank goodness I wore my good underwear!"

"Is that part of your glamour?" Indikaiya asked.

"No," Sorin answered, without offering any further explanation.

"My name is Carly," the brunette said.

"Like he cares," the redhead responded.

"Hey, if we're going to do it, I want him to know my name. This is Jane," Carly added, pointing to her friend. "And in case you're curious, the carpet does match the drapes. Natural redhead here."

Carpet? Drapes? Indikaiya was confused by that reference. No matter. It was clear these two humans wanted to lie with Sorin.

Could she blame them? He was an impressive specimen of manhood. Not human, not Warrior, but still very much a man.

Revealing nothing though she was unexpectedly bristling with a mixture of emotions she could not quite describe, she said, "It appears you have two willing partners just waiting for your attentions." Panting for it. "I will be happy to wait near the front of the store while you fulfill all their desires."

"That won't be necessary," Sorin said. His fangs retreated. His eyes no longer glowed.

Was that relief in her chest? No. She did not, could not care. She maintained her composure as she asked, "Are these willing women not the kind of sexual partner you prefer?"

He didn't respond immediately. And maybe his eyes did glow, a bit, as he said. "They are babies. Children. I want more."

"More what?" she asked, knowing as she did that she shouldn't have asked, realizing as the words left her mouth that she should've walked away before the conversation had reached this point.

"Indikaiya, Warrior woman, I want you."

CHAPTER NINE

Nevada walked down the stairs almost tentatively. She took easy steps, her hand barely brushing the bannister. It wasn't her first trip to the first floor of the mansion, but she'd been confined to her room for so long it still felt odd to venture far beyond it.

She wouldn't be in this house much longer, and that suited her just fine. Too much had happened here. Her world — the entire world — had changed since she'd been brought here against her will.

Nevada felt that change to her core. She wasn't the same person she'd been when Sorin had kidnapped her. She couldn't say if she was better or worse, but she was definitely different. The woman — the girl — she had once been had been so naive. Not stupid, not entirely clueless, but blind to too much of the world around her. That girl had lived in a bubble where if something didn't affect her, it did not exist.

She was glad to be moving to a new place. She didn't know exactly where they were going, but it didn't really matter.

The army was on the move, and she was part of that army.

After Chloe had left Nevada's room, Nevada had tried to meditate, to search not for a magical spell she might find in a book, but rather reaching for the inherent magic that had slept inside her for so long. What she'd found, what she'd experienced, had startled her. She hadn't thought that was possible, not after everything she'd been through, but in that meditation she'd found a connection to something, someone, some truth that rocked her to her core.

She'd already decided not to say anything to anyone, not just yet, because how could she be sure that she was right about what she felt? Maybe her imagination was running amok. Maybe she was closer to the breaking point than she'd thought was possible. Who was she kidding? It was a miracle she wasn't a raving lunatic.

Nevada swung through the kitchen and grabbed an orange soda from the fridge and a pack of cookies — chocolate chip — from the counter. It was a nice kitchen, and someone was keeping it stocked. Not *well* stocked, but no one was going hungry. Except maybe the vampires. Too bad no one left here really knew how to cook. That one conduit who'd stayed behind had taken on the job, but she'd already moved on, following her Warrior to one of the other outposts. Besides, she hadn't exactly been a great chef.

Nevada would be satisfied with cookies, for the moment. There were some leftovers in the fridge, but nothing she wanted. She'd love a steak and a baked potato, a big plate of grilled shrimp and veggies, shoot, even one of her mother's mystery casseroles would be heaven right now.

There were eggs and bacon. Those were easy enough to prepare, if she got hungry later.

With her drink and snack in hand, she headed toward the sound of a television in a massive den off the front entryway. A couple of Warriors and conduits, none she knew all that well, had gathered around a television to watch an all-news channel try to make sense of what was happening. Nevada remained in the doorway, ready to run if necessary. Lately she was always poised to make an escape. She trusted no one, felt safe nowhere. Well, maybe she trusted Rurik. Maybe she felt safe when he was around.

Nevada half listened to the newscast, as she replayed her latest meditation again. Could she be right? Was what seemed to be real — a rush of knowledge as if someone had crammed it all into her head in one painful blast — actual fact?

Chloe's daughter, what — who — Nevada believed was going to be a half vamp half human amazing creature, was the one who should be queen of the vampires. (Queen of the humans? Not so much.) If Nevada was right, the child would possess her mother's goodness and her father's power. She would know love and kindness and strength. She would be amazing.

One of the conduits glanced back. His eyes

widened when he saw Nevada standing there. She offered a weak smile, and he quickly returned his attention to the television. A wave of sadness wafted through her. The man was afraid of her. In his mind, a witch wasn't any better than a vampire. She possessed a power he did not. Even though as a conduit he himself had his own special ability, she could do things he didn't and would never understand.

Tough shit. What was happening here was too important for her to get her feelings hurt because not everyone liked her.

The war that had begun here in this mansion was about more than vampires being tired of staying hidden in the shadows. That ship had sailed. Once they've talked about vampires on Fox News and CNN there was no going back. Vampires had been exposed to the world, and they'd never be able to hide again. That's not what the war was about. Maybe once it had been, but not anymore.

No, this war was about the bitch queen vs an as-yet unborn powerful being that no one, not even the oldest vampire, had seen coming.

Nevada didn't think she'd be unborn for much longer.

Indikaiya considered exiting the department store, leaving Sorin to his silly enamored humans and whatever activities the threesome preferred. If she wasn't present he'd probably be having sex with them right now. Both at once, or one after the other. The vampire was walking sex, she knew that. In his hundreds of years he'd been with countless women, most of whom he'd also fed from. Had he left them damaged beyond repair? Turned them to his kind? Killed them? She walked toward the sunlight, head high, not looking back. She had come into this world to fight vampires, not tend to them. No matter how unexpectedly and disturbingly appealing they might be. No matter that she felt a soldier to soldier connection, which did come with the need and obligation to protect.

She stopped by the front door. Sunlight fell on her, and on the deserted street before her. Given the number of shops in the area she doubted this part of town was ever deserted in the middle of the day. Today people were wisely staying in. Hiding. Preparing for the worst. At least, she hoped so. Humans needed to be prepared for whatever might come next.

Her eyes fell on an establishment across the street. On the window there was a simple drawing of a cup and saucer, with wavy lines indicating steam. There would be food. She might walk across the street to see if anyone was there, and ask for nourishment. If no one was there, if the place was as deserted as this store had been when she and Sorin had arrived, she could surely find something. It was tempting. Rurik had filled many hours talking about food in this world. Pizza, hotdogs, french fries. She wouldn't mind tasting one or all of those before she returned home.

But her purpose here was to protect humans. Even those as silly as the two girls Sorin had fed from.

She turned on her heel and headed for the back of the store, following the sound of chattering female and lowered male voices. What were they talking about? Anything was possible. It had been a long time, but as she recalled there wasn't usually much chatter before or during sexual relations. If she walked upon an orgy she'd simply wait. Wait and watch and make sure Sorin didn't harm the women who had thrown themselves at him.

"No," Sorin said, his deep voice unmistakable. "These."

One of the women sighed. "You're not nearly as much fun as I thought you'd be."

Indikaiya found herself smiling, just a little, as she walked into an area of the store devoted to footwear. Most of what she saw was entirely impractical, and still, the shoes drew her attention in an unexpected way.

"Those just came in," the redhead — Jane — said. "They're part of a new fall collection. My supervisor will kill me if I filch a pair."

"A vampire will kill you if you try to run in *those*." Sorin pointed to the high heeled, insubstantial shoes on Jane's feet.

"Boots this time of year?" the other girl, Carly, whined. "It's just wrong, for someone whose job is fashion. You're a vampire, and you're nice. Nice and big and you look really strong. Stay with us and maybe we won't have to run."

Sorin moved so fast, he was a blur even to Indikaiya. He reached Carly in an instant, grabbed her by the throat, and lifted her from the ground. Those delicate shoes of hers dangled several inches from the floor. Her eyes widened, her face turned red. Jane tried to help. She beat against Sorin's back, while insisting that he put her friend down. He seemed not to even realize she was there.

Indikaiya controlled the impulse to assist the girls. If Sorin had wished to kill them, they'd be dead by now. He was a fearsome sight, strong and dangerous enough to scare even these women who had never known real danger.

"I am not like the others, but I am not, nor have I ever been, *nice*. I hope you never have to face another of my kind, but if you do you won't stand a chance as you are."

Indikaiya stepped forward to reveal her presence. She was quite sure Sorin had been aware of her location the entire time they'd been separated. Had he heard her breathing as she'd stood back and watched him interact with the girls? Had he felt her, as she sometimes felt him?

"Why do you care?" she asked.

The truth — and he knew it as well as she did —

was that no matter what kind of footwear these girls wore they did not have a chance against a monster of his kind. They were not fast enough, not strong enough. Soon enough, they would die.

Sorin placed Carly down. The girl wobbled on unsteady feet, swayed as if she might faint, and then lurched toward her friend.

"I don't fucking know," he said. "I shouldn't. I never have before."

The girls both scurried to Indikaiya's side. They had witnessed an aspect of Sorin's character which had been hidden from them before. Finally, for the first time, they were scared.

"He's right, you know," Indikaiya said, her eyes on Sorin's face. A fine face it was, she had to admit. "You should be better prepared when you leave this place."

One of the girls sighed, then said, "I'm a lover, not a fighter."

Indikaiya turned to look down at her. "Who says you can't be both?"

Nevada had not just made him remember the past, she'd cursed him. When he returned to the Potomac mansion he'd insist that she undo whatever she'd done to him.

Shit, by the time he left this department store, Nevada would not be at the mansion. No one would. They'd be closer to the center of town, closer to the action and headquartered in a place Marie had never been.

Sorin had a hard time admitting that whatever had happened to him had begun before the witch had cursed him. It had started with Phillip Stargel, the child — and conduit — he had been ordered to kill. Phillip was different. Not right, some would say. Special, others would insist. Complete innocence, that's what Sorin himself had seen in the child that day. The day he'd walked away from a kill, allowing a conduit to live.

When he'd allowed Phillip to live, Sorin had stopped being one of Marie's soldiers. He had changed sides at that moment, his thinking had shifted. No, he did not want to hide who he was any longer. He did not want to live forever in the shadows. That didn't mean vampires had to run the world. That didn't mean all those who opposed them had to die.

Indikaiya worked with the girls — who now wore heavy boots with their summer dresses — teaching them a few basic defensive moves. Neither of them would be capable of taking a vampire's head. Even if they'd had a couple of spare swords handy to give to the girls, to decapitate took a lot of strength.

With the girls' help, Indikaiya removed a large number of colorful blouses from a metal clothing rack. She studied the construction and then, with her capable bare hands, she dismantled it. It took

Sorin a moment to realize what she was doing. She hefted a length of metal from the rack, spun it about in a sort of test, and then she placed one end against the floor — there in the aisle where the floor was tile instead of carpet — and shaped the end into a crude tip. He could not help but admire the smooth motion, the sleek and feminine muscles in her arms, the determination on her face. She was well and truly unlike any woman he had ever met. And he had met a lot of women.

The Warrior fashioned two deadly spears. Carly ripped one of the discarded shirts from the ruined rack in two and wrapped it tightly around the end of her spear, fashioning a crude grip. Indikaiya nodded her approval, and Jane did the same. Heaven above, they were concerned about the *colors* used in this process.

Indikaiya instructed the girls how to hold the weapons, how to stand steady and how to lunge forward with strength and determination. She taught them how to go for the heart.

They still didn't have much of a chance of survival, but not much was better than zero, which is what they'd had when they'd foolishly come to work on a day when the city was at war.

Sorin stood back and watched. He watched Indikaiya, not the silly humans who had insisted on teal and purple for the grips they'd fashioned on their spears. Every move she made was well thought out, smooth and strong and yet still feminine. He could not imagine fighting such a creature in battle. How could any man even think of destroying someone so fine? Death would be better. Death at the hand of a woman without equal.

Not long into the lesson, they were interrupted. Sorin had been a little surprised by the quiet nature of the business. Sure, vampires were running loose in D.C., and chaos reigned, but not every resident would be content to hide and fight. These two silly girls were a grand example.

As were the three boys — teenagers from the look and smell of them — who walked into the store. They were all baggy jeans and ball caps and swagger. One of them said, "I told you no one would be here. We can take whatever we want!"

Fools, even more so than Carly and Jane.

"Like what?" another boy asked. "This is lame. Let's find a store with some electronics. TVs, maybe. I could use a new cell phone."

"My mom's birthday is next week," clueless boy number one said. "I can get her something nice here and it won't cost me a dime."

Fools and thieves. They would not last long in this new world.

"I gotta be home by dark," the third one — the only one smart enough to be nervous — said. "I don't want to run into one of those vamps."

"That's not even real," number one said. "Can't be. I bet it's promo for some vampire movie or something."

Carly and Jane walked around the corner and confronted the boys. Sorin and Indikaiya watched from a short distance away. In heavy boots, with those long spears and a new confidence, the girls were surprisingly impressive.

"No looting here, losers," Jane said. Her tone was actually menacing, as she brandished her weapon.

"Whoa." All three boys backed up a step. Two.

"We're just browsing," the nervous kid said.

"Dude, we heard you," Carly said. "You're a fucking looter. And by the way, the vampire thing is no joke. You'd better be in by dark, if you don't want to be some bloodsucker's midnight snack."

"You are so full of shit!" the boy looting for his mom's birthday said.

Jane shouted, "Sorin!"

Sorin obediently appeared behind the girls, moving unnaturally fast so that to human eyes it would look as though he'd popped out of thin air. He towered over the girls, glaring at the boys and showing his fangs, letting anger and hunger show in his eyes.

The nervous kid wet his pants. The legs of one of the others went out from under him. He dropped bonelessly to the floor. The looter, the one who had led his friends into this store, turned and ran.

"I don't wanna die, I don't wanna die," the kid on the floor said. The nervous one seemed unable to move.

Sorin didn't move or speak, for a long moment.

How had he ended up in this position? He was not responsible for every clueless human in the city. He could not become godfather, mentor, or general for every unprepared child who crossed his path. And still...

"Indikaiya, love," he said, never taking his eyes from the boys. "Could you whip up another couple of spears?

CHAPTER TEN

They left the store just before dark. Having fed, Sorin was stronger than he'd been upon arrival and apparently he could now withstand a good bit of dimmed light. Indikaiya glanced at him, looking for obvious signs of weakness and seeing none. Still, as they walked away — headed east as the young humans they had encountered in the store headed west — he took care to stay in the deepest shadows. Of course he stayed in shadow. It was his natural vampire instinct to avoid the sun, no matter that he had developed the strength to endure some of it.

Indikaiya had taken advantage of the abundance of goods in their hiding place and left the establishment wearing her own new pair of boots — which fit better than those she had confiscated back at the mansion — the denim jeans so many humans wore, and a leather vest laced up tightly to allow her full freedom of movement. Black leather and gleaming steel. That was her uniform for this fight. For this era. Her tunic, the one she had been wearing when she'd come into this world, was tucked in a black leather bag with a long, wide strap that crossed her body. She wasn't sure she'd be able to keep up with the bag once she began to fight again, but she hated to part with the leather shift. It was hers; it marked the time she'd come from, who she'd been when she'd been human.

It had not escaped her attention that she was now dressed much like her vampire partner, even though part of her reason for donning new clothes was to appear more human. She was tired of being mistaken for a vampire.

Partner. It had been a very long time since she'd thought of any man as a partner. And a vampire? She loathed them. They were the enemy; they were monsters who killed in order to survive. And yet...

She had lived for thousands of years, and she could still be surprised.

"Luca and the others will already be on the move," Sorin said.

"Duncan texted you the address on your electronic device so we know precisely where they're going." She was both amazed and annoyed by the cell phones Sorin and so many of the others carried. She could not imagine being constantly available — though in times of war it was convenient, she supposed. "We can join them there, yes?"

He shrugged broad shoulders. "We could. Personally I'd prefer not to waste precious darkness checking in with Luca Ambrus for orders."

Interesting. He'd fought with Luca, stood beside him, and yet his voice indicated that he had no love for the blood born. She would not ask him about it now, but later she would, if the opportunity arose. If they both survived the night. If she continued to feel as if they were true partners. If, if, if. Her voice was calm as she asked, "Do you have a plan?"

He glanced back at her, blond hair and black leather duster moving in a strange kind of harmony. It was fact, the vampire possessed an undeniable beauty. That did not mean she had to do more than make note and move on. So, why didn't she?

"My plan is to kill Marie," he said.

It made sense. Kill the so-called queen, and the vampire army would fall. At least, they could hope that would happen. Marie was old, she was blood born like Luca. She would not be easy to kill. But she was not invincible. No creature, in this time or any other, was truly invincible. "Do you know where to find her?"

"No." He grinned. "I suspect she's trying to find me. Maybe I should allow myself to be found."

"She will kill you." A few days ago she would have relished that outcome. His death would even have come as a relief to her. Now... her emotions were not easy to identify.

He winked at her, unconcerned. "She will try."

Sorin was not invincible, either. That thought shouldn't elicit any emotion within her, but as they walked down an ever-darkening street, it did.

***

"What do you think of our new headquarters?" Rurik glanced around the room he led Nevada into, as if he were searching for lurking vampires in the middle of the day. Nevada shivered; she glanced around as Rurik had. Maybe that's exactly what he was doing. Looking for vampires. When he relaxed, she followed suit.

The new place wasn't as posh as the big house in Potomac, but it would do. "Not too shabby," she said as she dropped the small duffle bag containing a few toiletries and a couple changes of clothes. "I'm here of my own free will and that makes all the difference." She'd expected a house, and that's what she'd gotten. An old, three story, historic red-brick building in a once fine neighborhood. Someone important had lived here a couple hundred years ago. Maybe even fifty years ago. She didn't have the details because she hadn't stopped to read the plaque that was posted on the small, only slightly overgrown front lawn.

But the house wasn't a home, not anymore. It was a library. A *public* library. Not the main one, of course, but a neighborhood branch on the west side of town. It would do. There was a kitchen/break room downstairs, and big spaces that had once been bedrooms and parlors that had been converted into offices and specialized rooms with shelves and shelves of books. Oh — the books!

"This room will suit you?"

"Of course."

Her new room was on the second floor in what looked to be the office of someone important. Main librarian or manager, she supposed. This was the logical choice for her. The vampires would prefer the interior rooms on the ground floor, or else the attic. Her room had a wide window that overlooked the street. Too much light for the vamps among them to be comfortable. The humans in their army were probably taking over the other spaces with windows. Maybe Warriors, too. Not that they'd spend much time in them.

There was big desk made of fine dark wood, basically smack dab in the middle of the room. Several of Nevada's own books, carried here by conduits and Warriors, were stacked on one end. There was an insanely tall pile of other magical books on the floor beside the desk. No bed, but the couch pushed against the window looked comfortable enough to sleep on.

Rurik walked to a narrow door — which she'd assumed was a closet — and pushed it open. "You have your own bathroom, but as this is one of only two showers in the building you will have to share."

"Not a problem." Rurik could use her shower any time. A picture flashed in her mind. A very fine picture. Rurik naked. In the shower, naked, soaped up. And as she'd already thought — naked. She glanced inside the small white-tiled bathroom. The shower was an ancient hand-held metal device over an even more ancient claw foot bathtub. Left over from when this house was lived in, she supposed, and too cumbersome to move when the building had been converted. Lucky for her.

Another appealing picture popped into her mind. Bubble bath!

"First things first," she said, turning her mind to business. "I need to cast a protection spell over this building." After all, the library had once been public, so there was nothing to keep out the vamps who were trying to take over D.C., and beyond.

She was good with protection spells. That had been the first thing she'd learned to do well, and it was now all but second nature.

Rurik didn't leave, as she'd expected he would. He sat on the couch. Afternoon sunlight fell over him, and again Nevada's mind went to...

No, she needed to be thinking of the spell she needed to cast, not shared showers and bubble baths that would probably never happen.

Nevada didn't need a book for this spell, not anymore. She knew it, in her mind, in her bones. She stood behind the desk, simply because it was a familiar position for her. Different room, different desk, same mindset. She placed her fingertips on the desk and closed her eyes, as she whispered words in an ancient language she had only recently discovered. She felt as if she were floating, though at the same time she could feel her feet firmly against the floor. Yes, her feet were on the floor, but her mind, her soul, they were elsewhere. They were a part of the universe, a part of the whole. There was darkness here, but she remained in the light. Always the light.

As soon as the spell took hold, she knew it. She felt it, deep down, and when she opened her eyes she saw that the air in the room was green and sparkly and fantabulous. The sparkly faded, but the protection spell did not.

"I'll have to invite the vamps who are on our side in tonight," she said, smiling at Rurik.

"Sadly, that number is small."

Nevada nodded, expecting Rurik to stand and head for the door and whatever battle plans or fight was on his agenda for this afternoon.

She didn't need a constant guard anymore. With the spell in place it wasn't like an uninvited vampire could sneak in. Marie and her ghouls couldn't sneak up on her here. She felt safer than she had in a long while, which was weird, all things considered. At the mansion, Rurik had had a habit of napping just outside her door.

He probably wouldn't do that anymore. Too bad.

Rurik didn't stand, didn't rush to leave her alone.

"If a person wasn't evil in life, why would they be evil when they're turned?" Nevada asked. Maybe Rurik would stay a while longer if they were having a conversation. She wasn't ready to be alone. "Chloe doesn't seem evil, and neither does Luca. Who I can remember now, by the way. Yay me!" She didn't give Rurik a chance to respond. "Sorin used to be pretty bad, maybe even evil, but now he's on our side." She had to admit, he was a confusing dude. She hadn't spent a lot of time around the others here, so she couldn't say she had a ton of experience with vampires. Still, she'd seen more than most. "Why aren't there more with us?"

"I do not know." Rurik didn't seem to be at all bothered by that lack of knowledge.

"Logically, you'd think there would be more decent vampires. Vamps who would fight with us instead of the psycho. They have to be out there, but how do we find them?"

Rurik did stand, then, slowly unfolding and rising to his full height of six foot plus. Damn, he was impressive.

"I will not stop to interview the vampires I fight tonight," he said. "My job is simple. Kill them. Protect the humans." He walked to her, and — in an unexpected move — lifted one big hand to cup her cheek.

Nevada stopped breathing.

"Protect you," he said, his voice lower than before.

And then he dropped his hand and walked away.

Nevada continued to hold her breath until she *had* to breathe again. It was breathe or faint!

She felt safer here, in this new place with a strong protection spell of her own making. And Rurik. Safe, yes, but she could not allow herself to get comfortable. She couldn't relax. It was time for her to step up. She was a damned powerful witch, and she could do something to help the war effort. She knew it.

More than anything, she wanted to make Marie sorry she'd ever heard the name Nevada Sheldon.

Sorin had done battle often in his long lifetime, but it had been a long while since he'd participated in war. He'd killed; he'd planned for victory; he'd known battle was coming.

He had not expected to be on this side of it.

If he thought about where he was and what he was doing, it would slow him down. So he fought, as any good soldier would, with everything he had. He swung his sword and took the heads of frantic vampires, one after another. Most of them were not skilled soldiers. They had expected to face only humans on this night, and all the nights to come. His presence surprised them.

They would be more prepared tomorrow, if they survived that long.

The Warrior woman who fought with him was impressive, in oh, so many ways. Indikaiya swung her sword as if it were light as a feather. It was not. She was fierce, and strong, and beautiful. No dancer who'd ever lived possessed such grace.

The vampires fought with swords and daggers and teeth. A few carried firearms, but not many. The humans carried guns and flamethrowers, for the most part. The sword was a weapon of days gone by, and very few of them were skilled with a blade of any kind. They were definitely not comfortable enough with them to face a physically superior enemy.

After facing strangers all night, Sorin finally found himself face to face with one of Marie's soldiers he knew. Edmund wasn't the brightest or the strongest of Marie's men, but he was loyal to a fault.

And so here he was.

"You!" Edmund shouted when he looked into Sorin's face. "Traitor!" He swung his own sword wildly. His weapon had a thin but razor sharp blade. Sorin easily danced out of its path.

"She is wrong, Edmund," Sorin said as he moved in closer. "Walk away." He did not want to kill this man he had once fought alongside. A man he had seen laugh. They had flown together, once, a long time ago.

Edmund did not walk away. He came toward Sorin again, blade singing, eyes blazing. Again, Sorin danced out of the way, but not before the tip of the blade sliced through his leather coat. They fought with no more words, their movements fast, their blades deadly. Edmund was more skilled than Sorin had recalled.

Soon enough, Edmund began to tire. Instead of continuing on, he turned and ran. Not away from the battle, as Sorin had suggested earlier, but directly toward Indikaiya, who was engaged in her own fight.

She did not see or hear Edmund coming.

Sorin flew, rising up in the air and coming down with his sword raised. He took Edmund's head when the vampire was no more than ten feet away from Indikaiya.

As Edmund went to dust, Indikaiya managed to take the head of her opponent. Only then did she turn and see Sorin standing there. Their eyes met, for a second, and then more opponents came at them and they raised their swords once more.

Indikaiya wished for a concise battle plan; she wanted the lines of this war to be clearly delineated. She was finally — if reluctantly — coming to accept that this was not that kind of war.

Battles small and large were being fought in this city, as they were almost certainly being waged in cities and towns around the world. If she thought about that too much she'd be distracted from this fight, and that would not be wise. For now, at least, her war was here, in this city under siege. Warriors and humans — and yes, a handful of vampires — were fighting a series of small battles against the vampires who wished to publicly and permanently take their place at the top of the food chain. These armies would likely never face off as they did in the battles of old. Instead they fought where they could, when they could, and won — or lost — one skirmish at a time.

For a while she had watched Sorin, half-expecting him to be a spy for Marie.

She'd seen him kill too many of his own kind to believe that to be true. She'd watched as he saved one human after another. At times it seemed he did so with some reluctance, but he was a good soldier. Perhaps even a good man.

Women, young and old, loved him, and she found that annoying. Not that she should care. Sorin was handsome and strong. It was only natural that weak females who didn't know any better might find him appealing.

Watching him fight even she found him appealing, for brief periods of time, and she was anything but weak.

The sun would soon rise. They had battled two small factions of vampires in a part of this large city that Sorin called Georgetown. In both instances, they had been joined by humans. Brave humans, who armed themselves and set out to protect their own lives, their own species. Some of them died, but many more survived to fight another day. To a man, they were initially reluctant to fight with Sorin, but once they saw him fight and kill, they changed their minds. He was impressive in battle, she had to admit. Effective. Sharp. Deadly.

In a war like this one, the humans would need every weapon at their disposal. Even Sorin.

Indikaiya had thought their night to be done. She needed sleep and food. Sorin needed... well, she didn't know or care what he needed, but even he seemed weary.

"If we hurry we can reach my place before the sun comes up."

"Your place? You have a place?"

Sorin shrugged. "I keep a small hideout, not far from here. An apartment. We were not close enough last night to make it before full daylight, but we have moved closer tonight. There's only one bed, but..." He glanced her way, and for a split second his eyes flashed that unnatural bright blue. "I'm willing to share if you are."

She glanced away from him, unwilling to allow him to see any reaction, no matter how small it might be. "As I am not restricted by the sun, I can continue on and join the others."

He stopped in the middle of the sidewalk, held out a strong hand to stop her, as well. Surely he was not going to argue about sharing a bed with her! No. That wasn't it. It took a moment, but soon she heard what he did.

A disturbance in the air.

The two vampires dropped down on either side of Indikaiya and Sorin. Instantly she realized these two were not like the others. They were older, more powerful. Physically stronger than any they had faced thus far. Many of the vampires they'd been fighting on this night were new, or fairly new. These two males were dressed in dark hooded robes that indicated they were not only *not* new, they had not adjusted to modern times in any way. They both had long hair, dark and unkempt, and their fangs were extended and frighteningly enormous. Their faces were not handsome, but were rough and angry, with large flat noses and small eyes. They looked enough alike to have been brothers in their human lives.

Back to back, she and Sorin drew their swords in a unified, clean motion. The creatures they faced were not afraid.

Indikaiya swung her sword, but her opponent was strong and fast. She caught a hint of a smile on a pug-like face before the attacking vampire spun away. It was the gleam of a streetlamp on steel that warned her that her new opponent was carrying a sword. She moved out of the way just in time, and spun around to see that Sorin was engaged in a similar battle.

For the first time since joining this war, Indikaiya was wounded. The sharp blade wielded by a monster sliced her arm, then her thigh. Neither wound was a killing one, and she had the strength to keep fighting. She got in her own strikes, but the creature she fought healed before her eyes.

It was well fed, ancient, and eager to take its place in the new world.

Sorin was suffering, too. He did have an amazing healing power, but he had started this battle exhausted and he hadn't taken his fill of the girls.

He bled. His injuries were not healing at the rate their opponents' were.

Death in battle was always a possibility. Even the best fighters fell. It was possible — very possible — that neither she nor Sorin would survive to see the sunrise. Her death would send her home, to another world where she would recover and then search frantically for yet another blood relative to invite her back into this world.

Sorin — Sorin would just be gone.

At that thought, she saw his opponent rise into the air and fly down swiftly, sword poised to take Sorin's head.

CHAPTER ELEVEN

Atlanta, Georgia

She'd tried to call her daughter a dozen times, and had gotten no answer. It went straight to voicemail, which meant the cell was turned off or the battery was dead, or maybe was in a rare area that got no service. Surely Chloe wasn't still on that camping trip; she'd never been a fan of roughing it, and *camping* was so out of character. Then again, staying away from the city wasn't a bad idea. Washington, D.C. was not the safest place to be right now. Maybe Chloe had been away from home when the madness started, and she'd decided to stay away. Maybe she'd lost her phone, or had no way to charge it, or... the other "ors" that followed were not so ordinary or pleasant.

Amelia Fallon hadn't slept in days. She'd dozed a bit the previous afternoon, but that fitful attempt could hardly be called restful. Her mind had been spinning with worry for her daughter. For the world! What she'd been seeing on the news couldn't be true. It was impossible. She kept telling herself that, but she was not convinced. Not entirely.

Her husband, Bill, busied himself in the kitchen,

making another pot of coffee and putting together an early morning snack. He had put on a calm face, for her sake she imagined, and he had tried to tell her that what they'd been hearing had been nonsense. There was a logical explanation for everything, they just didn't have that explanation yet. He was always so calm, so reasonable. She wanted to believe he was right. She didn't.

Amelia jumped when the doorbell rang. Who called at this time of the morning? It was far too early for anyone to stop by. Bill mumbled something from the kitchen, and she heard his heavy step as he headed her way. Like her, he was probably wondering what was wrong to bring someone to their door at this hour.

She opened the door to a young girl who looked frightened and lost. And so she should be, out at this time of day. "I'm… I'm…" The girl stopped stuttering, took a deep breath and continued, "Are you Chloe's mother?"

"Yes." Amelia opened the screen door wide. "Come in. I've been so worried. Chloe's not answering her cell, and the news from Washington has been so…" Alarming, unbelievable, impossible!

Bill entered the room, a cup of steaming hot coffee in one hand. "Who is it?" In his voice she heard a caution she had not felt, herself. Why should she be cautious? This friend of Chloe's was not more than a child.

The girl stepped inside, and as soon as she was

across the threshold her expression changed. Suddenly she looked older, and... meaner. At that moment, Amelia realized her mistake. Logical, reasonable Bill had been wrong; Amelia's worries had not been unfounded. Vampires! They were real, and they were *here*.

Amelia's brain reached for some semblance of control. Push away the fear. Accept reality. *Do* something. Could she order the vampire out? Was it too late? Before she could think to try, the girl — not a girl at all — flew across the room and tackled Bill. Her large husband went down like a rag doll, helpless. His coffee cup flew out of his hand and smashed against the wall behind him, splattering the dark, hot liquid against a pale yellow canvas. He grunted, struggled with the much smaller girl as best he could — but he did not struggle for long.

His throat was ripped open. Blood spurted across the vampire's face, into the air, and onto the carpet at his feet. Amelia's husband of thirty-six years was dead in an instant.

Her attempts at gaining control and taking action died as quickly as they had been born. She would be next, she supposed. Amelia was stunned, silent. She still stood near the front door, frozen in place. Dazed. The world narrowed, faded, went fuzzy. In a part of her mind she knew she should scream and run, but — it was too late for that. She had seen how fast the vampire moved, how deadly the monster was.

At this moment she would rather be dead than go on. She would rather not see and remember and accept that such things were possible in a world she had once thought safe.

But she did not die. The vampire stepped over Bill's body, walked to the couch, and sat almost demurely. The monster that looked like a girl licked her bloody fingers before saying, "Call your daughter, and tell her Marie said hello."

Sorin had realized this war might be the end of him, especially since he'd changed sides and made an enemy of Marie, but as it was coming at him — fast and ugly and sharp — he felt a rush of regret.

Regret was a new sensation for him. He didn't recall feeling it even in life, and as a vampire? Never. Life, however it was lived, whether for a few short years or an eternity, should always be without regret.

His sword arm was slashed to the bone. Flesh splayed, blood spurted. There was an instant and unexpected weakness as that arm fell to his side. He would heal, but not fast enough to gather the strength to fight the ancient vamp that was coming down upon him. Sorin shifted his sword to his left arm and prepared to fight on. He would not die standing on a D.C. sidewalk helpless as a human.

An arrow — no, a bolt from a crossbow — pierced the attacker's neck and threw him off balance so that the next swing of his sword went well wide. The hideous bloodsucker looked surprised by this turn of events. He landed on his feet near Sorin and spun to face the new attacker — the bolt through his neck largely ignored — just in time to take another bolt through the heart. With a sharp word in a guttural language Sorin had never heard, the monster turned to dust.

In the midst of the chaos, a ridiculously small dog began to bark.

Without sparing even a glance for the newcomer or the animal, Sorin turned his attention to the creature Indikaiya did battle with. Monstrous as they were, they died like any other of the kindred. Sword gripped in his left hand, he joined in her fight. The robed vampire seemed weakened by the loss of his companion. Perhaps they had been connected in some way. Mentally, spiritually. At the very least, he was distracted by the final death of his partner.

Indikaiya stabbed the attacker near the heart, barely missing her target. As she withdrew her sword with a frustrated grunt the small dog launched itself at the monster and clamped down on an exposed ankle. Sorin moved in and with one smooth stroke took the attacker's head. Again, dust as with any other vampire.

There was deep, complete silence, for a moment. A split second. Then the little dog sniffed at what was left of the monster. All Sorin heard was that sniffing, his own pounding heartbeat and Indikaiya's, and the faster, weaker heartbeat of the man who had — much as he hated to admit it — saved them. A nearby bird hidden in a thickly leafed tree chirped as if nothing had changed. Sunrise was coming. He looked Indikaiya up and down; he was not the only one who had been wounded.

"What the hell was that?" she asked breathlessly.

"Ancients, coming out of hiding to join in the fun."

"Are there more of those?"

"Not many." With that he turned to face whoever had been wielding the crossbow that had saved his ass. A Warrior, he assumed, perhaps someone Indikaiya knew.

What he saw standing on the sidewalk was a young man — a human — who was armed to the teeth. Crossbow, quiver filled with bolts, sword hanging at his side, shotgun hanging from a holster at his back. The heavy looking sack that hung on his hip likely held shells for that shotgun.

"You're one of them," the boy said, raising his crossbow in caution.

Indikaiya stepped in front of Sorin in an unexpectedly protective manner. "He is a vampire, that is true, but he's fighting on the side of right. He has disposed of many of his own kind on this night."

"And what are you?" The young man sounded suspicious. As he should. If he hadn't seen them battling these ancients with his own eyes, he probably would've killed them on the spot.

Sorin expected the little dog — which looked very much like a large rodent with long, tangled brown fur — to return to its owner, but instead the mutt stood at Indikaiya's side as if it belonged there.

"Long story," Sorin offered in a lowered voice. "You're a good fighter, well prepared and efficient. Fearless, perhaps. Foolish, most certainly. Would you be interested in joining others of your kind?"

"You mean, *people* fighting bloodsuckers?"

"Yes, people fighting bloodsuckers."

The eastern sky was lightening. Thank goodness the hideout he kept here in D.C. was near. "She will take you to…"

Indikaiya sighed. "I will not. I'm staying with you."

"Why?" He turned to look at her, and saw a determined expression.

She scoffed. "You know why, or you should." Indikaiya turned her attention to the human. "What is your name?"

"Kevin. Kevin Brown."

She gave Kevin the address of the new headquarters, and suggested that he ask for Jimmy. Jimmy was probably about Kevin's age, and he was also human, so that made sense. As much as anything made sense these days. "Tell them Indikaiya sent you. It will be daylight by the time you arrive there, so they shouldn't mistake you for a vampire. Still, it would be best if you approached with your hands visible and empty."

At that instruction, Kevin narrowed his eyes suspiciously. "You expect me to go into a strange house unarmed? I've seen my friends die horrible deaths, and I saw one turned into a... a... a monster." At that, he cast a glance at Sorin.

"You can continue on your own, if you prefer," Indikaiya said calmly. "You're a competent soldier."

"Competent?" Kevin all but shouted. "I'm a damn sight better than competent."

"Skilled, then," she continued without emotion. "You will live longer if you fight alongside other skilled soldiers, but of course that is your decision."

Kevin snorted, then asked her to repeat the address. She did so, and then he turned to leave, jogging away from the scene of the battle.

The mutt stayed put.

"Hey! What about your dog?" Sorin shouted.

Kevin looked back and grinned. "She's not my dog. Looks like she's taken a liking to her." He nodded at Indikaiya.

Sure enough, the mutt stood at Indikaiya's side like a teeny but determined guard dog. Sorin scowled down at it. The dog growled.

"Shoo, dog," Sorin said with a wave of his hand.

The mutt did not obey.

Sorin leaned down slightly. "Go. Away."

The dog launched forward and clamped down onto Sorin's ankle. Unlike the ancient, he was wearing boots, so the dog got a mouthful of leather.

Indikaiya laughed a little as she reached down and grabbed the dog. "She seems not to care for vampires. A woman after my own heart." The mutt whimpered a bit and then licked at Indikaiya's face.

In the midst of war, a ridiculous moment.

"You are fearless," Indikaiya said to the mutt. "I must give you a Warrior's name. Athena. Boudica. Perhaps Joan."

"Of Arc?" Sorin asked.

Indikaiya smiled. "Jett."

Ah, yes, she had come to love the music of the time. Some of it, anyway.

Sorin leaned in and checked the name on the jeweled collar. The dog snarled and then snapped. "Cupcake."

Indikaiya looked appropriately horrified.

"Just leave her here. Someone will find Cupcake, or else she'll find her way home."

Indikaiya glared at him. "We can't leave her here."

"Well, we can't keep her!"

"Why not?"

He had been in enough losing battles to recognize when he was met with yet another one.

Sorin took Indikaiya's arm — the one which did not grasp a small dog — and guided her down the sidewalk, then turned along a well-traveled grassy path that led to the rear entrance of an apartment building. The large building was three stories tall, and fashioned of the same red brick as the Council headquarters. There was a slightly overgrown flower garden and a couple of wrought iron benches near the rear entrance. Some of the apartments had small balconies. Others, just windows. Normally he checked to see if anyone was watching. Today, he didn't bother.

"You're hurt," he said as he positioned himself beneath his own third-story balcony.

"So are you."

"You should've gone with Kevin Brown to the new headquarters. Someone there could fix you up."

"I will heal."

"I don't suppose I can convince you to leave the demon dog behind."

Naturally, she shook her head.

Sorin wrapped an arm around Indikaiya, and for once she did not argue or curse. In fact, she leaned into him. Why was she being so agreeable? He understood very well why he wanted her here, what he wanted from her, but she had made it clear...

She answered the question he did not ask aloud.

"Like it or not, you are needed at this time," she said, sounding almost logical, speaking *almost* without emotion. "You have proven yourself, and unless I'm mistaken you are past the need for feeding."

She could not have surprised him more. He leapt, for the first time in a long while forced to expend great effort in order to do something that was usually so easy it took no effort at all. They landed on his balcony. He did not immediately drop his arm, and she did not push away.

"I do need to feed. Are you offering?"

When Cupcake bit his forearm — drawing blood, this time — and Sorin cursed, Indikaiya moved the mutt aside.

"I see no other option." Her eyes hardened as she took a step away from him. "Take more than is offered, and I will gut you." At that, she fingered the handle of one of the knives she wore.

"That won't kill me."

"No, but it will be very painful, I imagine, even for you."

Indeed, it would.

She would do it, too. Gut him. Hurt him. Turn that sword she wielded so well against him. In all his life, as a man and as a vampire, he had not known a woman like Indikaiya. He would not have even bet that such a woman existed.

He would soon feed on the blood of an Immortal Warrior. What would that be like, he wondered? He would not have to wonder long.

It was worth any number of injuries...

CHAPTER TWELVE

Indikaiya was surprised by the lair Sorin led her into. He slid open a glass door, pushed aside the drapes, and waved her in before him as if he were a gentleman. From the exterior it appeared that this building was well kept, charming to be sure, but hardly extravagant. The large apartment on the third floor, however, was a different matter. Sorin did like his creature comforts.

Stepping from the small balcony into the living space was very much like stepping from one world to another. Instead of battlefields there was luxury. In the leather and dark wood furnishings, in the paintings on the walls, in the small sculptures and fine colored glass. Instead of the sound of gunfire and metal on metal and the screams of humans and vampires alike, there was a deep and complete silence.

She wasn't surprised that the large room was dark. Heavy drapes covered the windows — and the balcony door, as Sorin entered and allowed them to fall behind him — but her eyes quickly adjusted to the lack of natural light. Sorin stepped past her and turned on a lamp, and she almost wished he would turn it off again.

In the dark, she could ignore that he was badly wounded. In the dark, she would not see the blood. Not all of it was his, but... most.

The small dog she had just collected burrowed into her, warm and fuzzy, panting a bit madly. She held onto to the dog a bit too snugly and stroked its matted fur.

Sorin nodded at Indikaiya. "You're hurt."

Had he been studying her own wounds as she had been studying his? "I will heal." Not as quickly as he did, but not nearly as slowly as a human. She moved the dog aside, catching it in the crook of one arm, and drew the strap of the leather shoulder bag over her head and dropped it to the floor. She studied the ugly gash on Sorin's right arm, waiting for it to knit closed before her eyes as his wounds normally did. It did not. "Why aren't you healing?"

He stepped toward her. "Considering the amount of energy I've expended tonight, it's been too long since I fed. I've been weakened." It was a hard admission for him to make, she could tell. "You know that. Otherwise you would not have offered your own blood."

Looking at him now, she had a fleeting doubt about her earlier offer. He could drain her in seconds. Maybe she would get in a nice stabbing wound in the process, but she'd be gone, whisked back to her own world to wait to be called again, before she could take his heart or his head. She was a Warrior, but she did not possess a vampire's speed.

She'd seen him use that speed often during the night.

Was he too weak to call upon it now?

The dog — she could not bring herself to call it by the ridiculous name of Cupcake — was exhausted, as she and Sorin were. Had this animal been in battle? Had her master lost his life fighting the beings this dog so obviously despised? They would never know.

Indikaiya grabbed a pillow from the sofa and placed it on the floor. The dog settled there with a sigh and was almost instantly asleep. They would need to find food for the animal, but first — sleep. For the dog and for her.

Sorin took her hand and drew it to his mouth. Here? Now? She held her breath as he placed his lips on her hand as if she were a fine lady in another time and he was a well-mannered gentleman. She doubted Sorin had ever been well-mannered, no matter what his station in life. He turned her hand over and exposed a scratch near her wrist. While she watched, barely breathing, he kissed the minor wound and then... and then he licked her.

The scratch healed before her eyes, as quickly and completely as his wounds did, when he was at his best. When he was fed and strong.

Her heart reacted to the sensation of his mouth on her flesh, innocent as the touch was. There was nothing innocent about the way he looked at her when he tilted his head to the side to smile and catch her eye. He stood, shifted her vest aside, and licked at a gash on her shoulder. His kiss took away the pain entirely, and she could feel the wound healing, inside and out.

Indikaiya closed her eyes. She was a Warrior, but she was also a woman. It had been a long time, a very long time, since a man had touched her in this way or any other. She was always separate from the others. Alone. She did not crave sex, and as for romance… she had long ago dismissed that notion as foolishness. Still, vampire or not, Sorin was a fine example of the male form, and he did have a certain charm.

She tried to shake off the thoughts of Sorin as anything other than a despicable monster and an unfortunate and temporary partner. If she considered anything more it was because she was as tired as he was, and her mind and body were playing tricks on her.

He brushed a few strands of hair away from her throat. Now that he had taken care of her injuries — most of them, anyway — he expected her to take care of his, as she had said she would. Indikaiya held her breath as Sorin kissed her neck. Just a kiss, for now.

She should be immune to his vampire tricks, to his unnatural magic. But at the moment she felt not at all immune to Sorin.

"Are you sure?" he whispered against her skin.

No. Yes. No. "Yes," she whispered, tilting her

head to the side to make sure he understood.

The sensation of his fangs entering her throat didn't hurt, as she'd thought it might. Instead the twinge she experienced was surprisingly pleasant. It was intimate, as intimate as the sex she had told him he could not have, not with her. Strangely enough, it was a relief when his fangs punctured her skin, as if she had been waiting, waiting, waiting. They had been partners for days, and now they were joined. One. She felt him not just at her throat but through her entire body, and she remembered what it had been like, so long ago, to lie with a man. With love, yes, but also for the sheer pleasure of the act.

Indikaiya imagined Sorin lying beneath her naked, filling her. She imagined him atop her, driving deep while she screamed his name. Heaven above, she could almost feel him, as if he were already there. She could smell him, feel his skin pressing against hers.

Shaking off the all too real sensations was difficult, but not impossible. In all honesty, though she pulled herself back from them — what choice did she have but to fight for distance? — those images did not fade entirely. They stayed with her, more like a memory than an imagining.

She thought of warning him again not to take too much, but she didn't. He knew. He understood.

They were linked, at this moment, and he understood everything.

Her head began to swim, just a little, and

instantly he withdrew. He kissed her again, and she knew the marks on her throat would heal. No one would ever know what had happened here. There was no choice about that. She did not want her fellow Warriors to know that she had offered her blood to a vampire. She definitely didn't want them to know that she was actually considering…

"You want me," he whispered, his mouth against her throat where he had taken healing and life.

She could deny it, but it was too late for that. "And if I do?"

"I am here for the day. You are free to leave, or you can stay."

He released her and stepped away, and she saw that his wounds were now healed. Blood remained, his leather jacket was sliced in several places, but there was no evidence on his flesh that he had been injured.

"I need rest, as you do," she admitted.

"We both need more than rest."

His jeans were worn so tight, she knew exactly what he needed.

Release, pleasure, connection with another human being. Neither of them was human anymore, but they had once been and some needs — needs she had not expected to experience here and now — remained.

Indikaiya did not understand how courtship worked in this modern age. All she knew was that she was not of this age, and would not pretend to be.

In Atlantis, the females had possessed much power. Like their males, they took what they wanted without artifice. They lived their lives to the fullest, in the years when life there had been so good. Before war. Before great loss.

There was so much loss in this world. So much pain. Was it really so terrible to take pleasure when it presented itself?

She began to work the fastenings down the front of her vest. "Remove your clothing," she commanded.

Sorin, for once, did not argue with her as she issued orders.

He felt good. So good. A diet of Warrior blood would agree with him, not that he expected Indikaiya to volunteer in any case that wasn't an emergency.

Of course, he had not expected this. Not at all.

He should not be surprised by the way this encounter had begun. Indikaiya was not a girl to be flattered and wooed. She did not need to be coerced or glamoured — he would not even dare to try. She was a woman and a Warrior, a being as powerful as he had ever been. When he'd tasted her he'd known that power, as well as her new and unexpected need for him.

She did not rush to remove her clothes, and neither did he. Still, neither of them dawdled. Eye to eye as they shed their tattered and bloodied garments, this was a new and much more pleasant battle.

Indikaiya had a fine body. Very fine. Firm and lithe, strong and soft, she was perfection. And she was not shy. There were no shielding hands over her breasts or her mound, no coy glances to the side as if she might be having second thoughts.

He dropped down in front of her, cradled her leg, and licked the cut on her thigh. The wound was not a serious one. It would've healed on its own in short order. But he could not bear to see any imperfection on such an otherwise perfect body. He did not want her to hurt.

And no, he did not mind at all licking her thigh, allowing his tongue to trail up to taste her, to kiss her until she shuddered. Only then did he shift away and stand.

"There's a bed in the next room."

"I expected nothing less," she said, walking past him with her head high, as if he hadn't just had his mouth on her. Damn, she had a nice ass. Long legs, perfect ass, small waist, shapely back with a braid — which was a bit worse for wear after a night of battle — swaying as she made her way into the bedroom.

Indikaiya stopped at the side of the bed, looked at him, and with a wave of her hand ordered him into it. Instead of immediately complying, he stood close to her and bent down to kiss her tempting lips.

She backed away from him before their mouths

could do more than brush lightly. "What are you doing?"

"I'm trying to kiss you," he explained.

"Kisses are for love, for romance. It is not necessary. All I want or need from you is this." She grabbed his cock, firmly but thank goodness not *too* firmly. When she moved her fingers, he almost embarrassed himself.

"As you wish."

She released her hold and gave him a gentle shove that sent him tumbling onto the bed. When he was there, on his back with his penis hard and poking straight up, she climbed on top of him.

Sorin had never been with a woman who did not need to be romanced at least a little bit. He had never been *ordered* to shed his clothes. No one ordered him to do anything. No one but Indikaiya. He liked it.

His Atlantean Warrior was strong and soft, beautiful and stern, and all woman. She knew what she wanted and had no problem commanding it. She was already wet as she guided him into her body, wet and hot and so damn tight he could've come then and there.

He did not. Sorin was nothing if not controlled.

She rode him, easy at first and then hard. Eyes closed, perfect breasts swaying, she rode. He had not expected to find this kind of beauty, this kind of connection, in a time of war. That was his last clear thought, for a while, as they swayed together and apart. There was only need, his body and hers, pleasure.

Indikaiya came with a gasp and a cry. That cry sounded almost — surprised. Surprised that she'd come so quickly? Surprised that he was the one beneath her? Her movements slowed, and as they did he grasped her around the waist and spun them both so that her back was against the mattress and he was on top of her.

He thrust into her once, twice, and then he caught her eye. "My turn."

"That seems only..." The word "fair" was so garbled it was barely intelligible, as he drove deep. She shuddered a little, finding pleasure again.

This was a woman he could spend all night with. No tricks, no glamour, just raw pleasure given and taken.

Sorin did know how to give. He definitely knew how to take.

Kevin Brown stopped well clear of the front entrance to the library. An old house, but the sign out front indicated that it was, or at least had been, a library named after a long dead politician. A fucking vampire had given him this address. A *vampire*. Anything could be waiting beyond those doors.

But he had seen the vamp kill two of his own kind. At this point, what did he have to lose? He couldn't continue to fight alone. His choices were easy. Run and hide, die within a matter of days, or join up with other fighters.

Kevin stood where he could be seen from the front windows. Any decent gathering place for those fighting the vamps would have some kind of lookout. Sure enough, he hadn't been standing there more than a minute when the curtain in the window to the right of the front door moved. Kevin nodded at the window, and held his hands up, palms facing forward. He would never do that at night, but by the light of day he could be without a weapon in his hand.

Not for long, though.

He shouted, looking at the now-closed curtain. "I'm here for Jimmy. A couple of kickass blondes sent me."

After a moment, the front door opened and a man about his age — which was twenty-four. He was really hoping to make it to twenty-five — stepped onto the porch.

"I'm Jimmy. Who sent you?" The man was obviously suspicious. Given all that had happened in the past week, he'd be a fool not to be.

"A couple of blondes. One vampire, the other… something else. She said her name was Indie something."

Jimmy relaxed, a little. "I wondered if they were still alive."

"Alive and fighting, as of two hours ago. They

gave me this address and told me to ask for you."

"Come on in." Jimmy stepped back into the library, leaving the front door open.

Kevin hesitated. What waited beyond those doors? He hitched his shoulders and walked forward. Shit, what did he have to lose?

He walked into the library, looked around cautiously trying to place the exits, the potential traps, the blind spots, and then he followed Jimmy to the east side of the main room and a door that opened onto a small interior conference room. He kept one hand on his dagger. The other was ready to draw the shotgun. Overhead lights illuminated the room but there were no windows. That in itself was alarming. He looked around, he studied those gathered there — men who were studying him just as intensely — and drew in a deep breath.

"Holy shit."

CHAPTER THIRTEEN

"You drink only from me," Luca ordered.

She should've learned by now not to argue with him, but she had not. "You need all your strength. I can't…"

"At this point, you would likely kill any human you attempted to feed from." His argument was based on fact, and was delivered in that way. Luca didn't lose his temper, he was a master of control. "Not feeding would drive you to the point where you'd not be able to resist the humans in our ranks, and there's no way to know what damage such severe hunger might do to the baby."

It was not Chloe's imagination that her strong, capable, two-thousand-year-old lover almost choked on the word *baby*. He was not unaffected by her condition. *Their* condition, if she were being honest.

He had not said so, but he knew she was worried. About her, about the child. How could she tell him that she was sure everything would be fine? She couldn't explain how she knew, why she was so certain.

So far, he had been her only food source, but it made sense to at least consider looking elsewhere for blood. A non-fighting human; a stranger; another vampire. Not that she wanted to bite into anyone else, but she was afraid if she continued feeding from Luca she'd weaken him. He didn't agree, but it made sense to her. She was stronger than she'd been even days ago. She was learning control, more every day. Wouldn't someone else do as well as Luca when feeding time came?

It was his argument concerning the health of their child that made her give in. She did as he instructed, drinking, working very hard to maintain control as she took what she needed from Luca's wrist. He stroked her hair as she fed.

This time he did not tell her when to stop. She stopped on her own, even though she wanted more. Even though a part of her wanted it all. She wondered if that hunger, that intense craving, would ever abate. Surely it would. How else could she survive? No. How else would those around her survive?

Not for the first time, she thought of her parents. She should've called, but what could she say? Would she ever see them again? Atlanta was safe, at least for now while the fight was focused here in D.C. As safe as anywhere else in the world, in any case. It was impossible to know where small pockets of rebel vampire attacks might've popped up.

She'd call her parents in a day or two. Where was her cell phone, anyway? So many ordinary things had been left behind. There had been a time when she would not have allowed her phone to go dead, much less be misplaced.

As much as she wanted to believe that the war was contained, that Atlanta and other places were safe, she did not. Not really. Maybe if not for the dreams...

She wasn't sure if the dreams were a part of her transition to vampire or if they came from the baby, somehow. Anything was possible. All she knew was that they were not ordinary dreams. There was a touch of reality in them. Horrifying reality.

A plumber and his wife in some rural location. Mike, that was his name. His own daughter had been turned, and his last sight had been... unthinkable.

A young girl in New York, the victim of a musician vampire and her own infatuation. For a while she had been thrilled, and then she had been shocked. Surprised. Dead.

These and so many others were human victims who had done nothing to deserve their bloody end. Nothing but to be in the wrong place at the wrong time. There was nothing she could do for them, or for others like them.

She and Luca had a small reading room to themselves, at least for a while. Luca sat in a fat chair, and she perched on his lap.

His wrist healed before her eyes.

"Do you remember when we went to see Ahron?" he asked.

Chloe shuddered. "Ugh, how could I forget? That dude is hideous."

Luca did not agree or disagree. "When we arrived, he welcomed the three of us. At the time, I thought he sensed Indikaiya."

"So did I. Do you think..." The baby. Had Ahron known, even then, that she was carrying Luca's child? That thought gave her a chill. They were trying to keep the baby's existence a secret, until they knew more. If Ahron had somehow sensed it... who else might have done the same? She was not yet fully up to speed on the abilities of vampires. All she knew was that they varied greatly.

Luca pulled her close for a kiss, but they had not gotten in nearly enough kissing when the door opened and Jimmy walked in. He was not surprised or embarrassed to find them in a rather compromising and intensely personal position. There was no time for such niceties.

"Duncan is asking for you, Luca. It's about tonight."

"I'll be right there."

Jimmy nodded, to Luca and then to Chloe, before closing the door behind him.

Luca sighed. "Being remembered is a pain in the ass. Everyone wants something from me."

She touched the enchanted ring he wore. "Eventually, you will be able to remove this, if you wish."

He caught her eye, and she saw a glimpse — just a glimpse — of the fear he felt. Not for the world, not for the kindred. For her. For what was coming for them. She had changed, the world had changed, but the power in his eyes remained much the same.

"Will I?" he asked. "Will the baby remember me? As we travel, we'll have the issue of you being remembered while I am not. There are too many unknowns."

He didn't say more, but the darkening of his attitude spoke volumes. One of the unknowns was their own survival.

Finally!

Nevada grabbed the stone she'd been concentrating on, ran for the door, threw it open on an empty second story hallway, and shouted at the top of her lungs. "Rurik!" She didn't wait for him to come to her, but hustled down the stairs and into the main room of the library.

He was running toward her, frowning, hand on the hilt of the sword that hung at his side. "What's wrong?"

Her wide smile must've eased his worry, because suddenly he stopped moving forward. He dropped his hand, and his expression shifted from one of concern to puzzlement.

"Nothing is wrong," she said. She kept moving, and they met near what had once been the check-out desk. A library. A haven. Her home, for now. Nevada tipped her head back and looked Rurik in the eye. She was so excited that she could do this for him! Well, for all of them, but mostly for him.

"You are flushed," he said, still a bit concerned about her outburst.

"Of course I'm flushed!" Nevada took a deep breath. It was time to explain. "I didn't tell anyone what I was working on, because I wasn't sure it would go anywhere. I still have so much to learn about this witch business. Anyway, when my family escaped from the mansion, I cast a temporary protection spell around them. I didn't trust the vampires to really let them go, the way they said they would." Trusting vampires was something she still had a hard time with. "That spell was a temporary thing. I knew it wouldn't last. Since I finished the sanctuary spell and the doodad for Luca, I've been thinking. What if I could come up with a longer lasting protection spell for the soldiers who are on our side?"

"For the humans among us?"

"Warriors, too," Nevada said. "I thought maybe I could start with you."

Rurik smiled at her. Surely he didn't intend for that smile to be more than a little condescending. It was. "I need no protection beyond my sword."

Really? She had worked herself silly to get this done, and he didn't want it? "It's not like this spell makes you invincible, or anything. It'll just give you an edge."

"I don't..."

"It can't hurt, and it might help." So much for gratitude!

He continued to argue with her. "I'm sure Jimmy and..."

Enough was enough. "Maybe you can't be killed, but I'm not ready for you to be yanked back into whatever world you come from." She slapped the clenched fist which grasped the stone to his wide, hard chest, quickly whispering the words that were necessary. She now understood that language as if she'd been speaking it since birth. The words were a part of her. Her heritage. Her gift.

She felt the spell form and slip into Rurik. She saw it, in a flash of sparkling green. Maybe he felt it, too, because he flinched. A little.

Spell cast, she dropped her hand and took a step back. She wondered if Rurik would be angry, but anger wasn't the emotion she saw in his eyes.

"You care about me," he said, his voice low.

Nevada felt the heat of a blush in her cheeks. "Well, yes."

"You wish to protect me in whatever way you can."

She wanted to protect everyone, but if she had to choose just one person to cast this spell on, it would be Rurik. "Yes," she whispered.

"I care for you, too." With that, he wrapped one long arm around her waist, pulled her in, and pressed his mouth to hers.

Nevada had been kissed, but it had been a very

long time. And she had never been kissed like this. The world went away. She felt the kiss to her toes.

Toes which were no longer touching the floor, since Rurik had lifted her with that one, strong arm. Nevada wrapped her arms around his neck and deepened the kiss. He moaned, deep in his throat.

Oh God, Oh God, Oh God. She didn't want this kiss to stop.

"Get a room, you two."

Their mouths separated, but Rurik did not put her down. She dangled in his arms, warm and snug and safe. Nevada looked beyond Rurik's shoulder to a grinning Jimmy.

"You'd better be nice to me," she said, still reeling from the kiss. She tried to hide her intense reaction, as she teased the first human among their ranks. Rurik's conduit. His blood.

"Why's that?" Jimmy asked.

Rurik placed Nevada on her feet and looked directly into her eyes. In those eyes was a promise of more. She wanted more. She wanted it all. And she was willing to wait, but seriously, she didn't want to have to wait long. If she had learned nothing else from this vampire apocalypse, it was that every day was precious. And that every day could be the last.

"Show him," Rurik said. "Show Jimmy what you have done."

She did.

***

Sorin didn't always sleep deeply, but for the past few hours, he had. He'd slept hard, with Indikaiya in the bed beside him.

She was not a cuddler. Just as well, since he wasn't, either. Tempted as he had been to wake her before leaving the bed, he had done her the courtesy of easing away with nothing more than a very gentle raking of his fingers across her back.

He stood in the shower with hot water pounding his body. The timing was off, but he could stand to eat again. War took a lot out of a man, no matter what species that man might be. He was hungry, but he didn't dare take another drop from Indikaiya.

Could a Warrior be turned? Could a Warrior and a vampire bond? He doubted it, but he couldn't be sure. Not that she would ever take his blood, and it took an exchange of blood for a human to be turned. Then again, Indikaiya wasn't human any more than he was. She was more. She was amazing.

Not that he would tell her so.

He'd realized all along that this revolution would bring great change to his life. It was a cosmic joke that the change was not at all what he'd expected. All this time he'd wanted to open the eyes of the blind, and yet it was his own eyes that had been opened. Everything around him looked different.

The world had not yet changed, not in the way

he had imagined it would, but he had. Whether or not it was for the better... the truth was, no one had ever made him want to be a better man. No one but her.

He should've been surprised when Indikaiya joined him in the shower, but he wasn't. Not really. She'd unbraided her hair, which fell like a wavy waterfall across her shoulder. Gorgeous. Sadly it was clear that she was here to bathe, not to play. She'd grabbed a washcloth on her way in.

She moved close enough to him to place her face in the hot spray, closing her eyes and sighing in delight. Sorin watched the water wash over her face and down her body, and he was hard again.

He wanted to take her away from this war and spend a week, a month, a *year*, making love. Just the two of them. No swords, no battles... no clothes.

But that was not possible. All they had was this too-short interlude. A moment. A reprieve that would not last nearly long enough. He intended to make the best of it.

"Have you ever had sex in a shower?" he asked, easing her around to face him. Her eyes opened. She was wary, but that wasn't new.

"I have not."

"Care to give it a try?"

Lucky for him, Indikaiya was not averse to trying new things.

***

Chloe was no longer growing larger and more obviously pregnant every day. Instead, it seemed that with every *minute* that passed, the child inside her grew.

How was this possible? She'd been hiding her condition with loose fitting clothing, but that wouldn't last much longer. She couldn't possibly be more than a few weeks along, if that.

Luca was... well, she would not use the word *alarmed* to describe him, not ever. He was forever in control, and nothing threw him off balance. But the very existence of the baby they had made puzzled him.

After his two thousand years of existence, she still managed to surprise him. That fact seemed to both please and annoy him.

He wanted to take her away, and if he insisted, that would happen soon. She loved him and he was her maker. That didn't mean she had no choice but to obey, but it added another layer to their relationship. Lover, maker, master, father of her child. Husband? Might as well be. No bond could possibly go deeper than the one they had.

If he insisted she would go, but she didn't want to. She wanted to be a part of the fight; she wanted to save the world.

Chloe had grown up with comic books and superhero movies, always wondering at the invincibility of the heroes. She herself had been anything but invincible, and as a teen and an adult she'd been keenly aware of her vulnerability. She had been fragile… until now. She had never felt so powerful, had never imagined she could be strong. Not like this. Why waste her strength hiding away while others did the dirty work?

Luca wanted her to hide because he wasn't sure what the others would do when they noticed her condition. If this child's existence scared him, what would the others think? Would any of them dare to go against him? Not if they had a lick of sense, but let's be honest. Some of them didn't.

The baby was growing much too fast. Did that mean the child would continue to develop more quickly after birth? Would she put her infant daughter to bed and after a few hours find a toddler in the crib?

A crib! With everything going on, she hadn't been able to give a moment's thought to ordinary new-baby issues. Like a nursery, diapers, onesies, stuffed teddy bears…

The truth was, this baby was a bundle of unknown. Dwelling on what might happen would drive her insane. One day at a time. One *hour* at a time.

And the child inside her kicked again. Hard.

CHAPTER FOURTEEN

Attacks had taken place all over the world, they knew that from the bits and pieces of news they'd seen. At the same time, Marie's recruits flooded Washington. This city was the center of it all, the initial and most important war zone. As darkness fell, there would be more battles. More humans would die.

Sorin sat in front of the television — an enormous flat screen mounted on the wall of the living room — and listened to one panicked reporter after another try to make sense of what had happened in the past week.

Several of them were still trying to find a logical explanation, but they were having a tough time of it. These reporters who dealt in facts — most of the time — found themselves smack dab in the middle of a horror story. The current news story was disjointed, the camera work sloppy and the reporter's words not as crisp and clear as usual. Instead of looking directly at the camera, the pretty brunette kept looking around her and behind. Up and down. Unfortunately for anyone with a tendency for motion sickness, so did the cameraman.

Sorin was about to abandon the television entirely when a new face appeared on the screen. He leaned forward in his chair and shouted, "Holy shit!"

His cry brought Indikaiya in from the kitchen, where she'd been hunting (unsuccessfully) for actual food. For her *and* the mutt who was at her heels.

She pointed at the screen. "Is that…"

"Luca, yes."

The blood born was being interviewed by an obviously nervous reporter, the young woman with a fixed waterfall of dark hair and a bright red dress that clung to her voluptuous body. Just a few moments ago, she'd said the words "mass hysteria." She seemed not so sure about that bit of the news at the moment.

"What does he hope to accomplish?" Indikaiya asked.

"I have no idea."

Together they watched a few minutes of Luca's unexpected press conference. He stressed calm. He explained about the sanctuary spell, how it had fallen and been reinstated. Sorin changed channels, and found that every network was showing the same interview. Luca was being watched around the country, around the world. The privacy he had valued so very much was a thing of the past.

Even a few days ago, this news conference would have been impossible. At the very least, it would have been a waste of time. In a quick phone call, Duncan had told Sorin about the spell Nevada had cast on a ring Luca now wore. If Luca removed that ring, would his old magic return? Or was that power lost now?

It was impossible to know. Luca even told those watching how to kill a vampire, much as Sorin had been doing these past few nights. Now everyone knew. The blood born also told them that not every vampire was in favor of this war, that there were some fighting to save the human race.

Damned few.

Sorin had never thought he would be one of those vampires. He'd never expected to be here, fighting alongside an Immortal Warrior, saving humans until one of them — or one of the kindred — ended him for good.

With a frustrated click of the remote, he turned off the television.

"Don't you want to know what else he has to say?" Indikaiya asked.

"Not really." He'd had enough of Luca Ambrus, blood born and savior of the whole damn world.

Sorin closed his eyes and listened. He heard the mutt's quick panting, Indikaiya's heartbeat, his own, and nothing else. Until her stomach growled.

He jumped from the couch and took her hand, leading her to the door. Not the balcony door, by which they'd entered the apartment, but the other, one he rarely used. He unlocked and opened that door. Beyond, the hallway was empty. Judging by the sounds and smells — or rather the lack of them — this entire floor was deserted. His neighbors had wisely fled.

He had seen — or heard — the woman across the hall carrying in groceries on several occasions. He'd smelled her cooking. She baked a lot. He'd enjoyed the smell, sometimes, but such aromas no longer had the power to make him hungry. Indikaiya, on the other hand, needed real food. She had fed him. The least he could do was return the favor.

His neighbor had also had a cat. Maybe the mutt would lower herself to eat cat food.

With the sanctuary spell in place, he couldn't enter the apartment. He couldn't even kick in the door. Instead he indicated the door with a wave of his hand. "No one is at home, but there will be food."

Indikaiya tried to turn the doorknob. Naturally, it was locked. She glanced at Sorin, then said, "My apologies to whoever lives here, but I have to eat."

She kicked the door and it flew open.

Sorin stood in the hall, just beyond the doorway, as Indikaiya walked toward the kitchen, which in this apartment was not a separate room but was a part of the large, open main area. The mutt followed, close on her heels. It was not his imagination that the demon dog glanced back and wagged a ragged tail as if to flaunt her ability to enter the apartment he could not.

218 | Linda Winstead Jones

There was no cat present, but there was a small bowl of dry food on the kitchen floor. Cupcake abandoned Indikaiya for that bowl.

"I have heard of these," Indikaiya called out as she rummaged through the cabinets. "Pop-Tarts. Rurik has a fondness for the frosted strawberry."

"Of course he does," Sorin muttered.

He watched and listened as she ransacked the kitchen. The refrigerator opened and closed, as did several cabinets. He wondered what had happened to the woman who lived here — or used to live here. Had she made her escape with her cat or had she become food for a vampire on her way out of town?

It annoyed Sorin that he couldn't walk into the apartment and help Indikaiya collect provisions. Something so simple, and he was incapable. That was one of the reasons why he had been so intent on Nevada taking out the original sanctuary spell, why he had fallen for Marie's prettily painted picture of freedom.

He was tired of standing on the outside looking in. He was tired of being forever separated from so many normal parts of life.

Of course, he had left normal behind seven hundred years ago.

His cell phone was charging in his apartment. He really should call Jimmy or Duncan — those two had kept him informed of the plans and progress until now — and see what the plan was for tonight. But all he wanted to do was fight. He didn't want to take orders from Luca Ambrus, didn't want to be assigned to a particular battlefield.

Indikaiya left the apartment with an armload of food and a rare smile. Again, the mutt was close behind. At least this time the dog didn't try to take a chunk out of his leg.

Sorin didn't care about the damn dog. All he wanted to do was fuck and feed and fight. With Indikaiya.

Marie put her frustration behind her and focused on the days to come. She'd expected the first phase of this war to be finished by now. The traitorous vampires and the damned Immortal Warriors had not entirely ruined her plans, but they had definitely interfered.

Still, she was nothing if not adaptable.

The long black limousine with the dark tinted windows had left Atlanta before full dark had fallen. Marie reclined on the rear seat. On the bench seat directly across from her, Chloe's mother slept. Of course she slept. Marie had drunk from the annoying woman almost until death. Almost.

Yet another part of her plan had hit a snag. Amelia Fallon had tried to call her daughter and had gotten no answer. Apparently she'd been calling for days without success. It was impossible to blackmail someone without making contact.

There was no need to be hasty. She needed to solidify her plan before moving forward.

Without Luca and Sorin in the mix, the war would certainly proceed more smoothly. Luca was a leader. Sorin, a fearsome soldier — and a betrayer. When they were punished and out of the picture, the war would take another turn. In her favor. As for the human Ahron insisted had to be eliminated… he would be easy enough to kill. She barely gave him a second thought.

The other two would not be easy, she knew that well. She would not underestimate either of them again.

By taking Amelia Fallon, she had a way to get to Luca through his woman. Perhaps it was just as well that Chloe hadn't died, after all. Beyond the annoying woman, Luca had no weaknesses. None.

Luca was all but hers. And she knew exactly how to draw Sorin out.

Nevada rolled over and into Rurik. A solid, warm, naked Rurik. The Warriors didn't sleep much, but they did sleep. Sometimes a couple hours a day, sometimes as much as four. The couch she normally slept on was far too small for Rurik, much less for both of them, so they'd spent the last few hours on the floor. It was hard, but there were pillows and blankets to make the area tolerable.

Rurik had been dozing, but as soon as she

touched him he was wide awake. Not startled, just instantly awake and aware. She smiled. He smiled. Life was good.

That was a thought she hadn't had for a very long time.

Very early this morning, after coming in from the fight covered in blood and dust, Rurik had made love to her in a way that convinced her that even though she hadn't been a virgin when she'd been kidnapped, she might as well have been. No encounter had ever been like that one. Nothing and no one had ever touched her as he had. It was more than the deep affection she felt for him, more than his skill in the bedroom. It was both of those things, and more.

Love, maybe. No, Rurik simply knew what he was doing. No — both. More. No, not love. That would complicate things far too much. Given the state of the world, what did it matter *why*?

She curled into him, soaked up his heat, wallowed in the feel of his skin against hers.

"I know it sounds silly, given what's happened in the past few weeks, but in the past twenty-four hours everything has changed," she said.

"Because we shared this hard bed?"

"That's one thing, but there's more. Luca, a vampire, held a press conference." She rolled over and on top of Rurik, resting there comfortably. "He put himself out there for the whole world to see. I never thought that would happen. Chloe is carrying a… I don't even know what to call her. A miracle, certainly. Will that baby girl save humankind or destroy it? I see her as a savior, I think she's important, but what do I know?"

"You know much," he said, his hand — so solid and warm and right — settling on her back.

"I don't know near everything," she said.

"No one is meant to know everything."

She leaned in and kissed Rurik. He was a good kisser. "I suppose there are some advantages to living in such close quarters," she said, taking her lips from his just long enough to whisper.

"Yes." He pulled her closer, tighter.

It was amazing how an orgasm could make her forget all the bad stuff in the world. For a while, anyway. It was awesome, it really was, but as Rurik rolled her over and spread her legs Nevada reminded herself that she'd have to be very careful not to fall in love with him. Tempting as it was, easy as it would be. When the war was over, he'd return to his own world. If her protection spell wasn't good enough, if his fighting skills faltered, he could be snatched back there in an instant. Tonight, tomorrow, any day any time. Maybe Jimmy could call him back, if that happened. Maybe not. Once Rurik was home for good, it wasn't like they could visit. Talk about a long distance relationship!

If the war had taught her anything, it was to live in the moment. She didn't know if she'd be around to see tomorrow. She didn't know what the world would look like if Marie won. She didn't even know what the world would look like if the good guys won! Not the same, that's for sure.

She had been working to find and develop more spells to aid the good guys or hurt Marie and her psychos. Preferably both. But she couldn't work all the time. Her brain and her body needed a rest. No matter what tomorrow might bring, she was going to push everything aside, for now. Everything but Rurik.

She could and would take pleasure when and where she found it. She would embrace joy, in small doses or large. She would learn to live in the moment.

Thanks to Rurik, this moment was fine.

Whatever peace this city had once known was gone. Only the most bullheaded of humans could believe that their opponent wasn't what they claimed to be. Vampires. Bloodsuckers. Creatures long believed to be demons.

Indikaiya kept her eyes trained straight ahead, trying to dismiss the fact that she had lain with one. She had not only laid down with Sorin in his bed, she had enjoyed it. She had enjoyed it so much she knew that if they survived this night she would lie with him again.

She was no stranger to pleasure given and taken. Indikaiya had had three husbands during her life in

Atlantis. One of them she'd truly loved. He'd died far too young of an illness that would've been easily cured in this new world. The other two had been husbands of political convenience. They had both been pleasant men she liked; she would not have married them otherwise, but there had been no real love as there had been with Nileas. She'd also taken lovers in the world she now called home, but… it had been a long while.

Her relationship with Sorin had her thinking too much of days long gone. Her life as a human had been more good than bad, more pampered than hard. A cousin had been queen for a while, which had put Indikaiya among a favored few. There had been golden days of music and plenty, when her children had been healthy and the husband she'd loved had been at her side.

But such wonder never lasted. Her children grew older. Her husband died and she was led into another marriage. And then another, after her second husband had taken ill and died. Good fortune for their island country led many to a quest for more fortune. Soldiers dressed in gold and blue sailed away from Atlantis; they became invaders, which in turn brought the enemy to their own shores.

Indikaiya had sent her daughters to live with a friend in Greece, putting them on a boat in the dead of night and watching them sail away. She could still feel the burn of tears in her eyes; she could still feel the heaviness of her heart. She had intended to join them, when she could. She'd planned to take her sons there as well, to escape a land which had once been so blessed but had been broken by those who were greedy and intolerant. The tears she'd shed that night, the heavy heart that had felt as if it could pull her to her knees... had she somehow known that she was seeing the girls for the last time?

Indikaiya had seen disaster coming, had dreamed of it, and she'd wanted to protect her children. Even though a part of her had wanted, so badly, to take her sons and go with them that night, she knew she would've been missed. And in all honesty, she was not a deserter. She could not have abandoned her home when she was needed, not even if she'd known how that battle was going to end.

A skilled swordsman, a fierce soldier for many years before the invasion, she'd led men and woman into battle, defending their shores. For two weeks, they had fought well, but the attackers had greater numbers and a burning zeal to kill. Indikaiya had died by an invader's sword, as had her third husband and two of her three sons.

If she had not sent her daughters away they would've been on the island years later when it was claimed by the sea — as her eldest son had been — and she would have no descendants to call her to this world.

The last few years of her life had been violent and uncertain, as this night — in another time and another world — was for so many. She remembered the terror, the panic, the will to survive. But tonight she also remembered love.

Her time with Sorin had nothing to do with love. That simply wasn't possible.

Indikaiya had attempted to leave behind the dog that had, for some inexplicable reason, attached itself to her. War was not for small and fragile creatures such as this one. She had planned to leave the animal in Sorin's apartment with a comfy bed and some cat food, but that had not worked. Cupcake — the undignified name still caused her physical pain — had barked and snarled and cried, and as much as she'd wanted to, Indikaiya had not been able to walk away from the crying animal.

Not far from Sorin's home, they'd passed an apartment building which was — unlike so many others — alive with lights and the sounds of people. Voices. Even unexpected laughter. Surely the dog would be safer there than in battle. Sorin and Indikaiya had both tried to send the dog in that direction. Cupcake had refused to go.

Indikaiya had to admit, she had been bested by a dog named Cupcake, an animal which weighed significantly less than a bag of sugar. At the moment, Cupcake slept in the bag Indikaiya had taken from the department store, along with the tunic, two bottles of water, and some food.

She and Sorin ran, side by side, toward smoke and fire and the screams of foolish humans. Foolish or brave? Soldiers — as well as ordinary citizens like Kevin Brown — had flooded into the city. They had come here to fight, and they had a fight on their hands. More vampires had come to the city, as well. True, they were showing themselves all over the world, but the initial battle, the one that would determine defeat or victory for the self-proclaimed queen, was happening here and now.

The battle they joined was taking place in a field. A park, a sign near the roadway proclaimed. Green grass was already stained with blood. The blood of humans and the ash of defeated vampires mingled to make a sickly, black mud. Sorin moved ahead of her, sword drawn, long blond hair flowing behind him. He'd disposed of his leather coat, which had been damaged the night before. Just as well. He no longer needed it to hide his sword. There was no reason, as anyone with any sense of self-preservation was always armed.

He moved up — unnaturally up — and then dropped down, sword swinging. Some of the humans feared him to be a new opponent, but as soon as Sorin dispatched two of his own kind in quick order, they celebrated his addition to the mix.

Indikaiya jumped into the battle as well. She could not fly, but few wielded a sword as expertly as she did.

As her enemies soon learned.

CHAPTER FIFTEEN

This mansion was hers, taken by brute force years earlier, so why shouldn't she reclaim it? Marie walked in through the front door like she owned the place. Which she did. One of her soldiers, one of the newer ones who wasn't particularly powerful but who did what he was told without question, carried the unconscious woman Marie had collected from Atlanta. They were directly behind her.

Glancing about, she wanted to scream. Tempting as it was, she did not. The battle that had been waged here a week ago had caused serious damage to this once beautiful place. Furnishings were in pieces. Once-spotless walls sported bullet holes, as well as sprays of now-dried blood. Someone had attempted to set the place to rights, but they had not done a very good job.

Allies, powerful kindred from around the world, were on their way. She should've gathered many of them before getting the war underway, but thanks to Luca and Sorin the timing had not been entirely in her control. Powerful vampires, friends, perhaps a worshiper or two, would join her here. They would help her put this war to rights.

Two of her most loyal soldiers had been sent to

collect the pieces she needed to complete her next move. They, too, would come here, to the place where her revolution had begun.

Outwardly, Marie remained calm. Even those closest to her could not be allowed to see her frustration. In spite of the failures, the chaos in D.C. was just as she'd imagined, and her experiments at long-term glamouring had paid off. She had many human soldiers who would do her bidding. They were weak-minded almost to the point of being simple, but they could, and did, fight. They could walk in the sun and they would never, ever betray her. If she asked them all to slice off their own heads, they would at least *try* to oblige her.

This next step... her next step would move this war forward by leaps and bounds. Ahron had promised.

Those who had wronged her were about to pay dearly.

This could not continue. Could not, would not. Indikaiya had been telling herself that for days, to no avail.

In Sorin's quarters, she fed and watered the small dog that had claimed her, patting Cupcake's back and praising her for a job well done. The poor dog needed yet another bath. As they all did.

Cupcake had not been content to stay in Indikaiya's bag during battle. She'd escaped, and nipped relentlessly at the heels of many vampires. Including Sorin, on occasion. If she had been a larger dog the vampires might've turned on her, but she was small and quick, and no self-respecting soldier would turn their backs on an armed enemy in order to see to the nuisance.

If anyone dared to attack Cupcake, Indikaiya would quickly end them. She was surprised by the intensity of that promise to herself.

When Cupcake was settled on her pillow, she and Sorin stripped, showered, and then fell into bed. Indikaiya enjoyed the sex, she truly did, but at the same time...

Her lover was a vampire. The enemy, a soulless being, a creature who needed the blood of the living in order to survive. Her purpose — in life and in the afterlife — was to protect humans. He fed from them.

He'd killed. She didn't know how many lives he'd taken, but he was far from innocent. He had been in Marie's camp for a long while; he had murdered conduits. Was the fact that he'd changed sides before the fighting started in earnest, that he was an invaluable asset, that he made her feel good — that he made her forget war for a while — did that mean she should forgive his past transgressions?

Was it her place to forgive them?

He slept. He must trust her completely, to sleep so deeply while she was in his bed. She needed to rest, had to, but her mind was spinning. With thoughts of Sorin, of war, of Chloe and her child. Lying next to him, she closed her eyes and willed sleep to come. As though that ever worked. Behind closed eyes she replayed scenes of last night's battle. She saw Sorin as he leapt and swung his sword with incredible power and killed his own kind without a qualm. She saw him catch her eye more than once. He smiled often, that brilliant, charming smile that had captivated women for hundreds of years. But he did not smile in battle. No, he was focused as he fought. Determined. Deadly.

And distracted by her presence. She had realized that last night, when he'd turned his back on a sword-wielding vamp to check on her battle status, to assure himself that she was unharmed.

The man confused her, so much. It was not at all like her to be confused. Good was good and evil was evil, and there was no gray area in between.

Yet here she was, washed in gray.

Sorin stirred. He rolled into her, above her. "You should be sleeping," he said as he spread her thighs.

"So should you." She lifted her hips as he aligned himself.

"How can I sleep when you need me?"

Indikaiya could not, would not, need Sorin or anyone else. She tried to tell him so but he filled her in one long, powerful, wonderful thrust, and words left her.

Sex, not love, she told herself as he brought her to the edge of release and then slowed, teasing her.

Pleasure, not need, she thought as he kissed her breasts and her neck softly before increasing the power of his thrusts and bringing her to the edge and over.

Her mind was no longer distracted by memories of battle. There was only this. His body and hers. The way he filled her. The way she responded. She should not, could not need or want him.

In spite of herself, she screamed and clutched at his broad shoulders while her body shook.

He shook, too. He needed her as much as she needed him, and she took some comfort in that knowledge.

She had not experienced real pleasure in a very long time. Her life was pleasant, but simple. Her life in a world far from this one had purpose. She was a Warrior, not a woman to be wooed.

"Can I kiss you on the mouth now?" Sorin asked, moving closer, edging in until his face was almost touching hers.

"No." He was so close they might as well be kissing. So close. He smelled so good. His lips were annoyingly tempting.

"Pity. It would be sweet."

"It would be unnecessary." And dangerous. Dangerous for her, if she allowed herself to think this might be more than sexual release. Dangerous, if she allowed herself to admit that she wanted to know what his lips tasted like. She tried to keep her voice calm, cool, detached, as she rejected his kiss, but she wondered if Sorin heard the slight tremble.

Of course he did. He missed nothing.

If he noticed, he said nothing. For that, she could thank him. But of course, she did not.

"Chloe is with child," she said.

Sorin's only reaction was a lift of his eyebrows that indicated his surprise. "That's not possible," he responded. Then he frowned.

"I did not think so, either, but I am not mistaken." She wasn't sure why she felt compelled to share the news with her lover, but it had been weighing on her and it felt good to say the words.

"The child won't survive," he said in a lowered voice.

"You're wrong. She's very strong."

He did not argue with her, but accepted her assessment. "What does Luca have to say about this development?"

"I'm not even sure he knows."

"He knows." Sorin rolled from the bed and headed for the bathroom. He returned moments later with a damp washcloth for her. "Nothing that momentous could get past the great Luca Ambrus for long."

It had been days since she'd seen Chloe and her vampire. It was likely Luca did know about the baby, by now.

"You don't like him."

Sorin crawled into the bed. He eased closer to her as he flashed that smile that affected her far too

234 | Linda Winstead Jones

deeply. "I do not want to talk about Luca while I'm in bed with you."

She turned her back to him, trying to create distance between them, then sighed as he ran one finger down her spine.

"Wake me if you have need of me again," he teased.

"And if you have need of me?" she responded, rolling over to face him, fully expecting him to laugh at the concept of needing anyone.

He lifted his head and grinned at her. "Indikaiya, I always have need of you." He placed his head on his pillow, closed his eyes and was asleep in moments.

Surely sleep would come for her now. Exhausted from battle, well loved, safe. Surely her mind would stop spinning. It did not, and long before the sun set she left the bed as quietly as possible, pulled on her clothes and gathered her sword *and* her dog, and left by way of the front door.

He'd heard Indikaiya leave, and had allowed her to go without question, without interference. To be honest, he was not surprised that she'd left. He was only surprised that she'd stayed with him as long as she had.

If he found himself in need of blood or fucking, there were plenty of other women available. There always had been, always would be. He could fetch himself a pretty woman who was enamored of his kind, who would not mind serving in all ways in exchange for his protection. Many of the kindred lived that way, most especially now, in time of war. Duncan and Isaac were both keeping human women who saw to their needs for blood and sex. They, unlike those under Marie's command, had consorts who chose to be with them, who could leave at any time.

As Indikaiya had left.

He told himself again and again that she would be easily replaced. As a partner in this war, as a lover, as a provider of nourishment. Others could and would provide what she no longer provided. He'd known many women and he would know many more.

But he admitted, to himself at least, that there was none other like her.

It was almost dark when Sorin left his apartment. He did not need to report to the library for instruction like a good and obedient soldier. He knew what to do. It wasn't as though skirmishes were difficult to find. They were everywhere, in this city and in others. He no longer bothered to carry his cell phone. Why should he? So Luca could call and issue orders? So Nevada could call to ask if he was still alive and kicking? Why did she care, anyway? Yes, he had saved her life, but she should hate him for everything that had happened before that.

He'd always liked New York. The lights, the people, the energy. No matter what the time of day, the city was alive. Did New Yorkers deserve protection less than those who lived in this city? They did not. It was doubtful that the war had reached Manhattan in full force, but he wasn't the only creature of the night who had a fondness for a city that never slept.

But he wasn't headed that way tonight. Tonight, he would fight here. Here, where he was needed. Here, where he might catch a glimpse of Indikaiya. New York wasn't going anywhere. Perhaps tomorrow...

CHAPTER SIXTEEN

Marie wasn't especially fond of having Ahron underfoot, but it made sense to keep him close. As an advisor and as a maddeningly unspecific psychic who occasionally came through with a bit of useful information. At the moment, he was necessary. She wasn't afraid of him, but at the same time she was wary. He seemed to be on her side, he *said* he was on her side. But was he? There were moments when she was certain this war was nothing more than much-needed entertainment for the ancient.

He was gleefully taken with the stock Marie kept in small basement rooms. For someone who was capable of going long stretches without feeding, he did enjoy snacking on the food supply. He was particularly fond of Chloe's mother. The Fallon woman had been edging toward madness before she'd become a favorite of the ancient Ahron. Now? Now she was a rambling basket case.

Marie was capable of fighting alongside the others, but she did not. She was surrounded by kindred who would die for her. Male and female, ancient and new, they believed in her and what she promised.

Which is why it was so annoying when Ahron

told her she was going about this war all wrong.

The ancient paced in Marie's own private chamber where none but he dared to confront her, hands waving about as he spoke. He had given up his loose robes for more modern clothing; a suit which still smelled of the human from whom Ahron had taken it before — or perhaps after — he'd fed.

"You struck too soon," Ahron said. "You should have waited. A year or two, ten perhaps. In our long lives, that amount of time is nothing."

"I had no choice," Marie argued. The Warriors had come in force, Sorin had turned on her, Luca had sided against her... what choice had she had?

"There is always choice." Ahron stopped in front of her. He was not much taller than she was. Perhaps he'd been a man of normal height in his day, but in this era he'd be considered short. No suit could disguise the fact that he was not of this time. His skin was so pale it was almost green. Unlined, unmarked, that face was oddly handsome enough, with even features and a touch of masculinity. But the eyes were ancient, and his long, thin hair was white. He sometimes moved like an old man. Other times he did not, she noticed.

"There is another coming," he whispered.

"Another what?" she snapped.

"Another queen. Better than you, smarter than you, and one day she will be much, much prettier."

Marie moved to strike so quickly, no one would

be able to counter her. No one but Ahron, who caught her wrist and held it to the side with surprising strength. He tsked, and smiled, and in that moment she was afraid. She had sorely underestimated him.

He could no longer be considered oddly handsome, not when he looked at her this way.

"Do not be angry, pretty girl. You have done what needed to be done. If you win, if you lose… it matters not. Our kind has been exposed. We are in the known world now, and cannot be denied."

His words struck a nerve. *If you win, if you lose…* "Will I win?" she asked, annoyed at the uncertainty in her voice, but wanting, needing, to know what Ahron saw.

"We will see," he said with more than a hint of sick humor.

A rush of anger, hot and powerful, burst through her. Somehow she was going to have to kill him.

She did not express her thought aloud, but with Ahron words were unnecessary. "Many have tried. None of them continue to walk this earth."

Marie took a deep breath, not because she needed air, but because she needed a moment to compose herself. "I apologize for my rash thoughts. You angered me."

"Of course I did." He released her hand and she let it fall.

Best to change the subject as quickly as possible.

"Tell me about this so-called queen you see."

"Oh, I think not." He smiled. That was never pleasant.

For a moment, Marie was afraid. Nothing scared her, certainly not this freakish old man! But yes, she admitted to herself, she was afraid of Ahron.

How might one go about killing a powerful psychic?

"You cannot kill me," Ahron whispered. "I will always see you coming."

New York would still be there tomorrow, and the next day, and next week. The majority of the fighting was here, where it had begun. Yes, there were skirmishes taking place elsewhere, and the fighting — especially up and down the east coast, judging by the little bit of news he heard — increased daily.

But Sorin did not leave. He stayed. He fought. It had been days since Indikaiya had left, and here he remained.

He found himself fighting alongside humans and Warriors. Some he had already come to know well. Others were new comrades. Each night he went into battle with no real expectation of survival. He watched his own kind fall and go to dust. He'd be a fool to think he was not just immortal, but invincible.

In the past few nights he'd fought with strangers.

Humans who had found a strength and bravery buried deep, who banded together to fight a superior force. To face death in order to maintain their freedom. D.C. was a large city, and the fighting was widespread. It was no accident that since Indikaiya had left he'd purposely sought out battles on the edge of the war zone, rather than at its center. He did not want or need the distraction which would be inevitable if he ran into those he had once called partners. Not only would he feel obligated to keep one eye on them, when the battle was done he might find himself inundated with questions he did not want to answer.

Tonight he saw a number of familiar faces, on this battlefield far from the headquarters they now called home. He knew she was here, long before he saw her. The damn dog's yap was unmistakable.

Jimmy. Kevin. Indikaiya. No one acknowledged him — if they even saw him. They were too busy fighting, as he was. Indikaiya cut down the enemy as efficiently and valiantly as any soldier among them. She was a vision, with that sword in her hand and that long blond braid dancing as she moved with a violent and powerful grace. She was once again dressed in the shift she'd worn when she'd come into this world, though she had kept her new boots. Modern clothing was wasted on her. No one would ever mistake her for human. She was like no other. It was in the way she moved, the way she swung that sword. It was in the intensity in her eyes.

Shit. He had missed her.

Sorin worked his way toward Indikaiya, his sword slicing through vampires and even the occasional human who had chosen — whether through glamouring or through a misplaced confidence in the vampires ability to win — to fight alongside them. They died differently, but they did die.

In the past two days they'd heard rumblings about the tall, blond vampire who'd been cutting down his own kind in new battlefields. In a way, Indikaiya was surprised. When she'd left Sorin she'd had no idea if he'd stay with the fight or walk away. She no longer believed it was possible he'd rejoin Marie. Even as she'd walked out of his door, she'd known full well he would not follow her. No, Sorin followed no one.

It was no mistake that he worked his way toward her, no simple coincidence. In the midst of battle, he was seeking her out, moving purposely toward her. Leaving him had been for the best, she told herself as she prepared to meet him face to face. Of that she had no doubt. He was a distraction of the greatest magnitude. He was a vampire! When she should be thinking of battle, of saving the human race, she instead thought of him.

Unacceptable. That was not her purpose, not in this life or any other.

She had tried very hard to distance herself from thoughts of Sorin, but she couldn't deny the wave of emotion that washed through her as she watched him fight. He was as fierce as any Warrior from any time; as dedicated as every soldier who had joined this battle. He'd not only discarded his leather coat, he'd apparently given off wearing shirts, as well. He fought wearing blue jeans and heavy boots, nothing else. His choice was practical, she supposed. Each fight left a soldier bloody, dusty, and torn.

Sorin was impressive in many ways, not that she would ever say so aloud, not to anyone. Worse than noting his impressiveness, she cared for him. Distance had not diminished that caring, as she had hoped it would. She was no longer a foolish girl who believed in love; she was a woman, a Warrior. And yet she cared for a vampire. Loved? Perhaps. Wanted? Definitely. That was a hard admission to make, even to herself. It had been such a long time since she'd felt anything beyond honor and duty.

These thoughts rushed through her mind as she fought a burly vampire with a shaved head and a short, thickly-bladed sword.

Sorin called on his unnatural speed to rush toward her. He flew up, arcing into the air with his sword raised and his hair flowing behind him. Indikaiya dispatched the bald vampire and then looked up, meeting Sorin's eye. Was she his target? Was he that angry with her? The thought was a fleeting one. He came down behind her with a swipe

244 | Linda Winstead Jones

of his sword, taking the head of the vampire that had been moving in on Indikaiya as she'd been admiring a man she should never admire. Or trust. Love? Impossible.

"Pay attention!" he snapped, his voice harsh and his eyes flashing blue, and then he turned his back on her to continue the battle.

She wondered how often in his long life he'd trusted anyone who held a sword enough to present his fine back.

CHAPTER SEVENTEEN

The battle waned; the few remaining rebels departed. A few flew. Others ran. A handful made it out alive. Others did not. Sorin noted, not for the first time, that Jimmy and Kevin were fine fighters, surprisingly efficient and effective for a couple of young humans. The last two vampires to die on this night went not by sword, but by shotgun and by crossbow.

The sun would rise in less than an hour. He needed to feed. He needed to sleep. There would be another battle tomorrow night, and another the night after that. He could see no end to this war, not until Marie was dead.

And yet instead of tracking her down as he had planned, he was busy fighting one battle at a time, watching over humans and Warriors alike.

He wondered how long the men he'd just admired would survive. He could not be the only one to note their worth in battle. The vampire rebels would be gunning for them specifically, and if they were targeted they'd be lucky to last two nights. Not that it was his responsibility to watch over them as if they were children. Both had gone into this war knowing how it would likely end for them.

Sorin dismissed all thoughts of the humans and turned his eyes and his mind in a more pleasant direction. He expected Indikaiya to walk away without speaking to him, but instead she stood there on the battlefield, feet apart, posture that of a soldier, sword down but still gripped tightly in her hand, and stared at him. Cupcake stood proudly at her side.

He stared right back. Dammit, he missed her. He would never admit to it.

If he told her he wanted to feed from her and fuck her, would she run? Of course she would. But would she run toward him or away?

He didn't get the chance to find out. This night's fight was over, so he was taken by surprise when one of the kindred — an Italian he knew well — appeared before him. Sergio had such a gift for speed, he could, and often did, seem to pop out of thin air even to a vampire's eye.

Sorin raised his sword and so did Indikaiya, who was still several feet away. When Sergio lifted his empty hands, Sorin relaxed. A little. Was it possible the Italian had come to join their side of the fight? A handful had. Only a handful.

"I have a message from our queen," Sergio said.

Nope, not joining the right army after all. Sorin's grip on his sword changed, as he readied himself to continue fighting, if it was necessary. He lifted a hand to silently instruct Indikaiya to remain where she was. She didn't care for the order, but she did stay in place.

Like him, she was ready to fight if necessary. Sergio looked at her, and at the men behind her, men who grew closer with each trudging, tired step. They were curious about the newcomer, but not alarmed. Not yet.

"You have not been answering your cell phone."

His cell phone, which he'd abandoned as unnecessary.

"I can't imagine that Marie has anything to say that I care to hear," Sorin said. "But you can give her a message from me." He leaned in, slightly. Sergio was fast, but he was also a small man, easily intimidated. "She can't win."

Sergio was not alarmed. He even seemed a bit smug. Sorin considered taking the vampire's head, now that he knew what side Sergio was on, but the Italian stopped him with a simple message.

Three names.

A time and place.

Three more names and a brief but dire warning.

Before Sorin had a chance to respond, Sergio was gone.

It was wrong, so very wrong, for her pregnancy to have progressed so fast! Chloe lay flat on her back on the long table in the interior conference room. Why hadn't her daughter waited for dark to decide to come into the world? Why now, well after dawn, when Chloe was not at her strongest? She had not seen the sun since Luca had turned her, but she felt it, a threat so close, so deadly.

She screamed, as another pain ripped at her insides. As the agony subsided she gave into the myriad of fears that flitted through her mind. What if the child looked like Ahron? What if her baby was a monster? Would the child need to feed on blood or milk or both? Would the baby, who had grown so quickly in the womb, continue to grow rapidly? There was nothing worse that facing the unknown where her child was concerned. She could prepare herself for anything, but when the possibilities were endless she was overwhelmed with what ifs.

Like any man facing impending fatherhood, Luca paced. He'd been pacing for hours! She could tell he was worried. He said all the right words — you'll be fine, the baby will be fine, I love you — but behind it all she heard his uncertainty. Even more, she felt it, she *saw* it, as if that worry were a physical thing, yellow and green and muddy.

Chloe screamed, and the walls shook. The pregnancy had progressed very rapidly. Could the labor not have done the same?

Nevada was present to deliver the child. Chloe trusted no one else. Not with this, not with her daughter. The girl should be terrified, she should be frantic with her own what ifs, but somehow the redhead was the calmest of the three of them.

Nevada could no longer be called a girl. She had faced monsters, faced death, and come out the stronger for it. She was a woman now, and a damned powerful one at that.

It was Nevada who had insisted that they have formula standing by. Just in case. Chloe trusted the witch; she trusted the woman's instincts, which, to be honest, went far beyond normal human instincts.

"It's time," Nevada said. Her face was a little paler than usual, and for the pale-skinned redhead that was saying something. Like Chloe, she had her doubts about this highly unusual pregnancy. She did not allow those doubts to slow her down in any way.

Luca stood beside the table that was serving as Chloe's bed. He held her hand. Nevada stood at the end of the table, with everything she thought she'd need at hand. Right outside the door, humans and Warriors waited. Like Nevada, they were nervous. No, they were more worried than nervous, worried about what might appear out of Chloe's womb. Some of them were frightened. They hadn't found out about the pregnancy until a few days earlier, when Chloe had grown so large that there was no hiding the condition.

No matter what, she would protect her child. Angel or monster, beautiful or horrific, Chloe would kill anyone who tried to harm the baby who was soon to come into the world. It was an empowering thought, and she embraced it. She would soon be a mother. A mother who would do anything for her child.

"Push," Nevada said.

Chloe did, gladly. She screamed as she followed her instincts and attempted to expel a brand new person from her own newly transformed body. The entire building seemed to shake.

"Again." Nevada licked her lips and positioned herself as if ready to catch a football. Chloe did as instructed, and her child, her daughter, came into the world. Just like that, it was done. Over.

Nevada busied herself at the end of the table. Chloe could see nothing, and she didn't dare move. Not yet. She wanted to know, but she was afraid. The fear melted away. No matter what, the child was hers.

The witch smiled and looked to the new mother. "She's beautiful." Nevada asked Luca if he wanted to cut the cord, and he declined. Instead he continued to hold Chloe's hand, wincing a bit.

Chloe looked down at their joined hands and realized that his was deformed.

"Oh my God, I broke you!"

"A little."

She released his hand. How many broken bones were there? What had she done?

"I will heal," he added.

Nevada presented them with a squirming bundle wrapped in a thin pink blanket — goodness only knew where the witch had come up with that soft bit of cloth, but she *was* resourceful — and Chloe was happy to see for herself that her daughter was indeed beautiful. She looked like any other newborn, a little wrinkled, a little red, with fat pink cheeks and very little fine, blond hair.

And then she opened her eyes.

Chloe gasped, and then she looked to Luca. "She has your eyes."

Gray, almost silver, they were piercing and unusual and powerful.

Her child. Luca's daughter. They were a family. Chloe had no idea what the future would bring for the three of them, but this moment... this moment in time was very fine.

Sorin stood in the deepest shadows of a side chamber of the Lincoln Memorial. The cavernous structure, marble and stately, made even him feel small. The columns were so wide, a small army could hide behind one. His nose told him there was no vampire army within these walls. Not yet, at least. An army was coming, he had no doubt about that. A few weeks ago this place would've been swarming with tourists. Today, it was deserted, but for him and his fellow soldiers. Even the road that circled the memorial was empty. Lifeless.

It was almost high noon, their assigned meeting time. Marie had been watching too many movies.

No, the self-proclaimed queen realized only a

very few vampires could withstand this much sunlight. Getting here had been difficult, and even within this structure, he could not find a corner of complete darkness. Luca should've been here, but when Sorin had left the library the blood born had been with Chloe, who'd been in labor for hours. It was no surprise that Luca had left this meeting with Marie to Sorin in order to be with his woman and child. It was his place to protect them, and that's what he was doing at this moment.

The blood born, who had always been a loner, a solitary figure, now had or would soon have a family. A woman and a child, as well as the joys and heartaches that came with those obligations.

Chloe — who had been ordered here as Sorin had been — would've been present to face Marie if she could. Even if she were not giving birth, Luca's woman was far too new to withstand the sun. She would not be able to function even in the shade, and the lightest touch of the sun would destroy her, now and for many more years to come.

Sorin was not as well fed as he should be for this confrontation. He felt queasy already. Not weak, not incapable, but not his best, either. He had fed since Indikaiya had left him, but not to excess. He'd taken what he needed from those willing to give it, but for the first time since becoming vampire he had taken no pleasure in feeding. He drank because he needed to function. That was all.

"We should not be here," Indikaiya said, walking

up behind him to speak in a low voice. Sorin had asked her to stay behind. He had *ordered* her to stay at the library to wait for the baby — her own descendant — to arrive, but she was stubborn. As stubborn as he was, apparently.

"At least you left the damn dog behind."

She bristled, a little, then ignored his comment. "If Marie wants a confrontation we should name the time and place, not her," she said. "There has to be another way. A negotiation…"

"I must be here," he said without turning to look at her. "You are here by choice. You're free to leave."

She scoffed. Yes, stubborn.

There were many large trees, summer green and full, to the sides of the memorial, some not far from the foot of the steps. He wondered if Marie was already there, waiting for the precise appointed time before emerging. No one knew why she had gone to such lengths to draw out Sorin, Chloe, and Jimmy. He could understand her anger with him and her tactical need to remove Luca — through Chloe — from the mix, but Jimmy? Why? Even Nevada, who on occasion had a bit of otherworldly insight, couldn't be sure. She only knew it was important that they go.

No matter what she'd said, nothing could've kept Sorin from this meeting, not after Sergio had whispered that name as he delivered his queen's message.

Phillip.

As instructed, their party was small. Sorin and Indikaiya, Jimmy and Rurik. If Luca wasn't otherwise occupied he'd be here, too, in Chloe's place. Surely Marie knew that none of the three requested would come alone. Would she come to this meeting prepared to face Luca and Sorin together? If so, she must be feeling very confident.

He should be afraid, but he hadn't felt true fear for a very long time.

"I will fight with you," Indikaiya said, one hand on the hilt of her sword.

"You will not," Sorin responded, his voice low.

"I will not stand by and watch..."

"Three humans are in danger today. I will get them to you so you can deliver them to the library."

"I am not a nursemaid!"

He looked her in the eye. Could she see his determination? Feel it? "Do this for me."

"Damn you," she said softly, then she stepped forward, tilted her head to one side, and offered her throat. "I will not allow you to do this at anything less than your full capability."

That throat, pale and perfect, was tempting. "I did not ask..."

"No, you did not," she snapped. "I'm offering. Be strong for this fight. You're more likely to save the humans you have come here to save if you've just taken in Warrior blood."

Not just Warrior blood, but *her* blood. They were connected, through sex and blood. Not bonded, not in the way a human and vampire could and sometimes did, but in their own way they had become one. He had not thought he still possessed the ability to be surprised.

He kissed her throat, bit down, and drank. Strength flowed through his body, and a new clarity filled his mind. It was as if until this moment he had been blind. As if he'd seen everything through a cloudy glass or a thick fog. The fog lifted. The glass shattered. This time and place, it was his destiny, his reason for existence. Seven hundred years, and now this...

He drew away long before he'd drunk his fill. There was so much he could say, should say, but instead he nodded once in acknowledgement and then he turned his back on Indikaiya.

It was unlikely he would survive this day. Marie would not have set up this meeting if she had not planned to win. He would do all he could to save the others. Perhaps, if he were very lucky, he'd managed to do what he'd been planning to do since this war had begun. Kill Marie.

What he would not do was burden Indikaiya with an emotional confession of love and caring. Blah, blah, blah. He would not be the soldier who went into battle after sharing his feelings with the woman he had come to love.

She had enough to worry about without that weight.

Noon came, and Marie — always punctual —

stepped from the side of the memorial, into the sunlight and onto the steps. She wore a wide brimmed hat, a long skirt, a long-sleeved shirt, and sunglasses, in deference to the sun she could withstand better than most. Sorin could barely see her face, but when he caught a glimpse of the lower half of her face, he saw her smile. Yes, she was confident. Behind her, the reflecting pool shimmered in the sun, framing her and the child with her. She held the hand of a little boy who didn't realize he was in danger, who didn't have any idea that the pretty lady who led him toward the memorial was a monster.

Marie did have a gift for sharing her most innocent face, when it was called for. She had shown that face to Phillip.

Jimmy cursed when two of Marie's soldiers appeared behind her. They did not seem to mind the sun at all, so they were human, either glamoured or choosing to be on Marie's side of this war because they believed she'd win and they wanted to be on the winning side, no matter what. Sorin was disheartened. If there were enough humans who'd fight for Marie, this war would be harder than anyone realized. One soldier held an older woman who favored Chloe. The other gripped the arm of a young woman with spiked, dark hair. As Jimmy tried to rush forward, Rurik forcibly stopped him.

"Don't give her what she wants," the Warrior said in a lowered voice. "Don't panic."

"That's Kate!" Jimmy argued.

Jimmy's Kate, Chloe's mother, and — for him — Phillip Stargel. The conduit he had spared. A special child incapable of seeing darkness in anyone.

Even Sorin.

The self-proclaimed vampire queen had found their vulnerabilities, their weaknesses. The army Sorin had joined was made up of people who would always have such weaknesses, while Marie and her soldiers had none. No heart. No love.

Marie climbed a few steps then stopped. She peered into the shadows beyond wide pillars, studied those she had called to this meeting — as well as those she had not — and her smile faded. "Where is Chloe Fallon? Does she hide in the shadows? Call her forth."

Sorin stood in front of the others. This was his mess, and even more, it was his calling. He was here to kill Marie. With her gone, the war could not continue. At the very least, the vampire rebels would be weakened. They needed a leader.

"Chloe couldn't make it," he said, taking a single step forward, closer to the sunlight. He didn't want to tell her about the child that would come into the world — or had already come — today. She'd find out soon enough.

"Luca?" she asked, and a trill in her voice told Sorin it was the blood born she really wanted here.

"He had other plans."

Marie turned her head and said something to

the soldier who held Chloe's mother. Sunlight glinted on a short blade. Before Sorin could even think of moving forward, the man slit the throat of the woman he held. Blood spurted. He released Chloe's mother and lifeless body dropped to the steps.

Any move forward would mean death for the remaining two prisoners. The man who held Kate also had a dagger in his hand. The blade was at her throat; a trickle of blood, red and sweet, marred the flesh there. Marie would need no weapon — and no more than a split second — to kill the child at her side.

"What do you want?" Sorin asked.

"It's simple, traitor. You for the child, Jimmy for the girl."

"I'm easily worth two humans. Leave Jimmy out of it."

"Perhaps you are, but I make the rules and I want you *and* the boy."

He studied the positions of the remaining players in this standoff. A quick listen, and he realized there were more humans nearby, ready to fight for Marie, if necessary. He could not see them from where he stood, but he heard their quick heartbeats, smelled their blood. What had she promised them? Life everlasting? He could hope they were all glamoured. That would slow them down. And if he killed Marie, her magic should die with her.

He knew Marie well enough to realize that she didn't intend for any of the opposing team to survive.

Sorin turned to Indikaiya and smiled down at her. He cupped her head in one hand and drew her to him for a quick, deep kiss. She had never before allowed him to kiss her on the mouth, and he wanted it now. Needed it as much as the blood she'd offered. "I'm glad I got to know you, Indikaiya. Woman, Warrior, lover. There is not another like you in any world, in any time."

There was fear in her eyes as she said, "You're about to do something foolish, aren't you? Don't. We can find a..."

Marie yelled, "Quit stalling! Do you want this child to live or not?"

Sorin looked into Indikaiya's eyes, one last time. "Be ready. There are more than these three."

"Sorin..."

He smiled at her. "No one lives forever."

With that he turned and walked into the sun. A ray hit his face, and the light was so strong it burned. He looked at Phillip, continuing to smile in spite of the pain.

There were worse fates than death, and no matter what the species, what he'd said to Indikaiya was true. No man could live forever. He'd had a good life, as a human and then as a vampire. Good and long and interesting. What more could any man ask for?

"Drop your sword!" Marie yelled.

"Let the boy go and I will."

She released Phillip's hand, and the child ran clumsily up the stairs. As promised, Sorin dropped his sword.

"My friend Sorin!" The kid ran straight into Sorin's arms, where he was caught. Without pause, Sorin turned and threw the child. Phillip squealed in delight, to find himself flying through the air. No fear, no alarm. He knew someone would be there to catch him, and there was. A waiting Rurik snatched the child from the air and set him on his feet.

Sorin turned his back on them, reached behind his back and drew a knife. He was entirely focused on Marie. He didn't mind risking his life, even losing it, if it meant he could end hers.

He heard Jimmy behind him, moving anxiously forward, and with a shouted word Sorin ordered the kid to stop. To *wait*. His time would come soon enough.

He was close now, very close. Marie looked at the dagger in his hand — unalarmed and unafraid — and said to the soldier who held Kate, "Kill her."

Sorin moved quickly. He changed directions, jumped up and flew toward the man who held Jimmy's friend. He slit the soldier's throat before the man could even twitch. Kate fell to the steps, stumbled forward, tried to stand and stumbled again, then rose up clumsily to run to Jimmy.

The sun burned, it ate at and through him, but for once Sorin didn't mind. He embraced the pain.

The man who'd killed Chloe's mother foolishly rushed Sorin, his own blade waving wildly in the air. He was as easy a kill as the first one had been.

Which left Marie and Sorin face to face on the steps of the Lincoln Memorial in the noonday sun.

CHAPTER EIGHTEEN

It all happened too fast. The child, the girl, the two humans who had aligned themselves with Marie — for whatever reason — and then the fight.

Indikaiya wanted to help Sorin, to rush in and help, but how? He and Marie fought, hand to hand and dagger to dagger. They rose in the air and then dropped down; they were a blur and then they were almost still again. The stillness never lasted long. It was as if she was offered occasional pictures, as if the fight paused for a second, just long enough to allow her to see. There was blood, so much blood, and she couldn't tell if it was his or hers. Sorin didn't have the kind of protective clothing Marie had worn, and each time she saw him he looked worse. Burned, in a way, as if the sun had chosen one small segment of skin after another to crisp.

Kate sat near the front of the chamber and cradled the little boy, Phillip. For a moment Jimmy allowed himself to touch Kate's hair, to sigh in relief, then the three of them — Jimmy, Rurik, and Indikaiya — rushed down the steps and toward the battle.

As Sorin had warned them, others were close by, waiting to attack. When the soldiers saw the trio emerging from the shadows, they ran forward, swords and guns drawn. Like the others, these were men who fought for Marie, not vampires. These glamoured humans had no problem with the sun, but they were not seasoned fighters.

None of them was a match for the two Warriors they faced. They were not a match for Jimmy, either, who had become a fine warrior himself. The enemy fell. The fight between Marie and Sorin continued. They moved unnaturally fast, clashing in the sunlight they both despised. They swept up and down the steps, leaving a trail of blood as they moved in a quick and violent dance.

As the last of the men fell, Marie and Sorin slowed. They were no longer a blur. They were now solid and all too clear. Indikaiya gasped at the sight. The opponents were bloodied and weak. Both were being affected by the sun in a way they had not been even moments before. Sorin swung his dagger forward, attempting to finish the job and take Marie's head. She saw the move coming, twisted to the side so that while his knife sliced her throat deeply, she remained whole and in this world.

The self-proclaimed queen fell down, then flew up, fingers curled and extended as if they were claws. With a burst of power and a primal scream, her hand thrust into Sorin's chest.

It came out with his heart.

In the split second while the heart she had taken from him still beat, Sorin turned his head to look at

Indikaiya. She screamed, unable to get to him fast enough, unable to do anything to help. And then he went to dust in the sun.

Nevada held the newborn close. Cradling the baby in her arms was an unexpected pleasure that wouldn't last. Chloe wouldn't let the kid out of her own arms for more than a few minutes. Like any new mother, Nevada supposed. Chloe's baby, who was just a couple of hours old, was swaddled in a pink baby blanket someone had swiped from somewhere. Bottles and formula and diapers had also been scavenged.

"Just when I think the world can't get any weirder, it does," Nevada cooed. The baby gurgled like any other might. Not that Nevada had ever held a two-hour old of any species.

The baby's eyes were freaky — like her father's — but it wasn't like she shot death rays. Those eyes weren't scary, just odd. Odd and beautiful. The kid cried, she cooed, she drank formula. She was pretty, too, like a picture of an infant on a jar of baby food. Thank goodness she hadn't tried to bite anyone yet, not that she had any teeth. All perfectly normal, so far.

But when Nevada concentrated on the baby, when she tried to see inside the child in any way, *normal* was not what she got. She still got queen vibes, big time. When Nevada reached deep, when she called on the witchy part of herself that had been sleeping for so long, she saw power and blood. Thank goodness, she also saw kindness and humanity.

One day this baby would drink blood like her parents, but for now, for a while, she was just a kid. Given the way Chloe's pregnancy had progressed, Nevada hadn't seen that coming. Maybe the fast progression of the pregnancy was due to Chloe's makeup, not the baby's. Whatever.

She should be scared, holding a human vampire hybrid of unknown powers and abilities, but she wasn't, not at all.

Instead she held the baby close and wondered if it was possible for a human to get pregnant by a Warrior. She and Rurik hadn't even discussed birth control. Maybe that was reckless, but seriously, they had other things on their minds. With everything that had happened, she couldn't say she was ready to bring a child into the world, but at the same time, Rurik's baby would be awesome. How could it not be? It? No, not it. He. Maybe she. Holding a baby, smelling baby smell and wallowing in baby softness, brought out every maternal instinct that had been lurking in Nevada's body. Those instincts were surprisingly strong, and insistent.

"Down, girl," she whispered.

She worried about Rurik, every hour of every day. That was a complication she didn't need, but there was no going back. She cared. She loved him.

He was, in a way she had never expected, a part of her. No one was more capable in a fight, but she knew who he'd be facing today, and she wouldn't rest easy until she saw him with her own eyes, whole and well and here, still in this world. She wanted them all to come back, she did, but more than anything else she wanted to see Rurik walk through her door.

Love is weird. That was her deep thought for the day.

She'd seen many men die, but Indikaiya had never been so instantly and deeply affected. Sorin was gone. There was no body to bury, no final touch of goodbye, no anxious fingers placed against the neck where a pulse should be in order to be sure that death had truly come. No, he was just *gone.*

She felt him still, on her lips and on her throat. What could she have done differently? How could she have saved him? She should've given him more blood, should've insisted that he be stronger when he faced Marie. No, she should've fought Marie herself. She should never have listened to his commands that she stand back.

The child Sorin had given his life to save tugged on Indikaiya's shift. "Where is my friend Sorin?" Phillip asked.

Indikaiya tried to answer, but she choked on the

words. Tears filled her eyes. She had not cried since the night she'd put her daughters on a boat and sent them away, knowing it was unlikely she would ever see them again. Jimmy held Kate tight. Rurik watched over them. Bodies littered the steps of this memorial.

Marie was gone. Not gone as Sorin was, not truly *gone*. She had escaped.

A breeze kicked up, and what was left of Sorin — dust, nothing more than dust — lifted into the air and flew away. Indikaiya watched that dust as it scattered and disappeared over the reflecting pond. He had always liked to fly.

"My friend Sorin…" Phillip began again.

Indikaiya took the boy's hand. "He has gone to a better place," she said, biting back the urge to declare bitterly that Sorin simply was no more.

"To live with Jesus, like my daddy?"

"I… I don't know," Indikaiya whispered. "Maybe. Maybe… yes. Yes, I'm sure of it. Your friend Sorin was a good man, and he will be rewarded with a fine afterlife." A kind lie, for a child who could understand nothing more honest or complicated.

The sun beat down on steps where Sorin had fought to save this child. Indikaiya ignored the bodies there, bodies of unworthy humans. She spared not a moment to mourn them. They had made their choices, and this was their just reward. She stared at a bloodstain on the steps, there where Sorin and Marie had fought. Not all that blood was his. He had wounded the vampire queen, had wounded her badly.

The sadness within her shifted, hardened, became something more. Something she could use. Anger. A need for vengeance.

Marie had to die, and at that moment, Indikaiya swore she would be the one to finish what Sorin had started.

CHAPTER NINETEEN

"My mother?" Chloe came out of her chair, the baby in arms. As if the infant sensed her distress, she started to cry. Not a normal "I'm hungry" or an "I need a new diaper" cry, but a screech that shook the walls. Chloe stopped where she stood, and noted that the entire library, which was always bustling, had gone silent. That cry had not been for her ears alone. Even Indie's yapping dog was silent.

Luca took the as-yet-unnamed baby from her and the screech ended. So much for convincing herself that her child was a normal human.

Chloe sat down, she listened as Luca explained what had happened. He tried to soothe her, to comfort her with words of logic. She knew he was right. She could not have been there. Not only could she not withstand the sun, she'd been in labor. Had her child come into the world as her mother had died? Perhaps Luca could have gone in her stead, but he'd been needed here. At least, she'd selfishly believed that she needed him. Still…

No, he would not have left her even if she'd ordered him to. He'd been here to protect her, and to protect their child. They were his priority, and nothing and no one would sway him. Not even her.

"My father?"

"He wasn't there. I don't know…"

But she did. Marie had only needed one hostage. Her father was dead, too.

"You should have been there," she said, accusation in her voice. "You could've saved her." If he had…

"Sorin did all that he could, I have been assured of that. He managed to save the other two, Jimmy's girlfriend and young Phillip, another conduit."

Why them and not her mother? Why couldn't he have saved all three? Anger welled up inside her again. She wasn't angry with Luca, she wasn't angry with Sorin. She was angry with herself for not reaching out to her parents, for not calling to let them know she was fine, even though she was not. Not in their eyes, anyway. Where was her cell phone, anyway? Sitting on a shelf somewhere with a dead battery, she imagined.

How had Marie found them? Chloe caught a sob in her throat. Why hadn't she even considered that her parents would be in danger simply because they were hers?

Her child would have no grandparents. Her mother would never know…

"I want to see Sorin," Chloe snapped, standing once more. "I want him to explain to me why he couldn't save her."

"Sorin is dead. Marie took his heart."

Chloe went silent and still, for a long moment.

Her knees — newly strong knees — shook in shock and surprise. She had no great love for Sorin, she really didn't even like him. But she had never considered that he wouldn't be a part of this war until the end. Whatever and whenever that end might be.

She would grieve for her parents for a very long time, she knew. For eternity, for whatever life she had been given, she would grieve. Eventually she might stop blaming herself, but that would take a while. A long while. Chloe stood and walked to Luca with an outward ease and calmness she did not feel deep inside. She took the baby from him, held her child close and shifted a small section of a blanket aside so she could see her daughter's entire face. It was perfection.

"Her name is Amelia."

After two days of wallowing in grief and anger, Indikaiya kept telling herself that she should not mourn a vampire. Should not, would not...

But Sorin was — had been — different. He'd fought for the humans. He'd gone into battle with Marie under the noon sun, knowing he would likely die, sacrificing himself for a small boy and a defenseless girl. No, not just for them, for the chance to take out Marie. For a chance to save far more than two humans.

He'd kissed her, before he died. She had denied

him that small pleasure, insisting that mouth to mouth was for love, not for the simple sex they shared. Simple. Not so simple. She should have kissed him more often.

Two things had made the past days tolerable. Cupcake, who seemed to sense Indikaiya's distress and did her best to offer comfort by licking and cuddling and sometimes whining, and music. Angry, passionate music, sung by strong women of this world and delivered via earphones attached to a small device Jimmy had given her. He called it an iPod.

Chloe was mourning, too. Her baby was two days old. As far as Indikaiya could determine, the child had come into the world during Sorin's epic battle. There was nothing Chloe could have done to save her mother. Nothing. And yet she continued to blame herself.

Indikaiya walked into the interior room where the threesome — Chloe, Luca, and the child — huddled together in silence. Whatever words they'd had to say had been said. She envied them their little family.

A vampire family. Had the world been turned entirely upside down?

Indikaiya studied the baby carefully. But for the unusual eyes, she appeared to be normal. Human. How was that possible? On the afternoon of Sorin's death, the child's cry had brought every being in this building to a standstill. Little Amelia might appear to be human, but she was not.

Through experimentation they had discovered that the child needed infant formula, not blood. After forty-eight hours the baby appeared not to be growing any faster than any other newborn. Chloe watched her daughter like a hawk, waiting for that unusual growth spurt, watching for signs of abnormality. Looking for ways in which her child was different from all others.

They had not attempted to move the child into the sun to see how she might react. She was too small, and potentially too fragile. Everything about baby Amelia was unknown.

These two unusual females were Indikaiya's blood descendants. Vampire or not, human or unknown species, they were her blood.

Chloe glanced up and caught Indikaiya's eye. Indikaiya nodded, then said, with no emotion in her voice, "The bitch is ours now. We will end her."

With that, she turned and walked away. No one would see her cry, not if she could help it.

Eyes closed, sun wonderfully warm on his face, he took a deep breath. Ah, that scent. No, *scents.* Fresh water, grass, a sweet shrub that bloomed in the spring and… his mother's stew.

Sorin opened his eyes and was almost blinded by the sun. His instinct was to cover his face, to search for the nearest shade or shelter, but he quickly realized that was unnecessary. He felt well, not at all weakened by the sunlight. He lifted one hand and watched the play of sunlight on his skin. He moved his fingers, slowly. The light wasn't at all painful. There was none of the nausea that sometimes accompanied his uncomfortable excursions into the daylight.

Memory came rushing back. He sat up, clapping a hand to his heart. Well, to the place where his heart would've been if Marie hadn't ripped it from his chest.

His heart beat, strong and steady and a bit faster than it had for a very long time. There was no blood, not anywhere on his body. His flesh had been burned by the sun as he'd fought Marie, but there was no sign of that damage.

He was naked in the sun, lying upon a grassy field that reminded him of home. Not D.C. or any other place he'd called home during his years as a vampire, but...home. Where he had worked and played as a boy. Where he had fallen in love and married and had children.

Where he had been a man, not a monster.

On alert, Sorin looked around. He was dead, he knew that. Marie had killed him. He'd realized his death was likely — perhaps even fated — when he'd met her in battle, but he had not expected this. He shot up, stood tall as he studied the landscape that was both familiar and foreign. What had happened to Phillip? To Indikaiya? To Jimmy and Rurik and...

"They are well, for now."

Sorin spun around to see a man in what appeared to be Roman dress walking toward him. "Who are you? Where the hell am I?"

"Not hell. Far from it, in fact. As for who I am, I believe you asked me to introduce myself when we met. I am the fucking lily-livered cowardly asshole you have been waiting to meet."

"Phillip's Warrior," Sorin said.

"Yes. He never did find my name, so here I remain while others fight against that which you once were."

Once were.

"My name is Halirrhothius."

"Seriously? No wonder the kid couldn't find your name. I don't suppose *Hal* would've done the trick."

The Warrior who had welcomed him into this world did not seemed pleased by that observation. "Not for the purpose of being called from this world into another, no."

Down to business. Sorin asked, "Why am I here?"

"You are here because you are a Warrior."

Instinctively, he shook his head. "Impossible. I'm no hero."

"With more than a touch of Warrior blood coursing through your veins, you died fighting for the human race. You sacrificed yourself for Phillip and Kate. If that is not a hero, I don't know what is." Hal shrugged his shoulders. "Of course, you can refuse to remain here, if you wish. There are other worlds beyond this one. The land of the dead is a vast and wondrous realm, for those who are worthy."

Worthy. Was he?

Sorin considered the offered option, for a split second. Apparently there was an afterlife for his kind — for the kind he had been. There was this world as well as others. How many others? If he left here would he be sent to a place of peace or of punishment?

"The word hero is not synonymous with perfection," the Roman said wearily.

"Neither word has ever been used to describe me."

There were worlds beyond worlds ahead of and behind him. Possibilities, wonder, redemption.

Indikaiya was of *this* world. That was a definite advantage to this strange place, but there was another. If he could find a conduit to call him back, he could finish what he'd started.

Another word that could not be used to describe him was quitter. As long as Marie lived, he had a purpose.

Sorin's stomach growled. He was hungry! Not for blood, but for food. Real food.

"Here." Hal tossed a pair of plain brown pants in Sorin's direction. "We have much to discuss."

***

It had been a long time since Nevada had cried. The world had been upside down, she'd been scared and furious and sad, but there had been no time for tears. Until now.

She'd been crying off and on for four days, since Rurik had delivered the news that Sorin was dead. Not vampire dead, but dead dead. Gone, forever.

"I am sorry," Rurik said. He knew why she cried, even though days had passed since he'd delivered the news. They lay, side by side, on the floor of her room. He held her close; she rested her damp face against his chest. "If I could have saved him, I would have."

Sorin was dead. When Rurik had told her, Nevada had felt as if the rug had been pulled out from under her, as if she could not find her footing. He wasn't supposed to die; his death had been startling in a world which had become one startling moment after another. She was a bit better now, but still she felt at a loss.

Rurik, who was so straightforward in all aspects of his life, could not understand her distress. Sorin had been a vampire. He'd kidnapped Nevada and her family. There had been a time when Nevada would've cheered at the news that he was dead. Maybe she was upset because Sorin's final death weakened the side of right in this damned war. Maybe she was upset because like it or not she had come to care for him.

"If I'd seen Sorin I could've cast a protection spell around him," Nevada said, not for the first time.

"It is not your fault he would not join us here."

"No, but I could've sent a message. I could have insisted that he come here so I could…"

Long before she finished the sentence, she grudgingly accepted the truth. That never would've worked. No one ordered Sorin to do anything. No wonder he had avoided headquarters all this time!

Rurik didn't tell her to stop sniffling, though she was pretty sure he was glad the tears had stopped. His hand settled in her hair. That hand delivered death to rebellious vampires each and every night. It was large and warm and capable. It was also gentle and kind, when gentleness was called for. "Sorin died a hero," he said, as if he thought that would soothe her, somehow. "He could not save Chloe's mother, but he saved Jimmy's Kate and the small boy, Phillip."

Poor Phillip, he kept asking when his friend Sorin was coming back. No one wanted to tell him that Sorin wasn't coming back, not ever. They talked around it, they told him Sorin was in a better place, but the child had a problem grasping the truth of it. He asked for his mother more often than he asked about Sorin, and they had no idea where she was. They didn't know if Marie had killed the woman or was holding her somewhere. The kid was surprisingly unflustered by the lack of concrete answers to his questions.

Nevada and Kate had been taking care of Phillip. It did help, to throw herself into whatever she could do to help, instead of looking back at those things she should've done. When Indie was around, her little dog Cupcake divided her time between the Warrior and the child, as if she were torn between them. Phillip did love that dog. Cupcake could ease Phillip's mind like nothing else, when he started asking about his mother. And Sorin.

Rurik cupped Nevada's cheek and made her look up at him.

She could not bring herself to tell him that she'd dreamed about Sorin last night. He was worried enough about her extreme response to Sorin's death, had even asked once if she'd been in love with the vampire. Love, no, but there had been a connection she could not explain. She had no desire to try to explain now.

The dream had been weird, but she'd been glad to see Sorin's face, even if it wasn't real. Eventually she'd forget the details of that face. The sound of his voice would be forgotten, too. It really had been a great voice.

Yes, one day her memories would fade, but she wouldn't forget anything today. She wouldn't forget tomorrow, either.

She looked hard at Rurik's face and did her best to memorize every line, the sparkle in his eye, the way his dark hair fell. One day he would be gone, too. Another man to remember. Another man who would just be gone from her life.

The world was so uncertain, she could not hold back. This was not a time to be shy or cautious.

"I love you."

CHAPTER TWENTY

Rural Virginia

Emily Sheldon busied herself scrambling eggs on the stove. The bacon was done, and there was toast in progress. Her parents should be back any minute. They'd gone out searching for neighbors and more food. And weapons, she knew, even though they hadn't specifically said so.

It had been years since she'd prepared a meal, but breakfast for dinner was easy enough. She and her family had just been here, in this deserted cabin, for a couple of weeks. She couldn't help but wonder what had happened to the owners. There was a small lake nearby, so it was possible this was a vacation cabin, simply not in use at this time.

But after all she'd seen, she had to wonder...

After moving from one place to another daily since leaving D.C., this was a place they should be able to stay for a while. It was off the beaten path, isolated and defendable. Her parents were worried that Nevada wouldn't find them here. Emily didn't know how to explain it, but she didn't share that worry. Her big sister would find them, when the time was right. Justin was just kind of lost, walking

282 | Linda Winstead Jones

around in a daze and sleeping too much. Emily was more worried about him than she was about her parents.

Justin slept on the couch, as darkness approached. None of them slept very well at night. Emily wasn't sure there would ever be a day when she wasn't afraid of the dark and the things that hid within it.

Her brother cried out, sharp and loud. Emily grabbed the skillet of eggs and ran into the room where he'd been sleeping.

There was no visible threat, no vampire, no monster who'd dared to come out before the sun set. There was just Justin, sitting up on the couch with his long hair in a tangle and his face flushed.

"What's wrong?" Emily asked.

Justin looked up at her with haunted eyes. "Dream," he said. "Bad dream."

She'd had her own share of bad dreams, especially since coming here, to this cabin. She didn't want to talk about them.

Justin, on the other hand... "I dreamed about *him*," he said as he sat up. "That bastard who kidnapped us. The big blond vampire."

A chill walked up Emily's spine. She'd been dreaming about Sorin the past couple of days. She hadn't dared to say anything to anyone. "What was the dream like?"

Justin caught her eye. "It was too damn real, like he was standing right in front of me."

Emily turned around and placed the skillet of cooling eggs on the small oak table where they'd been eating their meals. "Did he try to hurt you in this dream?"

Justin shook his head.

"Did he ask you for... anything?"

Again, that shake of a mussed head. "No. He was trying to speak but I couldn't hear him. Then he got mad and I woke up."

She had heard Sorin, in her dream.

The sight of the big vampire with the long blond hair still gave her chills. Even in a dream, even when she knew he wasn't real. She didn't want to see his face, didn't want to hear his voice. Emily sat beside Justin and took his hands in hers. "We will wish for him not to bother us, not ever again. Not in dreams, not in memory." She thought of blocking Sorin, of keeping him away, and it was if a gold shimmer surrounded both her and Justin. It was comforting, that shimmer. Her brother didn't comment, so maybe he didn't see what she saw. It was silly to think that a wish might keep away dreams, but at the same time... mind over matter was a thing, right?

Justin relaxed. His expression changed in an instant. "I had a bad dream, but I don't remember what it was about."

For a moment Emily was alarmed, and then she forgot, too.

***

Indikaiya focused entirely on the vampires before her. As she fought she mindlessly listened to the music. It was odd how at times the fighting and the music seemed to meld, as if they were one. As if they were connected. She loved the sensation of losing herself in the powerful songs, but when she was in battle she made sure one ear was free. She needed to hear everything, not just the music that seemed to drive her.

She lost herself in the beat and the power, and took her enemies' heads and their hearts with cold determination. She thought of Sorin with every well-placed swing of her blade.

She should have stopped thinking about him by now. He had not been the only soldier lost in this war. Humans had died. Worse, some had been turned into those monsters they fought. In Indikaiya's mind, that was the worst. Chloe had retained much of herself after the change, but she was an exception to the rule. So many of the baby vampires were beyond control. Beyond who they had once been.

Indikaiya's most recent regret had come when she'd had to take the life of a former police officer she had once fought alongside. He had become an enemy against his will. The final expression on his face had not been one of horror or regret, but of relief. Some of who he had been as a human had survived after all. Given time he, and some of the others, might've gained more control, become a vampire capable of choosing to fight for the humans instead of against them. Unfortunately, time was a luxury they did not possess.

Warriors, too, had fallen. Many had been sent hurtling back into their world, either to wait or to be called to this fight again.

It was a good thing they had not killed Nevada, when some had been thinking that would be the only way to reinstate the sanctuary spell. Her protection spells, delivered individually to humans and Warriors alike — including Indikaiya — did give them an edge.

Almost two months Sorin had been gone. Two months that moved by so slowly Indikaiya sometimes felt as if time had stopped. One day followed another, followed another.

She relished tonight's battle. Embraced it. Lately there had been too many nights when she didn't get to kill even a single vampire. Marie was changing her strategy. There were fewer battles in the open now, more sneak attacks on positions of power. Every night Marie and her army killed some humans while turning others. It seemed that for every vampire they killed, two more popped up to take its place. At this rate, the war would never end.

Marie. The vampire who had started this war had rarely been seen since the battle at the Lincoln Memorial. She had not been seen at all by any of

Indikaiya's fellow soldiers. There were days when Indikaiya remembered the moment when Marie had taken Sorin's heart. She remembered watching a man she had come to care for turn to ashes and fly away on a summer breeze. Scattered. Nothing. Gone. And she dreamed of sending Marie into nothingness. Summer breezes had passed, but she could hope to send the vampire queen off on an autumn wind.

Indikaiya was somehow certain that Sorin had hurt Marie in that last battle, perhaps more than anyone realized. She had been weakened by the sun, as he had been, and that last cut had been deep.

His death had been a great loss to their side, as well as a great loss for her. She missed him. Living in a large library teeming with other Warriors, humans, and a few vampires, she always felt alone. She should be accustomed to being alone by now. She had lived that way for most of her life as a Warrior.

Beyond the army and those civilians who were determined to fight, few humans remained in the city. She didn't blame them for getting out. There were reports now of open attacks in New York, Miami, and Atlanta, as Marie's army tried to take the east coast from top to bottom.

At times like this one, where the vampires seemed to come from all directions, Indikaiya wondered if this war would ever end.

This small band of vamp rebels dispatched, she

287 | WARRIOR RISING

and Rurik walked side by side toward the vehicle which had transported them — along with Jimmy, Kevin, and Duncan — to this site where the vampires had been spotted. She checked out each soldier. Duncan was fine. He had a few wounds that would be healed by the time they got back to the library. Jimmy and Kevin had to be more careful. They had minor wounds that would need to be tended. Rurik had a gash on one arm, but it wasn't serious.

No blade had touched Indikaiya. Not since Sorin had gone.

She looked back, spotted Cupcake sniffing at something on the ground, and called out a sharp, "Dog! Come!"

She was ignored. Indikaiya gave a sigh and then called again, "Cupcake!"

The dog responded to her name and trotted along to take her place at Indikaiya's side. Rurik laughed, but he stopped when Indikaiya glared in his direction.

Jimmy and Kevin walked just slightly ahead of the two Warriors and the dog. They had become great friends. Perhaps that had been inevitable. They were human warriors in an army of immortals. Their needs and vulnerabilities were unique among their fellow soldiers. They needed quite a lot of food to maintain their strength, and in the last month food had become an issue for the humans.

"I'm starving," Jimmy said, hitching his shoulder, adjusting his shotgun holster. "We'll need to make a food run tomorrow. I think all we have left is Spam and Velveeta." He made a low gagging noise.

"Hey, now," Kevin said with a touch of indignation. "Don't diss Velveeta. Velveeta is the cheese food of the gods."

Jimmy did not argue. "What about Spam?"

Kevin sighed. "Fry it up and cover it with barbecue sauce and it's not too bad. But the Velveeta... yummmm."

"I want a steak," Jimmy said. "A baked potato. Maybe a chocolate cake for dessert."

"You're killing me..."

Rurik slowed down and, with a hand on Indikaiya's arm, indicated that she should fall back as well. She did. The humans' conversation about food faded away. Just as well. They were making even her hungry! When the others were well ahead of them Rurik said, in a lowered voice, "Would you speak to Nevada?"

Like she had time to chat with a human! Indikaiya was a soldier, as strong as any man. Stronger than some. She did not have time for hand-holding, commiseration, and — she shuddered, recalling some recent overheard conversations — girl talk.

"Why? She and Kate have become friends. Whatever Nevada needs a female friend for, Kate will suffice."

Rurik did not take the suggestion. "Nevada has not slept the past three nights, because she keeps seeing and hearing Sorin. Even though it had been many weeks, she has not accepted his final death..."

Indikaiya stopped in her tracks. "What do you mean, seeing and hearing him?"

Rurik turned to face her. "Nevada is exhausted and grief-stricken, and that has led to these delusions."

Delusions? "Are you jealous that she cared for Sorin?"

"Not at all. She loves me. What she feels for Sorin is something else entirely."

Something else. Sorin and the witch he had kidnapped had always shared a strange connection. Not love, not friendship, but...

Indikaiya almost gasped, caught up in the thought that slammed into her.

It was impossible. Sorin had been a vampire at the time of his death. She might as well not even mention the first, outrageous idea that had popped into her head. Rurik would think she had lost her mind. Instead of responding to his request, she changed the subject. "It is beyond foolish for you to become entangled with a human."

He responded without hesitation. "My entanglement is no more foolish than yours."

Indikaiya instinctively stepped back and away from him. Shocked. Hurt. The pain she felt was intense and unexpected.

Rurik still had his entanglement. Hers was no more.

"My apologies." He gave her an almost formal bow. "I see the pain in you. I would not wish it for you."

She started to argue that she had no pain, none at all, but why lie? Did others see it so clearly? The possibility annoyed her. That hurt was private, for her alone.

Again, she changed the subject. "I will speak to Nevada when we return."

Rurik nodded. "I thank you. Perhaps sharing her grief with you will help her to move past it."

Indikaiya nodded her head, but she said nothing. Her mind spun with possibility, with wonder. With hope.

She was not convinced that Nevada was suffering from *grief.*

Sorin was beyond frustrated. He had followed the instructions Hal had offered, he had watched his world — his old world — from this one, unable to help. Other Warriors came and went, though none lingered. Some of them were suspicious of him, of his presence in this sacred place. A Warrior who had once been a vampire was unprecedented.

Time passed differently in the two worlds. It seemed as if he had been here for days, but there, where he wished and needed to be, weeks had passed. He was needed there. He had to get back.

He saw this through the eyes of his descendent. His conduit. Nevada. The others, her brother and sister, had blocked him, somehow. Just as well. He needed to concentrate on one conduit, and Nevada was in the thick of things.

Thanks to him.

"There has to be a better way," he grumbled. "Why do I have to be called? Why can't I just go?"

"Patience, brother," Hal said. "It is as it has always been. Do you not realize that I would be there if I could?"

His ability to watch, to see into the other world, was a gift he had picked up on quickly. He could turn it on and off at will. He rarely wished to turn it off. The more he knew, the more likely Nevada would be to realize what was going on and call him in.

He was ready. Sword in one hand, he waited to be called.

Tonight, Nevada paced in her room alone. He saw, he heard, as if watching a television with the picture fuzzy and the sound turned low. Sorin called her name and she spun around to face him. He could see her face; she saw nothing of him. The words he spoke were clear to him — precise and almost shouted — but to her, in her time and place, they were garbled. They were nonsense.

"Come on, Nevada," he grumbled. "You can do

this. You can hear me."

He was not blind to the fact that not so long ago he had passed his time killing conduits, and now, here he was begging one to listen. To hear.

The door to Nevada's room flew open and Indikaiya flew in. Blond braid flying, sword gripped in one hand, as always, she was a force of nature. God, he missed her. It had been mere days, for him, and yet it seemed much longer. For her, it truly had been longer. He reached out a hand, wishing he could burst through the film that separated them, wishing he could bridge the worlds to be with her again.

She and Nevada spoke, but he could not hear all. As his words had been for Nevada, these were garbled. Nonsense. Sorin fisted his free hand in frustration. Maybe he was not where he believed himself to be. This was hell, where he would forever see the woman he loved and yet not be able to touch her. To speak to her. Indikaiya looked over her shoulder as if she expected someone else to be there, though the room was small and it was clear Nevada was alone.

Nevada nodded her head, agreeing with whatever Indikaiya had said. She closed her eyes for a moment, she whispered a few indecipherable words, and then she looked directly at Sorin.

He reached out to her as she said, "Sorin, Warrior, please help. Please come into this world…"

He did.

CHAPTER TWENTY-ONE

Indikaiya had never been on this side of a trip between worlds. The lights, seemingly generated out of thin air in one corner of the room, were bright and beautiful. Blinding, almost, though she refused to close her eyes against the harsh glare as a human form took shape in the midst of the light.

Long blond hair. Plain clothing suited to another place and time. Tall leather boots. A massive sword.

Indikaiya held her breath, waiting. Waiting. She had grieved for Sorin these past weeks. She'd missed him. Longed for him. She'd loved him when he'd been a monster, and she would love him if he were a monster still.

But he was not.

As soon as Sorin was solid, Indikaiya dropped her own sword and flew across the room to jump into his arms. He caught her, as she had known he would. She grabbed his face in her hands and kissed him, long and hard. Deep and wonderful. He held her close with one arm around her waist, and he kissed her back. He was solid, warm, *real.*

"I did not think it was possible," she said between kisses.

"Neither did I." Sorin's heart beat faster than she recalled; he breathed.

"I missed you." It was an admission she would not have made a few weeks ago, not even to herself.

"Of course you did." He grinned. His eyes did not glow, but they did seem to brighten. They were lively. They were *alive*. Sorin was no longer a vampire, he was an Immortal Warrior, but in many ways he had not changed all that much. He was still Sorin.

He placed her on her feet, but continued to hold her close. Indikaiya leaned in, she placed her head against Sorin's chest and whispered. "I thought you were gone forever."

"So did I."

Nevada cleared her throat, reminding them that they were not alone. "Would someone like to explain to me what's going on?"

Sorin nodded to the witch, but he did not release Indikaiya. "I now understand why you smelled like my daughter. You are her descendent. You are *my* descendant."

"No way," Nevada whispered.

"I'm afraid it's true."

The witch drew back a little. "So you're my what, great-great... goodness knows how many greats... grandfather? And you just happened to kidnap me? Am I supposed to believe that was *chance*?"

"Chance or fate, I do not know."

"But..."

Sorin's posture changed, his expression hardened. "While I would love to extend this reunion, I have not come to offer suppositions. I am here because you called me. That is all the proof either of us should need. I have been able to view you from the other side, but you have no involvement in battle. The lack of knowledge on that front has been frustrating. How goes the war?"

The redhead blushed. "You've been *watching* me?"

"Now and then," Sorin admitted.

Indikaiya stepped away, turning her mind to business, though her heart protested more than a little. She wanted to hold Sorin a while longer. "Marie lives, though she doesn't show herself often these days. You hurt her, in that fight at The Lincoln Memorial. You almost took her head. I suspect you wounded her more than she thought was possible and she's been weakened. Most humans who are not involved in the fight have left this city, but other cities have begun to fall. The vampires have taken Richmond and are on the verge of taking Atlanta. We have no way of knowing how many smaller cities have fallen, but the vampires seem to be focusing their efforts on the East Coast, for now."

"Where is she?"

Even if they had not been talking about the rebel vampires, Indikaiya would've known who "she" was by the fierce expression on his face. "Our last intelligence says she's holed up in her Potomac mansion. It's heavily guarded, day and night. She has made good use of the human soldiers she glamoured or enticed."

Sorin wrapped her braid around one hand and gently forced her to turn her face to his. He kissed her, and she did not pull away. She did not protest or hesitate. She kissed him back, the way he deserved to be kissed. This man had made her drop her sword, for the first time since she'd fallen in battle, human and mortally wounded. He made her care, and want. She yearned for him.

When he drew away he grinned at her once more. "I know a way into that mansion."

Marie paced the chamber below stairs, where there were no windows, where no sunlight could ever shine. Normally she could withstand sunlight much better than most of her kind. Damn Sorin, she wished she could kill him again. The only thing that soothed her was imagining how delightful it would be to rip out his heart one more time.

She stood before the full-length mirror, turning her head and pulling her high necked blouse to one side so she could study the scar she continued to sport. Sorin had almost removed her head. Weakened by the sun and the exertion of the fight, he had cut her in a weak moment. She had only survived the wound because she was stronger than most. Even so, she should have healed more quickly. Instead she had an ugly scar that was fading at a maddeningly slow pace.

It was only the memory of Sorin going to dust that kept her from breaking the mirror and screaming until the mansion came down around her ears.

Ahron had a bad habit of walking into her chamber without knocking. Uninvited, unwanted, he wandered the mansion like an old man unable to sleep. She should've left him where he was, in that warehouse far from the city, but his psychic ability was incredible — if sometimes difficult to interpret. It had been his plan that had brought Sorin to her, that had led to Sorin's demise. It was too bad Luca hadn't been there, and as for the human Jimmy... she cared nothing for one more human in the fight, no matter what Ahron said.

Eliminating only one of the three she had intended to kill was a failure that stung.

Ahron rambled like an old man, on occasion. He rambled now. Words beneath his breath, cackling, muttered phrases in ancient tongues even she did not understand.

He had picked a bad time to interrupt her. The sun was up, so even here, away from the rays, she was weakened and more emotional than usual.

Ahron walked to stand beside her, to study his own gruesome reflection in the mirror. The smile he flashed for himself, or perhaps for her, was just short of insane. He dropped the smile and caught her eye in the mirror.

"He comes."

"Who comes?" Marie snapped.

"The heartless one. A ghost. Kindred and yet not. Son of a witch of old, hero and demon. He comes."

Marie sighed. "Your riddles are maddening."

"Not a riddle, only truth. He wants your head. You'd better hang onto it while you can."

For a moment, Marie was startled. Then she reminded herself that Ahron wasn't *always* right. No one was taking her head. She was safe here, with her glamoured army and the vampires who, like her, were tired of hiding. The mansion was well guarded. There was the back passage, but everyone besides her who knew about it was dead. If she asked her soldiers to guard that entrance as well as the others, then it would no longer be a secret. She enjoyed having a few secrets left.

"I'm leaving, soon," Ahron said, turning and walking slowly toward the door. "I have lived a very long time, that is true, but I would like to keep *my* head a while longer."

The sun was out, but that wouldn't stop someone as old and powerful as Ahron. He could leave at any time, and Marie wanted him gone. She had seen his great abilities as an asset to her army, to her strategies, but he was more of a nuisance than he was helpful. Yes, it was time for him to go.

As he reached for the doorknob, Marie asked,

"What do you see for me, Ahron. What does the future hold?"

He turned his head and looked squarely at her. He glared at her, and inside her, and through her, in a way no one else ever had. For a long moment, the ancient said nothing, then he whispered, "Goodbye, my queen."

Sorin's return came as a shock to everyone, but Luca's army was accustomed to facing the impossible. They all welcomed what he had to offer. A ready sword, a need for justice, and a plan.

A select few would be leaving the library within the hour. For the moment, for an all too brief time, he and Indikaiya were alone. As alone as they could be, in a building crawling with soldiers of three species. Four, if you counted Cupcake. They did not have the luxury of time or space, but to be here, to touch her... that was luxury enough. He took her hand and pulled her into a small room. Two walls were made up of floor to ceiling bookshelves filled with old leather volumes. There was a wide window on one wall. Sunlight streamed in. He did not mind the sun, not at all. He loved the light and the warmth on his skin.

They propped their swords side by side near the closed door. Sorin led Indikaiya into the center of the stream of light, where he kissed her, where he held her close. For today, at least, she had abandoned the modern clothing she'd adopted for this war, which made it easy to grab the hem of her tunic and push it high.

She gasped and spread her thighs. "We don't have much time."

He kissed her ear then her neck, where he had once bitten her. The feel of her, the sensation of skin to skin was familiar and yet new. She had not changed, but he had. He had been reborn yet again, not to darkness this time but to the light.

He whispered, "I regret to inform you that I won't need much time."

She laughed, briefly and with a throaty breathlessness. "Neither will I."

He lifted her, and she wrapped her legs around his waist. He filled her, and standing in the sunlight joined body and soul he made love to her. And it was love, unexpected and powerful. That love was a shift deep within him as important as the transformation from vampire to Warrior.

Until this moment, he had been alone in this world — one world of many — and he had not even been aware of the depth of his solitude. He had never needed anyone, but he needed her. He had crossed worlds not for the humans, not for Nevada, not to save anyone or anything. He had come back for *her.*

Indikaiya cried out, and he was with her. Pleasure so deep it had the power to wipe away the rest of the world, for a while, whipped through him.

He held her, was a part of her, needed her as he now needed air. And he whispered, as she held him close, "I love you."

CHAPTER TWENTY-TWO

These group meetings in what was essentially the center of the library had become so commonplace that Indikaiya normally didn't give them a second thought. They were necessary for sharing information, news, plans for the day, and sometimes for the week ahead. Today was not so commonplace. Sorin had returned. No one among them had considered his return even a remote possibility, and yet here he was. The humans in particular stared, wide-eyed, at the Warrior who had once been vampire. Especially Nevada, who had witnessed his reemergence into this world.

It was likely that everyone present — humans, Warriors and vampires — realized what had just happened. Not that they would have been so rude as to stand on the other side of the closed door that had, for a brief time, given them some privacy. They would not have made an effort to intrude, but still, they *knew*. Indikaiya straightened her hair with a casual hand, hoping it hadn't been too mussed during the quick tryst. Not that she had ever cared much for how her hair was styled. Not for a very long time. She *did* care what others thought of her. Even now. Especially her fellow soldiers.

Sorin was a Warrior, but he had once been a

vampire. A killer. A soulless being who had taken lives in order to maintain his own.

No, not soulless, as she had once thought all vampires to be. If he did not have a soul, a soul worthy of his new position, he would be as dead as she had believed him to be when she'd watched his ashes waft away.

A being with no soul did not love. A being with no soul did not care for others. Not for lovers or for those who needed the protection of someone stronger and more capable than they could ever be. Like Nevada. Phillip Stargel. All the humans who would serve vampires if Marie won this war.

Plans were made, as they were each and every day. Today those plans held an air of importance, of hope. Sorin's return was a boon to them all. Soldiers peeled away to prepare. Only a few remained behind.

They did not have much time, but Indikaiya did not rush forward to speed things along, as Sorin spoke to a still-stunned Nevada, and then to a young boy who was thrilled to see his friend again. Phillip held a content Cupcake in his arms. The dog that had always snarled and snapped at Sorin in the past sensed the change in him. Sorin even reached out and patted the dog's head. For a moment.

No, a monster did not care the way Sorin did, and had even before his death. A monster did not kneel down to face a child who simply accepted without question that Sorin had returned. A monster would not place a gentle hand on a child's face and gift that child with a reassuring smile. In his past Sorin had done monstrous things, but there had always been more to him. Much more.

"I'm going to teach you to say a name," Sorin said. "It is a silly, long name, the silliest and longest name I have ever heard, but it is the name of the friend you've been looking for and you need to know it."

Phillip nodded, and Sorin repeated the name, over and over. Such assistance was against the rules, but then all rules had been suspended for the moment, hadn't they?

When Phillip, still cradling Cupcake in his arms, was led away by a somber Kate, Sorin once again turned his attention to Nevada. They spoke — whispered — intently, and then Sorin placed a stilling and comforting hand on Nevada's shoulder.

Indikaiya shifted her feet as what felt like a shiver walked along her spine. Was that jealousy she felt? No, jealousy wasn't possible, not for her. Not only did she now understand the relationship, she also realized the depth of Sorin's commitment to her. He loved her. He had told her so. That shiver she'd experienced was likely caused by her impatience. She and Sorin had so much to discuss, so much to explore. This war, this world, had become a distraction.

She loved him, though she had not yet told him so.

When Sorin looked at her and smiled, her heart did funny things. Could she afford to be distracted from who and what she was by such a love? What would their lives be like when they returned, together, to the world that had been her home for such a long time? There were so many unanswered questions.

Only one thing was certain. Marie had to be taken out of this world as soon as possible.

If the vampire queen was somehow transported to another world after she went to dust in this one, her destination would not be a place for heroes.

Sorin would've preferred to go in alone, but instead he approached the entrance to the underground tunnel as one of a party of four. Indikaiya, Rurik, and Luca accompanied him. Jimmy and Kevin, along with a handful of other Warriors — human and immortal — would serve as distractions along the front entrance to the mansion.

While they fought Marie's human soldiers, the party attacking from beneath would take care of their queen.

When Marie was dead, those who had been glamoured by her would be free of her influence. So many of them had been under her long-term glamour for too long and would never be right-minded again. They might drop dead the moment that connection ended. As for all the baby vampires she had created, they would feel her loss, too, but in another way. They would remain kindred, but they would be weakened. They would lose their focus. Without Marie, the war should be done in a matter of weeks. Perhaps even days.

Sorin would've liked to leave Luca behind. They shared too much history, and Luca reminded Sorin too sharply of who he had once been, what he had once done. But with his ability to locate energy, Luca was essential to this mission. The blood born would lead them right to Marie.

He'd already confirmed that she was here, and on the lowest level of the mansion.

They allowed Luca to enter the tunnel first, as he was the least fond of the sunlight. Sorin savored the warmth of the sun on his skin and the bright light in his eyes. He loved looking at the way the light shifted through the leaves on the trees, the brilliant blue of the sky, the shadows he and the others created. The sun. He had never realized how deeply he'd missed it.

"She's mine," Sorin said as he watched Luca disappear into the darkness below.

"Not if I get her first," Luca responded.

"Now, boys," Indikaiya said with a smile as she followed Luca. "An expression I have heard used often in this world is 'ladies first.' Are you not all gentlemen?"

"I'm no gentleman," Rurik said as he went in

after the others. From a short distance away, Sorin heard a cry of alarm. Jimmy and his squadron were here; their presence was not a secret. It had begun.

This was it. Finally, the end had arrived. One way or another, the turning point in this war happened today. It was time. Past time. Indikaiya stayed close to Sorin, while she could. When the fighting began they would likely be separated. She reminded herself that it would be foolish to allow his presence here to distract her from her purpose.

This would be a fight to the death. Either the war with vampires would end and she and Sorin would walk to the other side together, or they would die fighting and be returned there in a flash.

Together, as partners and lovers. She could not imagine returning to her own world without him. He was *necessary*. It had been a long time, a very long time, since she'd thought of any man in that way.

Indikaiya had long been eager for this war to end for many reasons, but a new eagerness spurred her on. A new life awaited her, as well as Sorin. A real life, with love and laughter and... happiness. Happiness! What would come after the end of this war would be more than waiting for the next fight, more than living in limbo waiting for another chance to redeem herself.

And why did she feel such a need for

redemption? Why had she been so willing to fight for an eternity to save innocents? She'd fought during her own life and after. She was one of the oldest of the Warriors, one who had never even considered moving on to whatever might be waiting in the next world. She would not move on now, not even if she felt herself worthy. Sorin would serve a long while, she imagined. She would serve beside him.

Indikaiya allowed Rurik to pass her in the silent stone hallway. She edged closer to Sorin, not daring to speak. Vampire hearing made even the lowest whisper impossible. It was likely some would hear their very footsteps, no matter how quietly they moved along this passageway.

But she touched his arm, and in response he glanced down at her. She looked at him with what she hoped was love. Love and hope. She was ready. Ready to begin again.

Sorin nodded, as if he knew what she was thinking. Perhaps he did. He smiled. Before she could return that smile the alarm was raised and they all rushed forward, swords ready, hearts full. Vampires and Warriors here below; humans and Warriors above.

It was time.

He wanted this to be the end. He wanted, so desperately, to return to a normal life. If a normal life was even possible. Knowing what he knew now, having seen the greatest of atrocities, would his life ever be normal again?

Jimmy fought back to back with Kevin Brown. He didn't know what drove Kevin to fight so hard, but Jimmy knew what he was fighting for.

A life with Kate. A home. A world where walking after the sun set wasn't as dangerous as jumping out of an airplane without a parachute. He wanted kids, kids who would live to be old and happy and safe.

Some vampires would survive. Some should survive, those like Luca and Chloe, Duncan and Isaac, a handful of others who had come to their side. But seriously, he wanted bloodsuckers to be an endangered species. This uprising... the uprising had to end in a way that would discourage any other power hungry vamp from trying this again. At least in his lifetime. Maybe even his children's lifetimes.

Children. His mind could not go there. He might not survive this battle, much less live to be a father.

Jimmy didn't fight for his own survival. He had accepted the very real possibility of his own death long ago. He fought for Kate and those like her. He fought for all the humans who could not fight for themselves. And Kate... even if he didn't live to be a father, she should have the chance to be a mother. Watching her with Phillip these last few weeks had proven to him that she'd be a good one.

This was a battle like many others, even though it was taking place in daylight. He preferred to disable the glamoured humans, rather than killing them, knowing that if Luca and Sorin and the others were successful, the humans who had not chosen to be here, who had not chosen to serve monsters, might survive. But some of them had chosen this path, they wanted to live and fight among vampires. Sick bastards.

Men and women from both sides of the battle fell on a once normal street, in tall grass that had not seen a lawnmower in months, and along a sidewalk where kids had once skipped and ridden bikes and been pushed in strollers. Some of those who fell were wounded, others were dead. There were a few strong vampires among Marie's army, a very few who could withstand some sun but who kept to the shade as much as possible.

They fell, too, but not as easily as the glamoured humans.

A handful of Warriors fought here today, as they had fought for months. Jimmy saw two of them die and then disappear, very early on, but since that time they had been untouched.

Nevada's protection spell or skill? Both, he imagined.

The battle was waning, his side was winning, and then Jimmy spotted a new player. An old man, judging by the way he moved, head covered by a deep hood which was a part of the robe he wore, seemed to float toward Kevin. He stopped, turned toward Jimmy, and smiled.

In the darkness beyond the edge of the hood, eyes gleamed red.

Jimmy shouted, "Kevin, behind you!"

Marie knew they were coming. Of course she did. She had considerable powers. Sorin led the way, down a narrow hallway, into another, wider hallway where they had done battle in the past. It was here that he had made the decision to change sides. It was here that the shift in his soul that allowed him to leave the monster he had been behind and embrace the man he had been and could be again had begun.

Since he had changed, since he was no longer vampire, would Marie be able to identify his energy? Would she realize he had come for her? He hoped not. He wanted her to be surprised when she saw him.

The so-called queen did not lead her army. Instead she stayed behind and sent others to stop the invaders. That was her way; it had been from the beginning. She sent others to their deaths. In the darkness, her vampires could — and did — fight. Three vampires came around a corner with a war cry that echoed off the stone walls of this dungeon. With claws, swords, knives, and teeth, they met the raiding party of four that had come to end their rebellion.

Sorin had never fought as a Warrior until this moment. He could no longer fly — flight was the only power he would truly miss — but he retained his skills, and most of his speed. His strength actually seemed to be increased.

Marie's three soldiers fell quickly. If these were the best she had to offer, taking the mansion would be quick work. Sorin took the male in the lead, and Luca felled the behemoth of a monster that had been behind the leader. Together Rurik and Indikaiya took down the vicious female who had attacked like a bird of prey — from above, and with sharp talons. All three went to dust in a matter of minutes.

Sorin looked back and down to catch Indikaiya's eye. The male in him wished he had been able to leave her behind, to keep her safe, to protect her from battles such as this one. She was his woman now, and it was his instinct to protect her. But Indikaiya was a Warrior. She would never need his protection. That did not entirely erase the instinct, but he knew better than to try to send her to safety.

He accepted who she was as she accepted him.

They heard others — far more than three — approaching.

CHAPTER TWENTY-THREE

Ahron had not done battle in a very long time. He had not needed to battle. And yet here he was, throwing himself into the fray. In daylight, no less.

He'd left Marie when he'd seen that she would not succeed, when he had been washed in the knowledge that she was not long for this world, but he had not traveled far before he'd realized that he had nowhere to go. There was no longer a Council to protect him. No home other than an abandoned warehouse. No children to serve him. His children — human and vampire — had all died a long time ago. What life was there left for him?

He had not realized how much he'd wanted Marie to succeed, how much he'd wished for true freedom, until he'd seen, so clearly, that she was going to fail. He so craved the freedom to walk among all others of the world. Freedom to feed as he desired, to make new children, to *live*.

So he had come back. He had returned to participate in a battle he knew Marie's soldiers would lose. He would likely die here today, and he was not afraid. He wondered if Luca would be the one to take his life. It would be fitting that the strongest of his kind be the one to end him. Perhaps one of the Warriors would end him. They were impressive beings, he had to admit.

And yet, he had developed an irrational fear of a young human male. It was the reason he had told Marie the boy had to die, along with Sorin and Luca. He had made her think the mortal's death would serve her well, but he'd been thinking only of himself. No fear was truly irrational. In the back of his mind he had sensed the danger for a long while, and in the past few days it had only grown. He had hoped to change what he knew, had hoped Marie would be able to erase the possibility as she'd erased Sorin... but no.

If he hid, he would survive, but Ahron did not want to hide any longer. He would not go back to life as he had come to know it. A true death was preferable, and it was waiting for him. It would come today.

Before he met his death, he would take out as many of the annoying humans as he could. They should pay for ruining Marie's plans. They should not survive to see the world return to their rule, their supremacy.

The humans who fought on this annoyingly sunny day were well-armed. With swords and shotguns, they fought as soldiers will. For their lives. For victory. But they were merely humans, easy prey.

He set his sights on one who wore so many weapons strapped to his body that he should be crawling under the weight. Ahron delved into the human's mind. He had killed many vampires in the last few months. He would kill more, if Ahron did not take his heart. This was not the human he had come to fear, but was another who needed to be eliminated.

The well-armed human's blood would nourish an old vampire who needed nourishment. There would be no time to savor, but Ahron was fast. He had always been fast.

Another human — one Ahron instantly recognized as the boy, Jimmy, whom he had warned Marie to eliminate — called out a name. "Kevin!"

Ahron's target turned, and without hesitation fired a bolt from his crossbow. Ahron caught that bolt in mid-air, and then he caught Kevin's eye and smiled. His final hours might actually be enjoyable. The human turned his head and fought against the attempted glamour as he notched another bolt in his crossbow. The child could not harm him, Ahron knew. In an instant, this Kevin would nourish him, and then...

He was so focused on his prey that Jimmy's quick movements surprised him. The blade of a sword caught the sun, and Ahron turned just in time to avoid being cut down.

Ahron was fast, he was powerful, but he had not fought in a very long time, and these humans did not have the good sense to be afraid. Jimmy kept coming, and this time the sword sliced skin. The

316 | Linda Winstead Jones

wound was still healing when the other one, Kevin, put one of those annoying bolts through Ahron's eye. He fell to the ground, flailing like a wounded bird.

His eye would heal, even his brain would heal, but the damage, the damage to his body and brain slowed his response. Sunlight beat down, too hot and bright, into Ahron's one good eye. Another bolt went into his heart and he saw that blade again, reflecting the sun as it swept down to take his head.

He had been right to fear Jimmy. Marie had failed horribly when she'd allowed this insignificant human to live.

The last words Ahron heard on this earth were a breathless, disgusted, "Creepy fucker." His last thought before he went to dust was *Killed by humans. How embarrassing*.

Indikaiya fought her way through Marie's vampires, sword swinging. They were a good team, a fierce and dedicated band of Warriors — and yes, at this moment she considered Luca to be a Warrior — who cut through the enemy to make their way to their queen. Sorin had been right all along. Once Marie was dead, the revolution would fall apart.

She kept an eye on Sorin. She had seen him die once, and it had been devastating. If he was cut down today, if Marie or one of her soldiers ended him, he would go back to her world, their world, where she would see him again. He was Warrior now, one of them. He had been redeemed.

But she didn't want to watch him go without her. When this war was done, she wanted to walk back to their home side by side, perhaps even hand in hand. He was more than a lover, he was a partner. The other half of her, in a way she had never expected him or any other man to be. To find him here had been unexpected, even shocking. After all these years, to be surprised by anything was a miracle.

She did not miss that he looked her way more than once, checking on her, making sure she was well even though he knew — as she did — that she could not die, not in the true sense of the word.

The army before them thinned. Seeing their compatriots go to dust, those vampires who did not perish in the dimly lit hallway turned and ran. Some of them succeeded in retreat, but others did not. A young vampire ran to the end of the hallway and turned toward what Indikaiya knew to be the stairway to the house above. From just beyond that corner, he screamed. And then another vampire met the same fate. And another.

The four of them, their team, stopped in the middle of the hallway. Luca whispered, "Marie," and then, as if he had called her, the queen rounded the corner with a regal step. Her fine gown, bordering on ridiculous in this day and time, was covered with the ashes of her own soldiers, those she had punished for deserting her. She smiled, but when she saw Sorin that smile died. She stopped, stunned, but she recovered her calm quickly.

"I don't know how you managed this, but I will enjoy killing you all over again." And with that, she flew.

Sorin placed himself in front of the others. Marie was his. She had guided him, promised him power, promised him everything he'd ever wanted. She'd shown him how power corrupts. She unknowingly caused him to leave behind the monster he had become for the Warrior he was today.

And she had killed him. He owed her for that. He owed her for Jonas — the vampire she'd tortured and killed, a vampire without whom this war would not have been possible — and for Nevada, for Chloe's mother. He owed her for Phillip, for Phillip's mother, and for all the humans she had killed or glamoured beyond repair. He owed her for Melody, Sorin's own vampire offspring who had died early on in this war, a silly, bloodthirsty child who never should've been called a soldier.

What he owed her was justice. That was who he was now, who he had become. Justice.

He had seen her fight many times, so he knew how she would attack, what she would do when she reached him. Her eyes were on him; she seemed to have forgotten about or else foolishly dismissed the others. Mistake. Sorin took a stance that indicated he intended to meet her head on. His sword was held high and ready. His eyes locked to hers. She was coming for him; she wanted to kill him again. When she reached Sorin he ducked down, tucked the sword close to his body, rolled along the floor, and shouted a name.

He rolled up in time to watch Indikaiya swing her sword and take Marie's head.

Marie had time to scream in frustration, just once, and then she went to dust. It had happened fast, perhaps too fast, but it was done. The power in the mansion shifted instantly. He felt it. Luca felt it more strongly, he could tell by the way the blood born glanced up. Marie's children were now weakened. Her glamoured humans were free of her influence. The war was not over, but it soon would be.

Luca stepped over Marie's dust as if it were poison. "You could have warned us what you two had cooked up."

"It was not planned," Sorin said.

Luca scoffed. "Looked planned to me."

The four of them walked toward the stairway. A few vampires would need to be dealt with, before they could retake these headquarters. Sorin took a moment to ruminate on the fact that he was walking down the hallway side by side with Luca Ambrus. They had been on the same side for a while, but they had never been what anyone would call friends, or even friendly acquaintances. And yet now there was no animosity.

"What will you do now?" Sorin asked.

Luca did not hesitate to answer. "I'm going to take my family and go home."

"And home is..."

"None of your business," the blood born mumbled.

Scotland, Sorin thought, though he wasn't sure why. He had a lot to learn about being a Warrior.

As they reached the end of the hallway, four heads snapped to the side when they heard a meek call from beyond a closed door. Rurik shouted for the woman they'd heard to stand back, and then he kicked in the door.

Sorin smiled, and offered the woman in that room a hand. It was a very good day indeed. Though she would not remember him — he had seen to that — he remembered her well.

"Mrs. Stargel, Phillip will be so happy to see you."

CHAPTER TWENTY-FOUR

The war was over; she should not cry. Marie had been dead a week, and every day there were fewer battles. Fewer rebel vampires. The time for shedding tears was over, right? The world was safe, or at least as safe as it had once been.

Nevada turned her head and wiped her eyes when Rurik walked into the room. She didn't want his last memory of her to be one of her red-faced and puffy. Some women might look attractive when they cried, but she was not one of them.

She'd heard them talking. Tomorrow the Warriors would depart. They were no longer necessary.

How could she tell Rurik that he was necessary to *her*?

"Sorin has located your family," Rurik said, his voice sounding not much happier than she felt.

Good news. Maybe she felt a little better.

But not much. "I'm glad to hear it," she said, working to keep the tears out of her voice. "Where are they?"

"Not far. A cabin in Virginia, he said. He was quite annoyed that they seem to be trying to block him."

Emily had more than a touch of the same magic Nevada possessed. What about Justin? Which of her parents had witch's blood? She'd find out. After Rurik left.

He walked up behind her and placed a heavy hand on her shoulder. It was a soldier's hand, large and calloused, but it was also a kind and gentle hand. She lifted her own hand and placed it over his. After tomorrow she would not be able to touch him, not ever again.

"I love you," she said, whispering.

"I know," he answered just as softly.

I know? Really? How embarrassing! Then he said, "I love you, too. I have since I first saw you. You were traveling remotely and did not think anyone could see you, but I did. I will always see you, Nevada."

Forget about holding in tears! She turned, buried her head against his chest, and sobbed. "I don't want you to go! It's not fair!" As if life had ever been fair. "Can't I go with you? I'm no soldier, I know that, but don't the Warriors need a witch?"

"Impossible," he whispered as he stroked her hair. "You cannot travel to my world."

"But true love is supposed to fix everything," she said, her words garbled and teary. "That's what we have, right? True love."

He took her chin in his hand and made her look up at him. "True love is pain and joy in equal measure. It breaks worlds and fixes them. My heart is broken and yet it is also full."

Tears streamed down her face. "Isn't there a spell…"

"No."

"There has to be a way I can go with you!"

"No." He leaned down and kissed her tear-stained lips. "But if you will have me, I can stay."

Nevada held her breath. It had not even occurred to her that he might be able to stay with her! "Is it possible?"

"Yes."

She experienced a moment of ecstasy followed by… doubt. "You are an Immortal Warrior. How does that work?"

"If I stay, I will become human again. You and I will grow old together. We will make babies, and make a home. We will be husband and wife, and we will know all the joy and pain of a long but very human life."

She caught his eye and held it. "You would give up immortality for an ordinary life with me?"

"I would give up immortality for one more night with you. My love for you is that deep."

Nevada shook her head. "I can't ask you to…"

"Don't ask me to live a thousand years without you," he interrupted. "Even a week would be torture."

"Well, I wouldn't want to torture you." Nevada wrapped her arms around Rurik's neck and held on tight. She smiled. She kissed him. And then she pulled away slightly and whispered. "I should have known. True love always wins."

They were no longer needed. With leaders like Jimmy and Kevin in charge, the last remaining vampire rebels had been defeated in a matter of days. Or else they slunk back into darkness, where they would once again hide. It would be foolish to say the rebel vampires were no longer a danger, but with Marie gone there was no more risk that they would claim power.

It was discussed that perhaps Nevada, who had a gift for casting spells of remembrance, could cast a worldwide spell that would allow humans — or most of the them — to forget. But while ignorance might be bliss, it would be foolish to wipe away the knowledge that the danger of vampires continued to exist. Humans needed to know to be cautious about inviting strangers into their homes after dark.

Indikaiya stood, side by side with Sorin, at the edge of Arlington Cemetery. Warriors were buried here. Heroes. Soldiers. Row upon row upon row of precisely placed headstones stretched before them. She felt a reverence, as she often did when she stepped upon hallowed ground.

There were battle sites all around the city, scarred ground all around the world, but no vampire battle had taken place here. The stones were pristine; the grounds unblemished. In the distance, a small bit of fog had already begun to form.

It was in this way that they'd depart, as they were no longer required in this world. When a war was finished, the Warriors returned home to wait until the next time they were called. They entered their world through the sacred burial grounds of other warriors.

They would be remembered now. No more would the Warriors be forgotten.

On this crisp autumn morning, they had an audience for their departure from this world. Humans they had fought with, a few vampires who could withstand the early morning sun — Luca Ambrus included — Phillip Stargel and his mother. And Cupcake, of course. She would miss the dog, more than she'd imagined she would, but Cupcake and Phillip made a fine pair. They would be happy with one another.

Philip had hugged Sorin with all his might, when they had returned from the final fight with Marie with his mother, but most of his attention had been — rightly — for her. He did not seem to notice that his mother was pale and thin. She recovered a bit more every day, and soon she'd be herself again.

Nevada stood to the side, grasping Rurik's hand tightly. She'd hugged Sorin and Indikaiya moments earlier, and she'd shed emotional tears. Tears of loss, as it was likely they would never see one another again. She was not at all comforted to know that if he chose to, Sorin could watch her for a lifetime. Unless there was a need, she would not see him again. If she led a blessed life from this moment on, there would never be a call.

Indikaiya caught Rurik's eye and lifted her eyebrows in silent question. He nodded once. Once the decision was made, there would be no changing his mind. No regrets in a day or a month or a year. If he did not walk with the other Warriors back to their home, he would become human again. He would age, his strength would fade. Rurik had chosen Nevada over immortality. He had chosen her over his calling.

The witch was his calling now. Nevada was his purpose. He smiled, looking so odd swordless and wearing modern clothing. This was his life now.

Indikaiya turned her attention to the front, to the cemetery that awaited. She had so much to show Sorin, so much to teach him. Yes, they would return to this world when called, but until then — whether the wait was months or years or eons — they would have a life. A good life, together.

She patted the leather bag she would carry home with her. There wasn't much in it, just one small souvenir. She wasn't sure that the iPod Jimmy had given her would work in her world, but she was going to do her best to take Joan, Aretha, and Janis with her.

As they watched Warriors from every time imaginable enter the cemetery, the fog that had begun to form when they'd arrived grew and rolled toward them. Just a few feet away, a mist formed on the grass. That mist grew thicker and taller as more armed men — and a few women — walked into it and disappeared. It seemed to swallow them whole. Sorin took her hand and squeezed. She squeezed back, in a comforting way she had not even thought to offer in thousands of years.

"I have been reborn," Sorin said softly. There was a short pause, a deep breath, and then he said, "I'm not sure I deserve this second chance."

"If you had not earned it you wouldn't be here." She didn't mean to snap, but she had never been a coddler. Not even as a mother, a wife, a human with human frailties.

She glanced up, wondering if she'd hurt his feelings, but he wore a charming Sorin smile on his handsome face. "I love you," he said. It was not a romantic offering but was, instead, a statement of fact.

"And I love you," she responded. It was the first time she had said the words to him. It would not be the last.

Hand in hand, they stepped forward, following others of their kind.

"I wonder what the future holds, in this new world," Sorin asked as a tendril of mist wrapped around his ankle and crawled up his leg.

Indikaiya smiled, her heart soared, and as the mist swallowed them she said, "Let's find out."

LINDA WINSTEAD JONES

Linda's first book, the historical romance *Guardian Angel*, was released in 1994, and in the years since she's written in several romance sub-genres under several names. In order of appearance, Linda Winstead; Linda Jones; Linda Winstead Jones; Linda Devlin; and Linda Fallon. She's a six time finalist for the RITA Award and a winner (for *Shades of Midnight*, writing as Linda Fallon) in the paranormal category. She's a *New York Times* and *USA Today* bestselling author of seventy books. Most recently she's been writing as Linda Jones in a couple of joint projects with Linda Howard, and rereleasing some of her backlist in ebook format. She can often be found playing on Facebook, and information is always available at: www.lindawinsteadjones.com.

Linda lives in Huntsville, Alabama. She can be reached at:

lindawinsteadjonesauthor@gmail.com
https://twitter.com/LWJbooks
https://www.facebook.com/pages/LindaWinsteadJones
https://www.facebook.com/LindaHowardLindaJones

RECENT RELEASES:

Bridger's Last Stand
The Rock Creek Six: The Complete Set
Haunted Honeymoon
And coming soon,
the first trilogy in the Columbyana series:
The Sun Witch; The Moon Witch; and *The Star Witch*

For a complete list of previous and upcoming
releases please visit
www.lindawinsteadjones.com

CPSIA information can be obtained
at www.ICGtesting.com
Printed in the USA
LVOW10s1539181217
560168LV00035B/2500/P